Recent Titles by Janet Woods from Severn House

DIFFERENT TIDES

rges ma
is due fc
her reader
umber, tel

DIFFERENT TIDES

Janet Woods

This first world edition published 2014
in Great Britain and the USA by
SEVERN HOUSE PUBLISHERS LTD of
19 Cedar Road, Sutton, Surrey, England, SM2 5DA.
Trade paperback edition first published 2015
in Great Britain and 2016 in the USA by
SEVERN HOUSE PUBLISHERS LTD

British Library Cataloguing in Publication Data

Woods, Janet, 1939- author.
  Different tides.
  1. Governesses–Fiction. 2. Orphans–Fiction. 3. Dorset
  (England)–Fiction. 4. Great Britain–History–William
  IV, 1830-1837–Fiction. 5. Love stories.
  I. Title
  823.9'14-dc23

ISBN-13: 978-0-7278-8401-5 (cased)
ISBN-13: 978-1-84751-651-0 (trade paper)

Except where actual historical events and characters are being
described for the storyline of this novel, all situations in this
publication are fictitious and any resemblance to living persons
is purely coincidental.

One

Despite having been orphaned for several years, Clementine could still remember some details of her parents.

'My father's name was Howard Morris. He was an army officer and died at the battle of Waterloo. He was a hero. I was young when he died so I can't recall ever meeting him.'

The man questioning her was in his fifties, she imagined. He'd described his occupation as a lawyer and investor, and his name was John Beck. He looked down his nose at her with a faintly quizzical smile but she didn't feel intimidated since nature had provided him with a nose that was long. His eyes were kind.

'Quite. Now . . . do tell me about your mother, young lady.'

'Her name was Hannah Cleaver. She was not very strong and she died.' Clementine didn't like talking about her mother. She fell silent.

He waited a short while for her to continue. When no more information was forthcoming he looked at her. 'Can you tell us what your mother's occupation was?'

'She sang, I think. I only remember seeing her once after I was left at the school. I was about ten then. She looked ill. She said I'd have to earn my living when I grew up, so I should work hard and acquire the skills required to be a governess because it was a respectable occupation. She told me that both she and my father wanted that. A month later they told me she'd died in the workhouse.'

'That must have been a shock. Where did you live before you were accepted into the school?'

'There was no one close left on my mother's side, so we moved in with a distant relative of my father in Portland. My mother became his housekeeper. He was a minister in the church there.'

Clementine grimaced as she recalled an old man with a bald patch on his head – a man who had cuddled her and kissed her on the mouth when her mother wasn't there, and then kissed and cuddled her mother when she was there. His breath had been unpleasant, as if an attempt had been made to disguise its stink with peppermint. It had been their secret, he'd said, and she would be taken away from her mother if she told anyone. In her innocence she'd believed him.

She dragged her mind away. 'There was a typhoid outbreak and he died.'

'And then?'

It was summer and they'd trudged for many days. 'Our accommodation was needed for the new minister. We came to London because my mother had been offered a job as a housekeeper. When we arrived she was told they wouldn't employ anyone with a child to look after. She was offered work at night, and for a while I went with her.' Clementine closed her eyes, recalling a moment so reluctant to emerge that it died inside her mind almost instantly. Somebody had hurt her mother and there had been blood.

'One day she told me that my father had left money for my education and she took me to the school. She told me I must stay there, because that's what my father had wanted.'

The man's eyes sharpened and one peppery eyebrow rose. 'What was the work she engaged in?'

'I'm not sure.'

Although now she was older she could guess. She wasn't about to air those suspicions because she really wanted the position for which she was being interviewed.

The man at the window cleared his throat.

Her inquisitor glanced at the man, who seemed to be about half his age. He was seated, his head propped in his hand, and looking out of the window at the people scurrying in the murky gloom of the street below. The sky threatened rain, but it would wash the soot particles down from the sky and make London look dirtier, rather than refreshing it.

Then she realized he wasn't looking out, but was in fact observing her reflection in the glass. They hadn't been introduced yet. Was he her prospective employer?'

When their glances met and connected there was an impression of dark blue eyes and a wide, firm mouth. He was immaculately dressed in grey checked trousers, and a darker knee-length coat with a high cravat. A hat with a curled brim rested on the window-sill, a pair of leather gloves folded neatly on top of a stick with a silver handle that lay nearby.

Her gaze shifted back to her questioner when he asked, 'Did your mother perform in the theatre?'

'I've already told you I don't know much about her.'

'But you must have some notion of how she earned a living.'

'I cannot recall it with any accuracy. I was almost seven years old when we came to London, and that was fourteen years ago.'

Her mother had two best gowns that were used only for work. One was red and the other green.

Clementine had thought the gowns pretty then, the satin glowing in the candlelight, and as bright as the rouge on her mother's lips as she'd paraded around the small room that had accommodated them, talking gaily about parties she'd attended and of people she'd met. Clementine had never questioned that it had been less than the truth at the time because she'd been too young to know any better.

As she'd grown older the gowns had begun to reveal the despair of another life. The fabric collected stains and the armpits emitted a sour smell. The fabric rotted into holes. Clementine pushed the thought away, as she always did when it intruded with an alternative occupation. Because she'd loved her mother she could only bring herself to defend her. 'My mother had a lovely voice. When I was a child she used to sing me to sleep.'

'Did you earn money to help keep yourself at the school?'

'My father left an annuity to pay for my school expenses.' She looked down at her hands. 'When I was older the annuity ran out and so did my education. I taught at the school for a while.'

'How did your mother die?' he asked, alerting Clementine to the fact that this man already knew the answer to the questions he'd put to her and would draw his own conclusion.

She would tell him the truth as she knew it when she was small and embroider it a little to gain his sympathy. 'I was told she'd developed a cough and had grown very thin. A cold wind was blowing and there had been snow.' Tears gathered in her eyes. 'They said somebody had stabbed her and stole the money she'd earned. She's buried in Potter's Field.'

His voice softened. 'How did you end up in the workhouse?'

'When I was eighteen I asked the school to pay me a wage, but the request was denied. There was an argument.'

'And you came off second best. I understand you then sought shelter here, where you've been teaching the younger children their letters in return for your accommodation and food. You came here two years ago. Since then you've been recommended for two positions, both of which you took, and then absconded from. Why?'

She wished he hadn't asked. 'They were unsuitable.'

The mysterious man at the window spoke, his voice low, yet as soft as a purr. 'In what way were they unsuitable, Miss Morris? You copied legal papers for Argus and Shank, who are lawyers. It was regular work and you were in a position of considerable trust. Why did you leave there?'

He wasn't going to allow her to get away with half-truths. 'I worked there until I was dismissed. Then I worked in a shop as a clerk for a while, and I sewed seams for a gentleman's outfitters, where my stitching was pronounced unsuitable.'

The older gentleman said, 'My companion asked you a question. Why were the positions unsuitable?'

Her colour rose, but from anger this time. 'In a way I'd prefer not to discuss it with you, sir.'

'Are we to deduce, then, that you are a morally decent young woman, Miss Morris?'

Living in a workhouse amongst the most destitute of people, and being old enough now to suspect what had really constituted her mother's employment, Clementine couldn't pretend not to know what he meant. He had managed to corner her without even trying. She blushed, and her hands went to her face to cover it. 'Indeed I am, sir. It would be unfair of you to judge me, unless it's for myself alone . . . I attend church regularly.'

A muffled snort came from the man at the window. 'Thank you, Miss Morris.' He withdrew a silver-cased watch from his waistcoat pocket and gazed at it, before slipping it back in again, in a manner that suggested he might be losing interest in her as a candidate for the position. His eyelashes had a sooty darkness to them that matched his hair. 'I have a minute or two to spare if you wish to ask me any questions.'

'I do wish to ask a question . . . a personal one.'

'Do you, be damned? I must warn you, I'm not used to having my integrity questioned so you'd better have a good excuse for it.' The cornflower eyes that confronted her now had lost some of their warmth, and she hesitated.

'For goodness' sake, get on with it then.'

'It's nothing to do with your integrity, or lack of the same, sir. That must rest in your own estimation. It's because my previous employers proved unsuitable.'

'Ah yes . . . I see. So what's your question?'

'Are you a morally decent man?'

He gave a surprised huff of laughter. 'Well, that certainly answered my question. You're vexed because I embarrassed you, aren't you? Do you expect me to answer you honestly?'

'I did when you asked me.'

'Of course you did, but that is you, and this is me, and it might not be what you want to hear. Is there such a thing as an entirely decent man? Be careful how you answer though . . . if you spout religion I shall bite.'

Despite her resolve not to, Clementine threw caution to the winds. 'I asked you the question, not the other way round.'

'So you did. Who decides what's decent, or what's not in the person who sets himself above others to judge? How narrow or broad should that judgment be? Indeed . . . from where did it spring?'

'Are you suggesting I've based my question on personal experience?'

'You certainly have, Miss Morris. I find you impertinent because you are judging me on the foibles of your past employers.'

'I'm not judging you at all, sir. I merely asked you the same question that you asked me.'

'Allow me to put this to you, young lady. As a prospective employer, if I promise to refrain from making unwelcome advances towards you — as your previous employers seem to have done — will that satisfy you as to whether I'm a morally decent man or not?'

Her cheeks took on the intensity of fire. 'That will do perfectly well.'

'Do you want it in writing, signed, sealed and witnessed?' he asked pointedly.

'I will take your word for it and . . . trust you. Now I have answered your questions and you have answered mine and we are satisfied that we're reasonably decent, can we drop the subject?' He chuckled. 'Good Lord . . . what a provocateur you are turning out to be. I thought you were embarrassed, yet it seems I didn't shock you with my plain speaking. Perhaps I shall not hire you after all.'

She could have kicked herself for being so straightforward. She needed this position, whatever it was. 'I'm sorry, sir. It wasn't my intention to be rude, and I certainly didn't set out to provoke you. I just wanted to state my terms. I mean . . . I didn't want you to think . . .'

'Yes, yes . . . let's forget all that.' Without turning to his companion, he said, 'Miss Morris will do me nicely, John, since she has no intention of taking any nonsense from man or beast. I'm finding out more about you with each second that passes, Miss Morris. You're hired, if you are satisfied with my credentials, since you should be more than satisfied with the wage and conditions. I'll expect you to work for me for an initial period of at least one year, after which we'll assess our arrangement. Please try and curb your habit of breathing fire all over me every time you speak.'

She let out a breath slowly. 'I'll try. Thank you, sir.'

'May I just remind you that the workhouse will be under no obligation to allow you shelter again, as they have in the past. My lawyer, John Beck here, will settle up with this establishment and arrange your release. We are in business together.'

And whatever that business was, it seemed to pay well, for they were both well heeled.

'Mrs Beck has kindly offered you accommodation for a few nights, and she will take you shopping so you may purchase something suitable to wear. Your current garments will be returned to the institution. I'll collect you and your chattels when we're ready to travel.'

'New clothing?' Surprise filled her and she remembered her mother's gaudy dresses. 'What exactly will I be employed to do, Mr . . .?'

'My name is Zachariah Fleet. You will be entrusted with the care of my relatives, Sir Edward Fleet, who is a baron, and Lady Iris. The position is one of great trust.'

'May I ask if Sir Edward and his wife are infirm?'

He stared at her, his expression slightly startled, and then twisted a grin her way. 'Not yet, they're not. Edward is five years old while his sister is a year younger.'

'Ah . . . I see.' She tried not to laugh but couldn't help it. 'Have you considered I might be too young for such a responsibility?'

'Of course I've considered it. However, their mother was young, just turned twenty-two when she died. Nobody told her she was too young to be a mother, yet by all accounts she was a good one. The children will be grieving for both their parents, I imagine. John thinks an older and more experienced governess would do a better job.'

'I would want the same for my children, I think.'

'You can teach the children, which is a bonus. You might like to brush up on your own manners while you're teaching them theirs. You are too outspoken and that might upset some people.'

'Does it upset you?'

'Not unduly.' He sighed, and said to the lawyer, 'Perhaps you could go and make the arrangements for her release, John. I'd like to speak to Miss Morris alone.'

When the door closed behind the lawyer, Zachariah Fleet said, 'I beg your pardon, Miss Morris. That remark about your manners was uncalled for, since you have every right to question me, especially after your former experiences. Please don't be worried about the responsibility since you will have an older nursery maid who will be available to assist. Most of the servants are of a mature age, which is why I prefer a younger woman for the children. You appear to have a sensible head on your shoulders, and are not too talkative or frivolous. And I think you would welcome some responsibility.'

'What exactly is my position to be then?'

'Your role is to be a companion to the two children . . . an older sister perhaps. I want them to have someone they can trust – someone they can go to, who will treat them with respect and understanding rather than censure. What I don't want is somebody upright and rigid with disapproval and held together with as many stays as a spinster's corset. In other words I want my wards to enjoy their childhood in every way possible.'

'I see.'

'You're educated to a certain level. That's all the better because the children will benefit – and so will you. You will find plenty to keep them occupied in the country, and there is a small town nearby. I will visit as often as possible.' He gave a wry smile. 'I've had very little experience with children. For five of my early years I was raised by a cleric who beat me on a regular basis, whether I deserved it or not, so we do have that background in common, Miss Morris. I was supposed to follow in his footsteps.'

She tried not to laugh. 'I don't know why, but I cannot imagine you in a frock, standing comfortably in a pulpit spouting about the perils of sin.'

'Then we have that in common as well, since neither can I. One thing I would like to say, and I'll be blunt: if you stay here, in this city and under your present circumstances, we both know what the eventual outcome is likely to be, despite your shyness to admit that you're unaware of such matters.' He held out his hand. 'Shall we shake on it, or would that be considered an advance by you?'

His smile told her he was teasing now. His hand was warm and firm, his handshake brief, and he gave a little bow, as if she were a respected acquaintance instead of Clementine Morris, young woman with no means, no background she'd care to speak of – if she had one at all – and no prospects, except the one currently on offer.

The beatings seemed to have had a beneficial effect on Zachariah Fleet because he was mannerly, and without being foppish, she reflected as he picked up his hat, cane and gloves. But then, he wanted his wards to have more than just a governess. He wanted them to have an older sister they could turn to in times of trouble. It was a big responsibility; bigger than Zachariah Fleet could imagine.

Well . . . she could fill that role even though it might come at a price. Love was a commitment, and was hard to walk away from. Already, she felt the tug of the two motherless children in need, as if they were calling to her from afar like lost baby birds.

God knew, there were hundreds of hungry orphans in the workhouses. Mr Fleet's little chicks were lucky. They would never lack for anything material, and would be raised with all the love and care she could find in her. Then she would have to move on and her heart would probably break.

She told herself she should say no, but even a small amount of love was better than none to a child – and what else could she do?

'I'll see you in a few days' time then,' he said.

She nodded.

As they walked through the crowds back to John Beck's office suite, Zachariah said, 'You know, John, I feel guilty about not telling her she may be a distant relative.'

'Why get her hopes up when it might not be true. All you've got to go on is a rumour that someone called Howard Morris existed, and an annuity had been paid to a school for the orphaned children of army officers in his name, and on behalf of his daughter Clementine. You've always had a tidy mind, and that's what comes of your need to set the family papers in order. It might be for a different person altogether.'

Zachariah nodded in agreement.

'How many females do you know called Clementine who have fathers named Howard Morris? She's not on the family tree. She probably comes from the wrong side of the blanket and she's not your responsibility.'

'I remember the days when I wasn't *your* responsibility. I remember standing in front of you and my ears shrivelling from the lecture you gave me. And later, when you'd turned me into a man and I thanked you, you told me to repay you by improving the life of somebody who needed it on my journey through life. That person is Clementine Morris. What say you to that, John Beck?'

'That Julia and I did well at setting you straight.'

'So why the reservations? Clementine Morris was probably overlooked. Nobody paid much attention to keeping the family records up to date. The girl we interviewed attended the named school until the money ran out. That's no coincidence. Neither is the fact that her father was a distant relative of mine through my mother's side.'

'The blood connection is too distilled to signify.'

'All the better since the girl is alone in the world and she has nobody but me to turn to. She's already struggling to survive. I can either leave her to sink, or help her up. You know what happens to young women like her eventually . . . especially one so fair of face.'

'So, you noticed her looks. Look, Zachariah, you've offered her a decent position in your household, and given her more freedom than any other servant would be afforded. Forget that she might be a relative and leave it at that. Eventually she'll marry the gardener and have ten children to care for.'

Zachariah laughed. 'I like her . . . She's straightforward but she has a soft heart as well as being able to think for herself. Besides, I need her for Gabe's children.'

'They're your children now. May I make a suggestion? Marry the girl yourself, then you can take advantage of her services for nothing, as well as enjoy the comforts a wife brings.'

'I have no intention of marrying. I prefer my own company – and besides, I'd make a terrible husband, since I'm too argumentative. You said so yourself.'

John huffed with laughter. 'It seemed to me that Clementine Morris enjoys a good argument. Let things lie then. The less she knows about you the better. You don't owe the girl a thing except her wage. If you tell her you're related she'll try and take advantage of that. As the situation is now she'll be grateful to you.'

Two hours later Clementine found herself in a comfortable room in a more prosperous area of town. She'd been examined for lice and bathed. A maid had washed her hair with perfumed soap and she now smelled like a flower garden. The stench of bodily odour that permeated everything in the workhouse had been washed away and she felt all the better for it.

She stood now in a plain cambric petticoat in front of the fire. Under it she was as naked as the day she was born – and poor, for her discarded clothing had been consigned to the bag destined for either the workhouse or the rag-and-bone man. She'd discarded all the old items and would shortly be reborn in another skin. She welcomed the feeling of being clean.

Julia Beck was an elegant, mildly fashionable woman who eyed her up and down, but not unkindly. 'Your hair is so very pretty with that touch of auburn in it. It suits your eyes. I always think light-brown eyes can look rather ordinary.'

Clementine had never wondered if her eyes were ordinary or otherwise. She had good eyesight, something for which she was thankful. 'Yes . . . I suppose they are.'

The woman had meant no harm. She'd spoken without thinking, and she said hurriedly, 'Oh, my goodness, I didn't mean that to sound like a criticism. You will forgive me, won't you? I meant to add that your eyes are far from ordinary, though, since they are so large, and you have such a long sweep of lashes. I admit to feeling quite jealous.'

'You needn't be, Mrs Beck. I wasn't offended in the least, and I've always thought blue eyes like yours to be very pretty.' An image came to her of Zachariah's eyes, as blue as cornflowers in the field and reflecting from the workhouse window. He had a calm, direct sort of gaze, and was a man so very in control of himself.

As if she'd picked up on Clementine's thoughts, Julia said, 'You're young to be given the responsibility of Zachariah's wards, Miss Morris. I do hope he knows what he's doing.'

'Mr Fleet sounded very sure of himself to me.'

'He's certainly a confident man. Are you experienced with children?'

Having already gone through the questioning process with her employer, Clementine wasn't inclined to repeat the exercise to satisfy the curiosity of this woman, as nice as she seemed to be.

'Mr Fleet considered I was experienced enough to suit him.'

'Ah yes . . . Zachariah is very thorough. He would have had your background examined in advance of offering you the position. Still, he may have overlooked some things, such as languages for the children. The pair of them will need to learn French and the boy must be tutored in Latin as well. Then there are music lessons to consider. Oh dear, you have such a task ahead of you . . . boys are so different to girls.'

'I'll make sure to discuss these points with Mr Fleet when the time comes. Thank you, Mrs Beck. Your advice is invaluable.'

'Oh, do call me Julia, and I shall call you Clementine . . . such a pretty name for someone who was obliged to take shelter in a poorhouse, like a flower in a field of weeds. Was it very bad there?'

'Nobody likes having to accept charity but it's better than the alternative. As for my fellow inmates, they were no better or worse than me, and some of them had very pretty names. Poverty is a great leveller and I was grateful to have a roof over my head and a meal in my stomach.'

'Zachariah Fleet's sentiments too. Mine as well, but one wouldn't want to leave a legacy of poverty for one's own children and I count Zachariah as one of them, but don't tell him so. I didn't mean to pry.'

'I know, Julia, but when you've been poor all your life you like to savour a meal when it's offered to you.'

'I have some books you might like to borrow, since my children are grown up and married. There is one on social etiquette you might find useful. I bought it for Zachariah but he said he was as social as he intended to be. He can be such a rogue at times . . . and proud.'

'Thank you for warning me.'

Julia made a little humming noise in her throat. 'Thank goodness you have a figure that is well-proportioned and not overly heavy at the top or the bottom.'

This woman's mind is like a dragonfly that darts about from one thing to the other, Clementine thought.

So, Zachariah Fleet had taken the precaution of having her investigated in advance. Of course he had. He wasn't the type of man who left anything to chance, and probably knew more about her than she knew about herself. But why her, when there could be any number of women more experienced, and worthy of the position?

'What does Mr Fleet do to earn his living?'

'Oh, something to do with investment, I believe. I can never understand what these men get up to . . . The man is a genius where making money is concerned.'

A knock came at the door. 'Mrs Spencer has arrived, Mrs Beck.'

'Thank you, Cora, show her up.' A wide smile sped across her face. 'While you were in the bath I sent a message with your measurements and colouring to my dressmaker, and told her to send everything that she had ready to wear. It's so exciting. As soon as we have you looking decent we shall go shopping . . . I love shopping, don't you?'

Clementine couldn't remember the last time she had bought anything new, but she imagined that growing used to it wouldn't be hard.

Soon there were packages on the bed. The gowns were generally unfussy, but a feast of colour and softness. Julia picked out a plain undecorated gown in cream, with a lace trimmed bodice and puffed sleeves to be worn over the tight sleeves. 'You'll look elegant in this.'

Clementine did feel elegant, and to her shame she remembered the vulgar gowns she'd admired on her mother and knew they fared badly against hers. But she must not get above herself. She must remember that her current blessings must be paid for in kind.

She protested, but half-heartedly, because her longing for something feminine and pretty outweighed her good sense. 'This is too much . . . something grey and serviceable would be more suitable.'

'Zachariah gave me instructions . . . to avoid grey, brown and black, unless it's for outdoor wear, he said. He gave me a list, and will expect me to get everything on it, plus a few necessary items he's left for me to determine. We're not even halfway through it yet. We shall have so much fun over the next few days spending his money.'

'Julia, you are incorrigible,' she protested, half-laughing. 'I'm his servant, not his . . . well . . . his lady, I suppose.'

A glance slid her way, inquisitive and amused. 'You meant to say his mistress, didn't you? Let me tell you though, that would be a fine thing, my dear, were it Zachariah Fleet. He would surely be extremely discreet about such affairs. No doubt he has them, though not a glimmer of gossip has filtered my way. So annoying of him to be so secretive, but men have ways and means of going about such business, one supposes.'

Goodness, Julia is a gossip, even though there's no harm in it really, Clementine thought.

'Besides, he would not sully the family name by hiring his mistress to take responsibility for his young wards, for he wouldn't want the children corrupted in any way, shape or form. Now, I must stop gossiping.'

His mistress! Did he have one? Clementine pondered on the thought, but dare not ask her, lest it get back to him. She didn't want to lose her place because of an inquisitive tongue. And although she knew it was avarice, she didn't intend to lose all these wonderful garments before she'd had a chance to wear them.

Julia had a good eye for quality, and by the time her employer came to collect her a few days later Clementine had two trunks waiting in the hall.

'What do you think of her now?' Julia asked Zachariah when she came down the stairs.

The glance that washed over her was so quick that it only grazed an insult across her cheek in passing. At the same time he drawled, 'I hardly recognize you, Miss Morris, for you are quite the lady. I must congratulate you, Julia. She is a work of art and you're the genius who painted her.'

'I merely helped her emerge. If you'd oblige me with a second, more leisurely look you could perhaps make comment of the impression she has on you with more enthusiasm. How do you expect to attract a wife when you can't offer a decent compliment?'

'I've been telling you for years now that I have no wish to attract a wife.' He sighed. 'I'll indulge you if I must, Julia, though Miss Morris doesn't appreciate attention from men so a prolonged scrutiny from me would surely raise her ire, as well as her colour.'

'What nonsense! It just needs the right man to come along and sweep her off her feet. Isn't that right, Clementine?'

There was a moment of silence when Clementine's colour did indeed rise, and she hoped the ground would open and she'd disappear into the hole with a puff of smoke.

Zachariah chuckled. 'Well, Clementine Morris . . . you had plenty to say for yourself on the subject the last time we met. Have you suddenly lost your tongue?'

She didn't know what to say to that, so stood there, fighting off her embarrassment, until she sneaked a glance at him from under her bonnet and saw the amusement in his eyes. She laughed and shrugged at the same time. 'I would suggest that you've left your broom at home on this occasion, Mr Fleet. Julia, please stop your teasing else I'll never speak to you again.'

Julia kissed her on the cheek. 'I'll miss you, my dear. You must write to me for advice, and once a month so you can tell me all the local gossip, and let me know how you are getting on with Zachariah. Being a man, he can be difficult to manage at times.'

The exaggerated sigh he gave was accompanied by a grin.

Julia patted him on the cheek. 'As for you, dear man, come to dinner when you return. You can tell me all about the children. I approve of your young lady. You've made a good choice for your wards now we've tidied her up a little, I think. When will the children be arriving?'

'The agent expects the ship to arrive within the fortnight.'

'From where are they coming, Mr Fleet?'

'From Australia.'

Clementine was shocked into saying, 'Alone?'

'Good God, no! I'm not quite as irresponsible as that, though placing children in the company of people who are strangers to me does make me uneasy. They'll be in the charge of friends of their parents who they're already acquainted with, apparently. The ship will disembark passengers at Poole and my wards will be amongst them.' He gave Julia a hug. 'I expect to be back in London this time next month, Julia. Now, we must be off if we're to make the inn before nightfall without tiring the horses too much.'

'Goodness, you are too softhearted, Zachariah. Horses are born to pull carriages.'

'Try telling that to one who has decided to be stubborn about it.'

The servant took the trunks out to the waiting carriage while Clementine exchanged a final hug with Julia. 'Thank you for your hospitality; you've been so kind.'

Two solid-looking horses, a grey and a dark bay, waited for their riders to mount. She was relieved that the men were acting as outriders. She wouldn't have to share the intimacy of the close confines of the carriage with them. She grinned. They probably didn't want to share it with a female anyway, since they'd have to mind their manners.

She was practically lifted into the carriage by Zachariah's valet with a firm hand under her elbow.

'I'm Evan Bergerac, actor, singer, poet, temporary gentleman's gentleman and lover of beautiful women. At your service.' Evan gazed from under hooded eyes at her for a few moments then kissed her hand.

She withdrew it. He turned and exchanged a grin with his employer. 'I don't think she likes me.'

'She obviously has good taste.' Zachariah smiled at her. 'Evan is harmless.'

She wondered at the familiarity between them – as though they'd known each other for a long time.

One of her trunks was strapped to the back; the second took up most of the floor. The coach horses fretted in their straps, tossed their heads with imperious grace and stamped their hooves. Two coach drivers would travel with the carriage and pair, one to relieve the other. She would be well guarded.

Her excitement threatened to bubble over when the carriage began to move. She gave a final regal wave as they rounded the corner, for truly, she felt like Queen Adelaide in her carriage.

She doubted if Zachariah felt as grand as King William though. He was less fanciful than she.

The pace was leisurely and they made their first stop at an inn, busy with other weary travellers. After an early dinner they retired for the night.

Zachariah Fleet was in the next room, his bed in the same position on the other side of the wall, she guessed. Odd to think there was just a few inches separating them. She placed her hand against the wall and could almost feel his warmth as she whispered, 'Goodnight, Mr Fleet. I hope your dreams are pleasant.'

Two

Although her employer must have been more exhausted and aching than Clementine was, after he'd assisted her from the carriage he made no complaint. He just placed his hands on his back, did a few gentle twists and turns and then stretched towards the sky with a pleasurable groan.

He nodded towards the second coachman. 'I feel as though the grey has ridden me, not the other way round.'

To which remark the grey cast an eye his way and snorted.

Zachariah stroked the grey's nose to soften the insult and said to Ben, 'Rouse the staff, then alert the housekeeper.'

After a similar stretching action, Evan began to help unload the luggage.

Zachariah Fleet didn't look as though he'd travelled all that way astride a horse. He was almost as immaculate as he'd been when they started out, except his hat and coat were peppered with dust and he'd gathered a manly darkness to his jaw line where his beard pricked through his skin.

Removing his hat, he raked long fingers through his hair and then moved a short way away from her to beat himself around his shoulders with the hat. Dust flew in all directions.

When she laughed with the unexpected pleasure of the action, he smiled at her. 'Well . . . what do you make of your new home, Miss Morris?'

They were standing just outside the porch, but she'd already taken note of the features of the house from the carriageway on the way up. It was larger than she'd expected yet it was not a grand home by any means. Built of warm red brick, it was topped by grey slates. The windows were arched and leaded, with top lights of painted glass, as were the panels in the double oak doors.

The house was firmly planted at the top of a rise in a summer flowering meadow that was dotted with a few grazing sheep that resembled clouds propped on sticks, and it had a view that went on forever. The fields surrounding it were full of ripening corn that undulated in the soft breeze.

'Welcome to Martingale House,' he said.

'What a pretty name, and for a lovely home.'

'It was named after the architect who designed it for himself initially. Gabe and I were born here.'

'Gabe?'

'My brother, Gabriel, the late baron.'

'You mentioned you were brought up by a cleric.'

'I was, from the age of eight until I ran away. He was a distant relative on my mother's side who lived in Oxford. When my father died, my mother was persuaded by her family to send me there. They convinced our mother that the discipline would correct my overbearing ways.'

'You don't appear to be overbearing to me. Self-controlled would suit you better, I think.'

'I hope you mean that in a complimentary manner.'

'Do you?'

He smiled at that. 'The self-control was learned over time under John and Julia's tutelage. My family thought I was a bad influence on my brother.'

'Were you?'

'Probably. He was easily led and allowed others to think for him. Ask him a question and he'd never give an answer, just prevaricate until somebody answered for him. Gabe always lived for the moment, while I lived for the future, knowing it had to be better.'

His mood seemed introspective and she took advantage of it. 'You must have missed Gabe.'

'Yes . . . I did. I admired him, and envied him. He was so active, adventurous and heroic. I was dull and quiet in comparison. When the family turned him against me it was bitter. I ran away from my foster home when I was twelve. I didn't see Gabe for a long time, though I heard of him now and again.

'How did you survive?'

He looked troubled. 'By being dishonest for the most part. I hadn't realized that depending on myself for support was harder than it seemed, and there was no adventure in begging for the next piece of bread or stealing a purse and forever looking over your shoulder, scared to death in case you were recognized and sent to prison. You know what being a poor child is like.'

She had not expected a confession of a childhood so ill spent, and gave a shocked cry that drew a wry look from him. She found herself wanting to know more about him. 'How did you get to meet John and Julia Beck?'

'Through my manservant, Evan. I tried to rob him when I was ill and starving. He took me to a Quaker soup kitchen, but the place had closed for the night. John Beck was still there though. He took me to his home by my collar and I'll never forget the lecture I was subjected to when I finally recovered.

'Julia had a pot of broth on the stove. She told me I could join them for dinner if I took a bath, and she found me some clothes her sons had grown out of. Then she said I could stay the night, and if I had the urge to steal something would I please do her a favour and take the purple and green plant stand in the hall rather than anything else. I never moved out, and I regard them as my family. So you see, I'm not so perfect.'

He had captured her attention now. 'I don't recall telling you that you were perfect . . . just self-controlled. What happened after that?'

'With a loan from John I invested in property and managed it myself. The rents accumulated and I looked for other safe investments.'

'And that included the family home?'

'It wasn't exactly an investment. Six years ago Gabe sent me a message. He was in Marshalsea, the debtors' prison. He'd made unwise investments and was ruined. He could barely pay for food and his wife and baby were homeless. The remaining relatives faded away, except for Alice's half-sister and brother, who descended like carrion to feast on anything left over. They insisted Gabe was in their debt, and demanded the deeds to the family home and its contents to be handed over to them.'

'What did you do?'

'I threw them out. Gabe owed so much money he couldn't remember if he'd promised them the deeds or not. He got it into his mind that his debtors had hired somebody to kill him. He was worried about Alice and Edward, and decided to give up gambling and leave England to make a new life for his family. When I offered to buy the house he jumped at the chance, because he knew he and his family would always have a home to go to if they came back. The burden of Gabe's debts nearly brought me to my knees.'

Zachariah should have been the responsible older brother, not the irresponsible younger brother, she thought when he added, 'I bought the Martingale House deeds back with the intention of working the estate and placing it into Edward's hands as a going concern when he came of age. To that end I settled Gabe's debts and engaged Mr Bolton as estate manager. Gabe and I agreed on an amount of money he'd need to set himself up on a sheep farm. Alice was a scatterbrain, but she loved Gabe and her children. The estate is in my name now. Little Iris was born the year after they left. Gabe sent me a glowing account of their life at the time, and I thought he'd settled down.'

When he hesitated she prompted, 'And then?'

'That was three years ago. I heard nothing more from him until a letter arrived from somebody called Sheridan, who said he was Gabe's friend. He told me Gabe had lost his life trying to save Alice when she was swept away by a flooded river.'

'Where were the children then?'

'Staying with the Sheridan family apparently . . . though I fail to see why. When he wrote, Sheridan told me about my brother and sister-in-law's demise, and said they'd bring the children home with them, as arranged, along with Gabe's goods and chattels. He said they were Iris's godparents.'

'But you're not sure?'

'I only have instinct to go by.'

'And his sheep farm?'

'I doubt if there was a sheep farm. Gabe could be very evasive. I think he had fallen into his old habits and had gambled nearly everything I'd given him for capital away.'

She placed a hand on his sleeve, quickly removing it when he looked down on it with some surprise, as if it had flown through the air like a bird and landed there to rest. He was a man who didn't like being handled. 'I'm sorry.'

He misinterpreted, and so had she. 'It's me who should apologize. I shouldn't have told you all this.'

'Why not?'

'It isn't really relevant, and I don't usually tell strangers my business.' The grin he gave was shamefaced.

'We're no longer strangers, and I won't repeat it.'

'Thank you. I thought you might have refused to take the job since you'd be buried in the country.'

'You could have employed someone else.'

He hesitated for a moment, then said, 'Nobody else would have been suitable. It's a responsible position and you will be secluded in the country.'

'I think I shall like that.' While he was in this softer mood she took the opportunity to ask, 'Why did you choose someone as young as me to offer the position to?'

'I sought you out and chose you specifically.'

She waited for him to clarify his statement, then when an explanation wasn't forthcoming she sighed and said, 'Why?'

'Your name came up at the board meeting of the workhouse. You had the qualifications I'd been looking for. The matron was less than enthusiastic, but she supplied you with a reference.'

'Did she say what she thought was wrong with me?'

His eyes lit on her, slightly contemplative. 'Yes, she did.'

After a few moments of silence, she sighed. 'Is that all you're going to say?'

'For now.'

She thought about it for a few seconds. 'I don't think my disposition needs any improvement.'

'Neither do I,' he said, and laughed. 'Actually, the matron was less than enthusiastic about losing you, since the children liked you. She said you resented taking charity when you were perfectly capable of earning your living, if someone would employ you in a decent household and pay you a living wage.'

'She's right. I'm not humble enough to feel grateful about it.' That reminded her that she hadn't thanked him. 'You've been too generous, and I've been neglectful . . .'

'There's still time to delight me with a scintillating display of good manners.'

'I thought I just had. Thank you for your generosity, Mr Fleet.'

'It was more necessity than generosity. That gown you were wearing at the workhouse, if you could call it a gown, was appallingly unbecoming. The alternative was to gaze on something too dreary for words.'

She felt aggrieved by the ironic reminder and stalked off towards the door, knowing that if she'd been a dog her bristles would be pricked up as high as they'd reach. All the same, she had been rude, and it was worth thinking about. She came to a halt at the step and turned to face him.

'I'm curious to know what my station is. If I wear rags and earn a little money writing letters, I'm a ragamuffin. If I get a job as a maid, then I'm nobody. If I'm dressed in fine clothes and look after children, I'm a nursemaid. If I teach them I'm a governess. If I do none, or all of these things and I have a husband, I'm respectable. If I remain unmarried, I'm a spinster to be pitied. If my husband happens to have a business, I'm respectable. If he has a title then I'm admired and sought after. Yet I'm the same woman. Who am I really?'

'You are everything you mentioned with the addition of being what you feel. That's what makes you what you are. Tell me, Clementine . . . do you like yourself?'

'In the main, I do. I do make mistakes but I try not to dwell on them.'

'You're an intelligent young woman who is as self-possessed as I am. You can be whatever your circumstance expects from you.'

'And you have a glib tongue when you want your own way. Shall we go in, Mr Fleet?'

'Call me Zachariah when we're alone together,' he said, and laughed, his casual manner taking her breath away.

'I'd rather keep the relationship more formal.'

'Be as formal as you wish, Clementine, and I'll be as formal as I consider the circumstance requires. We'll be going inside shortly, after the housekeeper recovers from the shock of having visitors and gets her clean apron on. Right now she'll be scurrying through from the servants' quarters. I should have informed them of our arrival.'

'A well-run house should be kept in readiness for visitors.'

'Who told you that, Miss Prim and Proper?'

'Mrs Crouch.'

Zachariah gave a delicate rise of an eyebrow in enquiry.

'Mrs Crouch hired me as a maid, but followed after me with

a dusting cloth and a bucket and mop, cleaning the same things I did. Her husband used to berate her for it in front of me. I felt sorry for her . . . she just needed to feel useful. It was quite a relief when I had to leave.'

'Why did you have to leave?'

'Her husband kept pinching me.'

'Where?'

'That's immaterial.'

He laughed. 'Did you reprimand him?'

'No, but Mrs Crouch did . . . and with a poker. Then she threw me out. She said I'd enticed him.'

'And had you?'

Clementine found it hard to prevent her hand from moving in defence of the spot where most of the injury had occurred, though she'd been covered in bruises in other places from his sly pinches. 'I was only seventeen and nobody would try to entice a fat, ugly toad like him, except a female fat ugly toad.'

She ignored his smile, since the incident hadn't been funny, and turned her head away to look up at the building with tears clouding her eyes. 'It's a nice house, if a little forlorn.'

'Living here should suit you then. I'm sorry I laughed,' he said gently. He allowed her to compose herself and then said, 'The sensible course would have been to let the staff go, and then board the place up when Gabriel left. I rarely come here and it cost a fortune to buy back the furnishings that had ended up in the marketplace.'

'Why didn't you board it up?'

'I'd never experienced the urge to become a family man and have the responsibility of an estate to uphold. I kept hoping Gabe would reform and come back. Now I'm saddled with it . . . and with two children who need to be raised into adulthood as part of the bargain. Luckily, the surrounding land is productive and the market gardens have been kept in order. Besides, anything that's neglected usually deteriorates and loses value.'

'The whole episode has become a challenge, hasn't it?'

He looked surprised. 'Yes . . . that would be the truth, though I hadn't thought of it that way before.'

'Do the sale of the produce and the rents cover the household costs?'

He smiled. 'My goodness, you are a practical little creature. It makes a good profit since the estate manager is hard working and honest. That profit needs to be invested properly and built on. There's something sad about a family home that has no family to occupy it.'

'A family without a home is just as sad. This house has you . . . and now it will have Edward and Iris. They will grow up here and marry, and the family will renew itself.'

'It will give me a goal to work towards. Odd really, to think I've done my best to maintain the family home, yet I was never welcomed here. I was born here, but the estate has never needed me before. I feel tolerated by it, though I should feel triumphant that I'm finally the master of it. I'm coming to the conclusion that a house owns you rather than the other way around.'

'Do you feel no pride of ownership?'

'The house will still be there after I've gone, and another will own it. I'll be pleased to have you living here with the children. Perhaps playing the country gentleman in this house will suit me and I'll grow to like it.'

She liked the thought of that too, and hoped it would come about.

A knock at the door preceded a woman's appearance. She was neat, but out of breath and still tying up her apron strings.

Clementine exchanged a faint smile with him.

'Oh, it's you, Mr Fleet,' the woman said. 'I thought you had a key. We keep the door locked during the day in case someone wanders in. I'm sorry we're so disorganized, but we weren't expecting you. Have you news of Sir Gabriel and Lady Alice?'

'Yes, I do, Mrs Ogden. Perhaps you'd assemble the staff in the hall. I have something to tell them and would like to get it over with as soon as possible.'

Her hand went to her chest, as if to keep her heart in position. 'Surely not bad news.'

'I'm afraid so.'

'The milk was curdled this morning, and there were two crows knocking at the kitchen door last week. That's a sign of bad news coming, so I knew something was going to go wrong. It's made me feel downright queer, it has, what with that other pair coming all la-di-dah and saying they were from the bailiffs and they owned the place on account of an IOU they waved under my nose. They were taking possession.

"'Not till I hear it from Mr Fleet, or Sir Gabriel himself," says I, and the baron is in some place called Australia where he's doing missionary work . . . at least, that's what the master said they'd be doing, though it sounded a bit queer to me at the time, him not being all that fond of praying.'

Zachariah strangled a laugh, but didn't interrupt her to say that the bailiffs had been in the right, as Gabe had taken a sizeable loan out on the house before he'd left for Australia – one he'd omitted to tell Zachariah about.

'Anyone could write one of those papers and put a signature to it. Likely I could do it mesself if I could write, and call myself mistress of the manor. Mr Bolton sent them packing too. "Go and see Mr Fleet in London," he says, and we haven't seen hide or hair of them since. Now here you are on the doorstep . . . the wonder of it.'

Zachariah took the opportunity to intervene when the woman paused for breath. 'The staff, please, Mrs Ogden.'

'Yes, sir . . . at once, sir.' The woman bobbed a curtsey. 'I'll send the stable lad to fetch Mr Bolton. He'll be doing the accounts, I reckon.'

Clementine gazed with interest around the hall. She'd been presumptuous about the state of the house. It was well maintained and had been kept clean and tidy.

The servants were soon lined up, faces grave or scared, some fearing that they might be forced to seek new positions, no doubt. The estate manager arrived, out of breath and with the stable lad in tow. The lad smelled strongly of dung. Both removed their hats and shuffled awkwardly, as though they were unused to being inside.

Mrs Ogden flapped her starched white apron indignantly at the stable hand. 'Take those stinking boots off and throw them into the porch, Bob Munday. The very idea, tramping the stable muck all over my clean floor.'

Turning red he scrambled to obey, exposing hose that were ragged, and equally dirty. He shuffled back into line, trying to look inconspicuous.

There were cries of distress when they were told the bad news, and a couple of the women began to weep or dab at their eyes.

He introduced Clementine. 'I expect you're wondering who this young woman is. Her name is Miss Clementine Morris. The children – that is, Sir Edward, and Lady Iris – are on their way home. Miss Morris will care for them and in my absence you will defer to her in all matters regarding the children. I would ask you to treat her with respect. I will appoint one of you to be the nursery maid. If anyone wants the job, please step forward.'

Nobody did. There was a shuffle of feet and the servants looked at each other, then a robust-looking woman stepped forward, looking self-conscious. 'May I speak, sir?'

'Do you have questions?'

'Begging your pardon, sir, and no offence meant, isn't Miss Morris a little bit young for the position? I mean . . . would we have to take orders from her?'

'Where the children are concerned, yes.'

Clementine looked at her employer. 'May I?'

When he nodded, she smiled at the woman. 'I wondered the same thing, but Mr Fleet has assured me that the late mother of the children was young, and because of that he felt they might respond better to a younger person. Also, I have some experience of teaching.

'As for giving you orders, it's obvious that you know your jobs and carry them out well, Mrs Ogden, so why should I want to interfere with that? It was suggested to me that someone called Polly might be interested in becoming the nursery maid, since she's had experience.'

Mr Fleet raised an eyebrow. 'Ah yes . . . Polly would be a good choice. I was going to suggest her myself.'

The initial suggestion had come from the coach driver who had educated her with a few bits of gossip when they'd stopped. He'd told her Polly was pleasant and obliging.

A comfortable-looking woman with a big smile stepped forward. 'I looked after young Edward when he was in his cradle, and just before they went off on their travels. He would have grown a fair bit since then, I reckon.'

'And now there are two of them,' Clementine said.

'Poor motherless little orphans,' Polly said, and tears tracked down her cheeks.

Clementine put a stop to such maudlin thinking. 'The children have much to be thankful for and we must dwell on the positive rather than the negative. With Mr Fleet's permission you may show me the nursery, if you wouldn't mind, Polly. I'm sure he's got more important things to do than sort out domestic matters.'

She followed Polly up the stairs into the nursery, leaving her employer to talk over arrangements with Mr Bolton and the key house staff. There were two adjoining rooms for the children and a playroom that would double as a classroom once they were settled in. Across the hall was a sizeable room for a nursery maid.

'Shall I have your luggage brought up, Miss Morris?'

'We'll wait and see what arrangements are made by the house-keeper. I rather think that the nursery room will be allocated to you, Polly.'

A wide smile sped across her face. 'It will be an improvement on the one I've got now. It's as small as a dog's belly button.'

Mrs Ogden bustled in to assert her position. 'Polly, I've spoken to the master and he's agreed that you're to have the nursery maid's room, as is right and proper. The children will be unset-tled to start with and may need attention during the night.' She sniffed, as though she regarded Clementine as an upstart. 'The master said you can have the guest room underneath, Miss Morris, so you're not too far away if you're needed, though I'm sure Polly can manage the children by herself.'

'Thank you, Mrs Ogden, but Polly and I are quite capable of organizing the children and the nursery routine between us.'

Mrs Ogden shrugged. 'Very well, Miss Morris. I've told the men to bring your trunks up if that's all right with you. Polly, you've got nothing to do until the children arrive, but don't think you're going to laze around doing nothing. Your new position doesn't start until the children are here, so you can make Miss Morris's bed and unpack her trunks, and then the nursery can be scrubbed nice and clean. The bed linen will need washing too.'

Clementine sighed at having created so much extra work for them. 'Can I be of help?'

'Dear me no! The master was quite adamant that you're to be regarded with as much respect as if you were the mistress of the house.' She hesitated, and then said. 'It seems odd, with you being so young.'

The same notion had occurred to her several times. 'The decision to hire me doesn't seem odd to Mr Fleet, and that's all that matters.'

'Yes, Miss Morris.'

'Good. When you go down, perhaps you'd serve some refreshment in the drawing room. It's been a long journey from London and I expect Mr Fleet would welcome something . . . and so would I.'

Her employer smiled wearily at her when she entered the drawing room, leaving Polly to arrange their domain. 'How are you coping?'

'Better than you, I think, sir. The housekeeper appears to feel threatened.'

'She got on well with Alice . . . my late sister-in-law. I expect she regards you as an upstart. Would you like me to speak to her?'

'I'd rather you didn't. Mrs Ogden has had the rug pulled from under her feet, and I can understand that. She will learn to live with it in time. I don't want the staff thinking they can run to you with every little complaint.'

'I admit that would be tedious.' He ran a hand over the prickles on his chin and he sighed. 'I apologize for my appearance. I'm in desperate need of a shave. I must go and seek out Evan, though I expect he's tidying himself up first.'

'You do look a little piratical. I'm equally dusty from the journey. Let's have some refreshment before we do anything else. That cake looks delicious.'

'Yes . . . we have an excellent cook here,' he said with a smile.

It was a week before Clementine settled in and the staff had grown used to her. Mrs Ogden thawed once she realized that Clementine's presence didn't put her own position in jeopardy. By his actions, Zachariah had made clear to all that her status was almost equal to his own. She took breakfast and dinner at the same table as him, and used the drawing room.

He looked pained at the times she questioned this arrangement, and said, 'You must grow used to it.'

Toys, books and other amusements appeared, as though Polly had raided the attic.

A basket of clothing for each of the children was delivered and unpacked. Clementine held up a miniature gown of white muslin with blue ribbons. 'I had a similar gown when I was small, only my ribbons were green.'

Zachariah smiled, saying a little wistfully one day over breakfast, 'I wonder if Iris will look like her mother. There's a portrait of Alice with Gabe that was completed just after they wed. Would you like to see it after we've eaten?'

She nodded.

It was hanging on the study wall, a room that was the domain of the master of the house. It was a gloomy and unwelcoming place. There was a similarity between the brothers. Gabriel had a more careless, rakish look to him and was smiling, but there was something insincere about it. The brothers had the same blue eyes, but where Zachariah's glance was direct and sometimes disconcerting, Gabriel's eyes were slightly hooded and seemed to have shifted sideways at the moment the stroke of the brush was applied.

Alice was pert, petite and pretty. Also blue-eyed, her gaze was fixed on her husband with an expression of adoration mixed with mischief.

'How sad for the children that their parents died,' she murmured.

He gazed down at her. 'We've all experienced such sadness in our lives, including you. I doubt if circumstance makes the grief any less.'

'I doubt that too. Would you mind if I moved the painting on to the nursery wall in the day room? It might comfort the children if they think their parents are watching over them.'

He nodded, 'I'll move it myself.'

'Thank you. Nothing will be familiar to them and it will be hard for them to adjust, but at least they'll have that.'

'You seem to know a lot about children.'

'I've seen them come and go at the workhouse. You're a nice man, Mr Fleet, and I expect you'll turn out to be a good father to your brother's children once you get used to each other.'

He had that surprised look on his face again. 'I haven't had much to do with children, and I'm terrified. Fathering is beyond my capabilities, I fear. I was thinking of buying them a gift . . . a sort of bribe. Can you suggest something suitable?'

'Perhaps a dog might be just the thing. It will give them something living to love and be responsible for.'

'Of course! It's settled then. They shall have a dog apiece . . . a perfect substitute for parents, don't you think?'

'No, I don't think that, and you're making a mockery of me.'

'Not of you, Clementine, because the children's parents didn't possess a responsible bone in their bodies while they lived. This must be the ultimate betrayal, to leave two children alone and penniless when they deserved more.'

'You're being too hard on them. Your brother and his wife didn't expect to die, and the children's poverty is merely a consequence of it. You have the means to give them a future.'

'You're mistaking me for a saint. In fact, it has just occurred to me that you are a romanticist.'

'While you are a cynic,' she retorted.

'Hmmm . . . it could be an accurate assessment at this moment. Actually, I feel more than a little angry on behalf of the children.'

'Anger is wasted on the dead.'

She wanted to touch him, to run her fingers through his unruly hair and soothe the tension and anger from his brow. It was the only thing about him that seemed to be revealed. 'I'm sorry, I shouldn't have said that.'

'Why not when you're right? Anger must be mastered, not fed. The truth is, my brother made a mess of his life and, as usual, left it to me to sort out. I resent it, but there's nothing I can do about it.'

She drew in a deep breath. You will sort out the mess, no doubt. As for resentment, the children might come to resent it too.'

'Why should they?'

'Children react as their emotions demand. They might resent you for being alive while the father and mother they loved are dead.'

'Why should they react to something so illogical?'

'Because children act on instinct rather than reason; didn't you?'

He laughed. 'See . . . you have taught me something already. Would you have me emulate my brother? I have no intention of doing so.'

'You wouldn't be able to replace him, Zachariah, but Edward and Iris could grow to respect you as much as you came to respect John Beck. Would you want to change places with Gabe?'

He gazed at her, his smile coming and going. 'I would prefer to manage my own life than the remnants of my brother's. You called me Zachariah.'

'I know . . . but you invited me to when we first met.'

'And you got on your high horse and you refused.'

'I thought the horse might prove to be too high to dismount from easily, so I changed to a lower horse before I became stiff with my own pride.'

He laughed. 'It was a ruse to divert my threatened bout of self-pity, wasn't it?'

'If so, it worked. But you haven't answered my question.'

'Would I change places with Gabe? Of course not; life is already too short.' He placed a finger over her mouth when she opened it. 'There, there, Miss Clementine, let us not argue, but dance around each other until one of us trips over their own cleverness and falls off the carousel.'

'I'll try and catch you before you suffer injury.'

'And I'll probably squash you flat. By the way, you look lovely dressed as a lady . . . and you were right . . . nobody would be able to tell that you were plucked out of a workhouse. As for the children, I'm sure they'll adore you.'

The thought gave her a thrill of apprehension. What if they grew to love her – would she be able to leave them when the year was up? Would she even want to?

She shrugged. She doubted if she'd be given a choice . . .

Three

A month passed before word arrived – four long weeks in which Clementine tried to hide her anxiety. Her employer remained calm. He wasn't a man who worried unnecessarily or flustered easily, it seemed.

She settled into the house, and while Zachariah spent most of his time in business meetings or poring over maps or account books, Clementine familiarized herself with the district, taking occasional forays outside on foot while the weather was at its best.

The countryside was dappled with sunshine and shade. Fruit ripened and the days were perfumed with the soul of summer in a way that filled her heart with joy. Sometimes the air was lively, at other times it was still, moist, and almost languid, so it hummed as the bees went about their work.

Clementine watched as each field of corn was harvested, and wagons filled with wheat rumbled past her, pulled by a plodding horse that she suspected of knowing its way home by heart.

If she was lucky, a man with wise nut-brown eyes and weather-worn skin might tip his hat as he passed and say, 'G'day my lovely, a nice one, isn't it? The good Lord has blessed us . . . indeed he has.'

When one morning the message arrived from the shipping office they were having a late breakfast together. Zachariah smiled when he read it. 'The ship lost some of her rigging in a storm, which slowed her down. She's berthed at a shipyard in the Isle of Wight undergoing repairs.'

'Where are the passengers?'

'They've been transferred to another packet, which they estimate should arrive about . . . goodness . . . in about two and a half hours!' Zachariah consulted his watch. 'We must hurry. I'll tell the stables to ready the carriage, while you get your bonnet and shawl.'

Excitement pricked at Clementine. 'I hope we have a sunny day to welcome the young man and his sister home when the mist rises.'

They were soon ready and the house was a hive of energy as people ran to and fro.

Zachariah was astride his horse and he gazed at her as she hurried through the front door with Mrs Ogden waddling after her, flapping her apron in agitation. 'Your ribbon isn't tied properly, Miss Morris. Your bonnet will fly off.'

Clementine had a quick vision of her bonnet sprouting wings and flying up into the sky, and she laughed. 'I'll fix it before we get to Poole. Do stop fussing, Mrs Ogden. We're in a hurry.'

Zachariah's smile charmed Clementine. 'That gown you're wearing is pretty, and it suits you.'

She liked it too. It was cream and the bodice and sleeves were decorated in rosebuds. The matching bonnet had green ribbons. Colour mounted to her cheeks. He'd never said anything so personal before and it was as if he had just noticed she was alive, and she was a woman.

'Thank you,' she murmured, and gained entrance to the carriage with an unladylike leap, like a startled frog going into a pond. Her bonnet fell to the ground. Zachariah reached down and lifted it with his cane before flipping it through the door on to the seat opposite.

He gazed at it and smiled. 'I'll go on ahead in case they're early.'

The mist was thin and vaporous, and it rose in wisps from the ground and hedgerows to cling to the vegetation in clusters of small liquid beads. Pretty crystals of hanging light trembled on the spiders' webs. They were an enticing lure for any unwary insect drawn into its false glitter.

Clementine loved it here. The countryside drew her in and she could feel her roots clinging to the earth, making her feel part of it, as if she'd come home. Had her father's spirit come home from Waterloo? Perhaps her parents were together again.

'Give me the wisdom to care for these little orphaned children,' she whispered, and then as an afterthought, 'And it would be very helpful if you could help me to handle Zachariah Fleet. He's so very aggravating, at times.'

Shafts of sunlight began to spear through the mist, and then the nebulous vapours thinned and evaporated into the sky. They had left the farmlands behind; some fields that were still waiting to be stripped undulated before the breezes like waves upon the sea. The air was drenched with golden dust as the field workers went about the harvesting.

To her left was a wide tract of undulating heath. To her right stretched the outer reaches of the harbour. The tide was in and the water reflected the sky on its grey and purple surface. When the tide was out the water disappeared, leaving a surface of piquant rippled mud behind. There was an island in the middle of the harbour they called Brownsea, and not far ahead, a quay where the ships tied up. Their masts stretched tall into the sky and swayed back and forth. There was no sign of Zachariah up ahead, but when they reached the quay he strode from the shipping office and helped her from the carriage. His eyes went to the bonnet and he grinned. 'I'm glad to see you managed to tie your ribbons.'

The ship had just berthed and passengers came ashore. There was a small crowd of them, the rest of them destined for London. A couple appeared pushing two children across the gangplank before them. Mindful of the danger a small gap of water between quay and ship presented, a seaman stepped forward and lifted them across to solid ground. The couple joined them.

The children were thin and pale, apart from bright fever patches on the girl's cheeks. They clung together, shivering, though the morning was not cold, and looked around them, bewildered, as though they'd just woken.

'Edward.'

The boy's pale blue eyes settled on Zachariah and there was no recognition in them. The man he was with took a grip on the boy's shoulder and gazed sourly at Zachariah. 'I expected to deliver them to the house.'

The girl's nose was running and she sniffed loudly.

'I think Iris has a fever,' Clementine whispered.

Zachariah handed her an immaculate handkerchief. 'Take this; you might need it.'

'I'll get them settled into the carriage and start out for home while you talk to the couple who were with them. Would you ask them if they've been in contact with any infectious diseases?'

As they crossed to the children Iris began to cry. 'I don't want to go to the workhouse. We'll be good.' The woman grabbed her arm and shook her, hissing, 'Be quiet, you little rat.'

When the girl shrank towards her brother, anger ripped Clementine apart. She would have liked to slap the woman's smug face, but she could only go as far as to intervene by pulling her hand away and thrusting the woman aside. 'Leave the child alone.'

'Who d'you think you're talking to?' she said.

Hands going unbidden to her hips, Clementine looked the woman up and down. The woman's face was pale and her mouth mean and tight. A quick glance told Clementine she might be

big enough to bully children but she wasn't too big for her to
throw into the harbour if the need arose. 'Enlighten me.'

There was a soft chuckle from Zachariah, then he drawled,
'Don't start a brawl on the quayside, Miss Clemmie. It's not lady-
like.' He stepped between them and said to the woman, 'I'm the
children's legal guardian, Zachariah Fleet. I have papers with me
to prove it. This young woman is the children's governess.' He
nodded in Clementine's direction. 'Take my brother's children to
the carriage if you would. They're shivering.'

'I'm thirsty,' Iris whimpered, and Zachariah instructed the coach
driver to purchase some ginger ale from a vendor.

This time the man detained Edward, and with a tight grip
anchored him to the spot. 'You're not taking these youngsters
until you've settled what you owe us,' the man said. 'They've
been sick for the past couple of days so that will cost you extra
. . . and I've got an account to be settled for your family's burial.
And then there's money in IOUs to settle.'

'I imagined there might be. I take it that you are Thomas
Sheridan and this woman is your wife, Emily Sheridan.'

'That's right.'

'Well, Mr Sheridan, there has been no suggestion that your
accounts won't be settled. I've just been through them with the
agent, who received them yesterday in the Royal Mail packet.'

The man and woman exchanged a glance, which wasn't lost
on Zachariah for his eyes narrowed and he said, 'Come now, I'm
a businessman. You surely didn't expect me to hand over cash
without question and proof of expenditure?'

'There have been extra expenses since then.'

'Of course there have,' he said pleasantly, 'and we shall discuss
them. What's wrong with the children? Have they been ill for
long?'

'A couple of days, and it's just a cold in the head.'

'Have they seen a doctor?'

'There was no medical officer on board, and besides, it's only
just started. They do nothing but whine, and the girl tells lies,
so don't you believe a word they say. Gabe and Alice spoiled
them when they needed to be disciplined.'

'Your opinion of my brother and sister-in-law's parenting is of
no interest to me whatsoever. I'll examine your more recent

claims and we'll settle up in the shipping office.' Zachariah beckoned to the carriage driver. 'Sort out which luggage belongs to us, Stephen. Mrs Sheridan will oblige you by helping, no doubt.' He strode off towards the agent's office, expecting the man to follow.

When he didn't, Stephen cracked his knuckles and stared at the man. 'Let the bairn go, Tiger, else there will be ructions. I can guarantee you'll come off the worse for offering me the encouragement.'

The man did as he was told, but he offered Stephen a challenging stare, saying, 'Don't you brats move an inch while I'm sorting this out, else it's the workhouse for you.' He hurried after Zachariah.

Clementine took Edward's grubby little hand in hers and offered him a cup of ginger ale. 'Come along, young man, drink this down and let's get you both into the carriage while your luggage is being dealt with.'

Edward dug his heels in and fear leapt into his eyes.

'If we move he'll beat Edward when they come back, and they'll take us to the workhouse instead of Mama and Papa,' Iris whispered.

Stephen cracked his knuckles again. 'I'll throw Mr Sheridan into the harbour before he gets to you, young sir.'

'And I'll throw his wife in after him and a fish will bite off her nose,' Clementine threatened.

The woman hastily moved off towards the luggage.

The giggle Iris gave turned into a cough as she nudged Edward and took the ginger ale. The pair of them gulped down the contents of the cups, which were then handed back to the vendor.

Soon they were on their way. The children were quiet, and they huddled together. Iris's eyelids began to droop. Clementine laid her down and was about to tuck a rug around her when Edward snatched it from her hands and covered Iris with it himself. The poor child was hardly out of infancy, yet he was doing his best to look after his sister.

For a while Edward stared a challenge at her, but he was unsettled, and obviously unwell, and trying to fight off sleep in a swaying carriage became impossible. Eventually he gave in and sank into a corner. His eyes drifted shut. He grunted in a sleepy protest when she gently lowered him on to the seat and pulled a knee rug over him.

'Poor lad, it's quite safe to sleep now. Nobody will hurt you,' she said, and she gently kissed his cheek.

'Mama,' he whispered, and she wondered if anyone had told them that their parents were dead – indeed, did they even know what the word dead meant?

The children smelled peculiar, as if they hadn't been bathed for some time. They would be a host to parasites too, she imagined.

Her skin began to crawl and she felt the need to scratch.

The poor little creatures were wearing thin shifts and very little else apart from scuffed boots and a rag around their shoulders. Tears filled her eyes. She sniffed back a sob, glad that nobody was there to observe her weakness.

When they reached Martingale House the second coachman came from the stables and helped Stephen with the luggage: three trunks that were taken upstairs.

'Mr Fleet wants them placed in Sir Gabriel's room.'

Zachariah didn't sleep in the master bedroom, but in a room on the other side of the staircase and one floor below hers.

There was a smaller trunk, securely locked, of the type that looked as though it might contain personal items, or firearms.

'Where shall I put this one, Miss?'

'With the other two, please, Stephen. I imagine it will contain personal items and Mr Fleet will open it at his leisure.'

Polly arrived, her smile beaming over the children like sunshine. 'Hello, my dears. Come along with me. We'll soon get you settled.'

Polly had anticipated the children's needs. The pair dipped oatmeal biscuits into cups of creamy milk, still warm from the cow, and then gulped down the milk, leaving foamy moustaches along their upper lips.

Though they were bewildered by everything going on around them they didn't protest when their dirty clothing was removed and tossed aside.

Polly chatted as she busied herself, giving angry little spurts of information like steam spouting from a kettle. 'Look at those

poor little motherless youngsters. Thank goodness they have Mr
Fleet to take them in.'

'There was nobody else, I understand.'

'Bless the goodness of his heart, especially after what they did
to him.' She fell quiet for a moment. 'Sir Gabriel had a temper
on him sometimes. He liked having his own way, and he wasn't
quiet like his brother is. Mr Fleet is a kind man in his own way,
and always polite. He's a deep one, though. You can never tell
what he's thinking, and from what I've heard his family cast him
out.'

Although she shouldn't encourage Polly to gossip, Clementine
couldn't help but ask, 'Why?'

Polly lowered her voice. 'I heard that he was born a caulbearer,
and because he was quiet and different, and was as clever as a
cart-full of monkeys, they were scared that he had some sort of
power over them.

'What's a caulbearer?'

'Someone born with a veil of skin over the face, so they look
as though they have no features. The midwife cut it away so he
could take his first breath, though his mother and father wanted
it to stay in place so he would suffocate. They never took to
him, and eventually they sent him away to live with a relative, a
church cleric who promised to drive the devil from him.'

Poor Zachariah, no wonder he had nothing but scorn for the
church. 'That's merely superstition, Polly.'

'Could be, but why else did his parents cast him out?'

She found herself leaping to Zachariah's defense. 'Because they
were bad parents, that's why.'

'Everyone in the house knew he'd been born with a caul. We
just weren't allowed to mention it.'

'And I'd rather you didn't now, especially in front of the
children.'

Edward kept gazing around him, and Clementine sought to
refresh his memory so he would develop a sense of belonging
here. 'This used to be your nursery when you were a baby. Polly
looked after you then.'

Her words brought no response from Edward.

They were placed in a bath of warm water already prepared
for them, then soaped until they were covered in lather and

smelled faintly of lavender oil. Once rinsed off, Clementine examined them for lice, and was pleasantly surprised. She cracked the few adult fleas that scurried through the children's hair seeking refuge. 'I think they picked these up on the way over from the island, because I can't see any eggs.'

'Look at them bruises, poor little loves,' Polly said.

'You must remember they've been a long time on a ship.' She looked at Edward and smiled. 'Did you fall over on the moving deck much?'

Edward hadn't talked so far, except in his sleep. Now was no exception. He just stared at her.

Iris gazed at the door, whispering, 'Mr Sheridan said he'll cut Edward's tongue off and eat it if he talks.'

'Mr Sheridan isn't here.'

'He'll know, and he'll come when it's dark. He said so.'

Edward clapped a hand over his mouth and gazed through terrified eyes at her.

'I won't let anyone hurt you here.' She took his hand from his mouth and wrapped a towel around the boy before giving him a hug, though she measured a certain amount of resistance in him. She released him, inviting instead, 'If you whisper in my ear, nobody can hear you but me. Tell me if you remember anything.'

The boy put his mouth against her ear, but although he grunted and made some hesitant noises, no words came out.

Clementine decided not to push him. 'Don't worry, Edward, I know your voice will come back without you even trying, and when we all least expect it to. It will be a wonderful surprise. I'm going to snip some of your hair off so it's just below your ears. It's nice hair, curly like your uncle's.'

'Is mine curly?' Iris asked.

'Not as curly as Edward's, and yours isn't as dark. It's pretty though. It looks as though it's been painted with sparkles of sunshine.'

Looking pleased by that description, Iris came over to where Clementine was going about her task. 'You've got spots,' she told Edward, matter-of-factly, 'and I've got some on my belly. They itch.'

Polly said, 'Goodness, look at those bruises and sores. Shall I go and ask Mrs Ogden for some salve, Miss Morris? She's good at doctoring.'

'The bruises will go away by themselves, though a little witch hazel might help them along. I think the children may be suffering from chicken pox. If so we must use something to soothe the itch, aloe perhaps.'

'What's your name, Miss?' Iris asked.

'Clementine.'

The girl giggled. 'Lemontime is a funny name.'

'It certainly is. After you've eaten you can go to bed until the doctor has examined you.'

'Will our mama and papa be there when we wake up?' Iris blurted out, looking up at her with eyes as watchful as those of Zachariah. 'Mrs Sheridan said they'd be waiting for us.'

Edward looked towards the door and began to quiver, like a little dog eager for a walk.

Curses on the Sheridans, Clementine thought. 'When your uncle arrives home I'll ask him to come and talk to you about that. He shouldn't be too long.'

Zachariah arrived home an hour later and Clementine went downstairs to intercept him. He'd just placed his hat and gloves on the hall table.

'My apologies for being late. My business with the Sheridans turned out to be more complicated than I expected. You look serious. Are there problems with the children already?'

'Several. The biggest one is that they haven't been told their parents are dead, and expected them to be here waiting for them.'

'I see . . . Did you enlighten them?'

'I thought that particular duty should be yours, since you are their guardian.'

The sigh he heaved was heavy. 'Yes . . . of course it should be. I hadn't considered that they might be unaware of the circumstances.'

'Also, I believe they've been badly treated. Edward, in particular, is too frightened to speak. Iris is the more confident of the two.' She described Edward's reaction, and recounted what Iris had said. 'Edward believes Mr Sheridan will come in the night and cut off his tongue and eat it if he talks – so he no longer talks, though he tried.'

Zachariah sucked in a breath and his hands curled into loose fists.

'Now who feels like starting a brawl?' she said softly.

'You're right. The children are young and impressionable and they need someone to protect them. What else, Clementine? I can see you're not done.'

'The third problem is that both children seem to be suffering from an infectious disease. From the nature of the blisters I think it could be chicken pox rather than smallpox, and a mild dose at that. The symptoms are not too severe, but it's best to make sure so I've sent for the doctor to come and examine them. I hope you don't mind.'

'Not at all; you must do what you think is in their best interest. Mr Bolton will take care of the accounts on my behalf. We shall also consult with the doctor about Edward's lack of response. It may be that he just needs to grow used to us. I will speak to the children about their parents afterwards. They'll be upset, I imagine.'

'Yes . . . but small children are resilient, and they adjust to their situation fairly quickly. Whether they live in poverty or luxury, and especially when they're sad, they're needful of any kindness and affection that's offered to them, even if they don't respond as well as you expect them to.'

'That's something we've lacked in our own childhoods, so we should be experts in knowing what to provide. We shall have to make sure they have plenty of both. I'll be kind to them and you can supply the affection.' For a moment Zachariah's eyes gazed into the distance, his vulnerability all too apparent as if he was trying to recall what affection and kindness felt like. Then his gaze shortened and his eyes slid towards her. His voice was unsure, salted with his imagined inadequacy to carry out such a task. 'I'm not used to children and I can't promise to be perfect, but I'll do my best.'

Clementine felt like hugging him, but doubted he would appreciate such a gesture from her.

Four

The doctor endorsed what Clementine had suspected.

'It's chicken pox. Use a soothing lotion, and try to prevent them scratching the scabs off when they form, else they'll be left with scars.

'As for the other business . . . there's nothing physically wrong with the boy's tongue or mouth that I can see, and no reason why he shouldn't talk in time. Give him plenty of activities to keep him occupied, both mental and physical. Encourage him by singing around him, and he may join in. Singing does wonders for children with speech impediments. I also advise you to keep to a routine. It will build him up and give him confidence.'

But first the children had to learn that they were orphans. And judging from Zachariah's face he wasn't looking forward to telling them. 'I'll fetch the picture of my brother and his wife and we'll go up together,' he said.

When they got to the nursery he propped the painting against the table with the back towards them and cleared his throat when the children gazed expectantly at him. 'There's something I must tell you, and I can't express how sorry I am that it's necessary. Your mother and father won't be returning home again. They have lost their lives in an accident.'

Edward stared at him.

'I thought I lost a doll once, but Edward had hidden it and I found it again,' Iris said.

'It's not that sort of lost, Iris dear. Your parents are dead . . . I'm afraid.'

'What does dead mean?'

Zachariah gazed an appeal at her.

'They've gone to be angels in heaven,' Clementine said.

'Why can't we go to heaven and be angels as well?'

'Because you've got healthy bodies to live in.' And before Iris's curiosity prompted more questions, Clementine added, 'We will all go to heaven one day.'

'My body's got itches. So has Edward's.'

A quick glance showed Zachariah's eyes filled with amusement, even though the situation should have been serious. He told them, 'They'll go away in time if you don't scratch them. Now, listen carefully while I tell you what has been arranged. This house used to belong to your father, who was also my brother. You will live here and Miss Clementine will be in charge of you, with Polly helping her. I work in London and travel a lot, but I will visit here as often as I can to find out how you're getting on. Do you understand all that?'

Edward nodded and Iris said, 'Yes, sir.'

'Good . . . and because your father was my brother that means we are close kin, and you may both call me Uncle Zachariah. I've got a painting of your father and mother here. Would you like me to hang it on the nursery wall? That way you'll see them every day while you're growing up, and you won't forget them.'

Iris gave a little cry when he turned the portrait around and her voice choked up, though she had a puzzled expression. 'Is that our mama and papa? Mama is pretty with all those jewels on but Papa's hair is funny and he looks stern. His eye looks odd.'

'Your mama and papa were much younger when that was painted. It has a date on the back and it was painted before Edward was born.'

'Perhaps he was wearing a wig when this was painted.' Although the family resemblance wasn't marked — in fact it was too slight to really signify — it was there. Clementine said, 'You look a little like your mother, Iris.'

'But they don't look like our mama and papa, do they, Edward? I want my mama . . . I miss her,' she said, sounding so miserable that tears pricked Clementine's eyes. 'That man said they'd be here waiting for us.'

Clementine remembered the ache of losing her own mother, and she'd been older than Iris. 'I know, darling. Perhaps the artist wasn't very good.' She drew the girl into her arms and rocked her back and forth while she wept. After a little while Iris relaxed and Clementine knew she was asleep.

Edward had turned away from them and had pulled the covers over his head. Zachariah gently patted the boy's back while he tried not to cry, but eventually he gave into it, releasing sniffs and sobs.

Pulling the covers back, Clementine stooped to kiss his wet cheek. 'Try to be strong for Iris, my dear. You're too young to lose your parents, but you have your uncle, and you have me and there's Polly. It's all right to cry, Edward. Will a hug help you feel a little better? That's what your mother and father would have done, I expect.'

When the boy nodded and scrambled from under the covers it was Zachariah he hurled himself at.

For a moment Zachariah looked almost panic-stricken by the contact, then he placed his arms awkwardly around the boy and patted his back. 'If I could bring your parents back to you I would. They loved you, Edward. You must always remember that.'

Clementine wondered when Zachariah had last hugged anybody, when he gave her an appealing look that stated he needed help. His expression quickly turned to exasperation when she ignored it and smiled at him.

Edward clung to him like a little monkey to its mother. Suddenly the boy gave a series of long, shuddering sobs.

'Oh God,' Zachariah whispered, but after a while his eyes closed and his fingers caressed the boy's scalp through his silky hair.

'It will be all right, Edward,' he whispered. 'I loved your father, too, and he sent me you both to be cared for. Now you must rest, so you'll recover quickly from your illness. It's been a long, busy day, and we have many things to do together before I return to London. One of them is a surprise, but it can wait for a week or so.'

Edward looked up at him and Clementine could see the question trembling on his lips. She held her breath, willing him to ask it, but he didn't. Instead, he reached up and tentatively touched Zachariah's face.

Zachariah smiled and gave him a final squeeze. 'Into bed with you now. Polly will stay here with you.'

The children recovered rapidly from their illness and life took on some normality as they edged into a routine.

So her charges wouldn't get bored, Clementine divided the day into sections. The mornings were spent doing easy lessons that consisted of drawing, or shaping their letters on a slate and repeating the sounds they made, for they were hardly out of infancy. Once they gained mastery of the chalk and slate she intended to progress to a pencil and she'd introduce other subjects. The afternoons were spent being more active, exploring the countryside and playing games. She told them a story each night before they slept.

Edward still didn't speak, and he had bad dreams where he thrashed around and called out, but it was more noises than words. Sometimes he shouted out the name Jonas, and he'd wake, wide-eyed and trembling. Since Polly was a sound sleeper it often fell on Clementine to provide comfort for him. She'd hold his little body in her arms, rock him back and forth, and sing him a lullaby until he relaxed again.

On the last day of the children's confinement it was as fine a morning as could be. The children were lively and couldn't keep still. Who could blame them when the sun was shining outside and the countryside was begging to be explored. Zachariah came into the nursery in the middle of lessons. He was dressed for the outdoors and wore riding boots. 'Good morning everyone.'

'Good morning, Uncle Zachariah,' Iris said, and Edward gave him a wide smile.

'I think it's time we picked up the children's surprise, don't you, Miss Clemmie?'

'They're supposed to be having lessons, and I'd be obliged if you'd stop calling me by that ridiculous name. The children are picking it up.'

He ignored her complaint. 'Here's a lesson for you.' He picked up the chalk and wrote a word in large letters. 'Can either of you tell me what that says?'

Iris puzzled over it, her forehead screwed up in concentration as she mouthed the letters. 'It's GOD!' she shouted. 'Are we going to church? I hope not. It smells like pepper there and it makes my nose itch until I sneeze.'

His mouth twitched. 'Not until Sunday, I believe, and only then under duress, because Miss Clemmie insists it will be good for our souls. You almost got the word right, Iris. Clever girl.'

Iris gazed proudly at everyone at the compliment. Like all children she responded to praise.

Whether Zachariah knew it or not he didn't have to try very hard to attract the affection of the children. They would miss him when he returned to London. She'd miss him as well, she thought, and gave a faintly surprised smile. Now, who would have thought that?

Edward gave a snort and the expression on his face was suddenly alert. He was almost quivering with excitement.

'Edward knows what it is.' Zachariah ruffled his hair. 'I knew a mind reader in London and he taught me how to do it.' Closing his eyes he placed a hand on Edward's forehead. 'Think of the word.' After a few seconds he opened them again. 'You're thinking the surprise might be a dog.'

Edward vigorously nodded his head.

'Well done, Edward. You're right. Polly, fetch their capes and hats if you would.'

'Yes, sir.'

'You can get yours on too, Miss Clemmie.'

She knew she was fighting a losing battle when she told him, 'The doctor said they're not out of quarantine until tomorrow.'

He placed a finger over her mouth with just enough pressure to form her lips into a kiss-shaped pout around it. His blue eyes gazed intently into hers and his voice was a quiet drawl. 'I insist.'

If she parted her lips she'd be able to draw his finger inside and bite it.

He withdrew it with a smile, as if he'd truly read her mind, leaving her shocked by the blatant exposure of her own thoughts.

The carriage was waiting for them, the hood folded back so they could enjoy the day.

Twenty minutes later they stopped outside a cottage where the front garden was awash with summer-scented flowers and the air was thick with the frantic hum of bees around the roses, as they gathered the last of the pollens and carried it back to their hives. The side gardens were crammed full of vegetables.

The cottage stood in the middle of the village, and people came out to lean on their fences and gossip together when the carriage came to a halt. She imagined that most of the men living in the village worked for Zachariah.

A woman opened the door and bobbed a curtsy, her smile wide and welcoming. 'Come in, Mr Fleet. You as well, Miss.

I've been expecting you.' Her eyes widened as her glance went to the children. This is never Master Edward, the young sir who belonged to Sir Gabriel?'

'It certainly is, Mrs Mason.'

'My goodness, he's grown tall since I last set eyes on him, like a stick of rhubarb . . . though he was an infant then, and kicking up a stink as the reverend gave him his name. He's grown, all right.'

'Yes . . . well . . . he would have. This is his sister, Iris.'

'You're a pretty little miss, and called after a lovely flower with purple petals that grows at the edge of the pond. Though some be all golden, so when they come out together they look right royal.'

Edward had edged closer to Zachariah, while Iris smiled and said graciously, 'Thank you, Mrs Mason.'

Zachariah allowed Clementine through with the children first, then he removed his hat and bowed his head to enter through the low doorway.

Inside, the spotless little cottage smelled deliciously of baking.

'Will you take some refreshment before the children get acquainted with the pups? It doesn't do to rush these things and they're having a sleep.'

In anticipation of the event Mrs Mason had already spread the table with a spotless white cloth and her best blue-and-white china. Before too long the table was laden down with freshly baked scones, and there was clotted cream and strawberry jam to spoon on to them. Steam curled from the spout of a brown earthenware pot and there was milk for the children.

Edward and Iris tucked into the scones and soon wore creamy moustaches and expressions of bliss. They tried not to appear too eager or impatient as they waited for the adults to finish, but they exchanged looks and now and again forgot they were supposed to sit still, and jiggled about. In the back room one pup yelped.

Edward's gaze went to the door when others joined in. Mrs Mason smiled. 'It sounds like they're waking up. Would you like another cup of tea, Mr Fleet? A surprise is always better for the waiting.'

'I think not, Mrs Mason. We'd best get on before the children burst out of their skins.'

The woman filled a bowl with warm water and picked up a clean cloth. 'We'll wash those hands and faces before you see the pups lest you get dog hairs stuck to them. I've put two aside that I thought might suit. They're the smallest of the litter and just the thing for young children . . . But that's not to say that they're not strong and lively.'

Edward reached for Clementine's hand and clung to it with a sticky tightness. He wasn't ready to trust strangers. 'I'll wash their hands, Mrs Mason,' she said. 'Perhaps you could fetch the pups in.'

The dogs were plump little creatures, with pointed ears and soulful faces. The brown one had white socks and a matching patch on its back. It immediately pounced on Iris, full of energy.

'It looks as though that one's chosen you,' Zachariah said.

Iris began to giggle as she fought a losing battle with her pup trying to lick her face. She tickled its belly.

The second one was black and wiry-haired, and one of his ears flopped. 'He has long legs so I do reckon he's going to be a gangly dog that can run like the wind.'

The pup gave growling yaps when Edward picked him up, but it was all for show because its thin tail wagged furiously.

Clementine exchanged a smile with Zachariah at the sound of laughter coming from the children.

'My dog smiles so I'm going to call him Happy,' Iris said. 'What will you call yours, Edward?'

Still absorbed with his puppy, Edward gazed at it, his head to one side, his expression contemplative. It was a look he'd adopted from Zachariah. The boy was going to miss his uncle when he returned to London.

'Well?' Iris said.

'Shush, Iris. I'm thinking.'

'You spoke,' she said.

He gazed round him, gave a secretive little grin and lowered his voice. 'Of course I did . . . how else can I call my dog to heel? I'm going to teach him to bite Jonas.'

Iris gasped. 'You're not to say that name in case the orphanage comes to take us away . . . remember?'

Fear came into Edward's eyes. 'I forgot. I'll call him Wolf because he looks fierce.' He placed the dog on the floor a few inches from his feet and crouched, his hands held out. 'Here, Wolf . . . come.'

The pup wobbled along for a few steps and flopped on to Edward's feet. 'See, it's easy. They can't hear me from where they are.'

'Who can't hear you?' Zachariah asked him. 'Who is Jonas?'

Edward's voice was a murmur as he answered, 'Nobody.'

Iris said, 'How did you make Wolf do that?'

Edward gave a modest shrug.

Determined not to be outdone, Iris copied him. 'Come to me, Happy.'

Happy rolled over on his back and waved his legs in the air.

When Zachariah exchanged a smile with her, Clementine realized how clever he'd been by finding a practical method to trick Edward out of his state of solitude. First the mind-reading trick, then a gift that demanded he use his voice . . . and all done so casually. She wondered if Zachariah had noticed the exchange about the name. Of course he had; he didn't miss much.

'I should congratulate you for helping Edward to find his voice,' she said, when he escorted her to the carriage. 'Was it planned?'

'The dog was. The mind-reading . . . well, let's call it a gift.'

She laughed.

'You don't believe me?' He placed a hand on her forehead and gazed into her eyes. 'Think of something.'

She tried to but could only think how blue and guarded his eyes were and wondered why the wry twist to his mouth was just one-sided. Her breath seemed to leave her body as her glance was suddenly absorbed into his, as if a window had opened and invisible forces had pulled her through it. Her mouth tingled and she wished he'd kiss her, though she knew he wouldn't. She wondered desperately what it would feel like if he did.

Panic filled her and she felt angry – at herself and at him. She was a servant, nothing more, but he made her feel as though she was his equal. She would be glad when he went back to London.

'Hmmm . . . perhaps not,' he said with a chuckle, as if he really had read her mind, and had found her lacking in everything he desired in a woman.

Twisting away from him she ignored his hand and scrambled into the carriage unaided.

Five

The season slipped quietly into autumn and the landscape covered itself in a cosy patchwork quilt of warm colours.

Seated astride his grey, Zachariah gazed at Martingale House. He'd already stayed longer than he'd intended to and it was time he left. There were business matters to take care of in London. He wanted to take stock and sell off some of his more risky investments.

Cotton prices in America had plunged, and the wheat harvest had been poor. He also had investments in overseas railways. Luckily most of his wealth was in gold or property, rather than paper. He liked to get things settled in a timely manner lest an opportunity to profit from it was lost.

Unlike Gabe, who had gambled for the pleasure of the risks involved. Zachariah knew when to apply caution, when to stop and wait until markets improved. He suspected there would be a recession in America before too long and that would have an effect on his own fortune. The upside of that was the property market would contain some bargains.

There was a sense of reluctance inside him to leave. He'd not expected to discover such a strong sense of duty in being responsible for two orphaned children. He admitted it had been a painful trait to recognize in himself. Edward in particular had formed an attachment to him. Odd when the child hardly knew him. Zachariah had offered him very little encouragement. Iris was a sweet child, outgoing and dainty.

He could see only a passing resemblance between the children and their parents – or had that been a defence? That bothered him somewhat. They hadn't seemed to recognize Gabe and Alice in the painting. Then there was the name that had slipped out. Jonas. '*I'll teach him to bite Jonas*,' Edward had said, evading Zachariah's question. Also their manners were slightly rough, though they were improving.

He shook himself, willing himself not to look for faults.

Clementine was smoothing the rough edges from them. Circumstances made children change to suit their environment, so they wouldn't make themselves noticeable by being different. He'd expected the impossible, two fully trained children complete with impeccable manners – children that wouldn't cause him a moment of trouble. They would be trotted out in their Sunday best every time he visited so he could smile his benevolent-uncle smile on them and bask in their adoration. What he'd got was a pair of underfed strays who were strangers to him, both of whom were bewildered and afraid to trust anyone.

Iris was fairly confident, though tended to look to her older brother in times of stress. Even at her young age she displayed some of the outgoing feminine charm that he hoped would stay with her. That, she'd inherited from her mother, except the girl had an intelligence that needed nurturing, so she didn't grow up empty-headed. Clementine's influence would ensure that Iris would contribute an informed opinion to a conversation in the years to come.

Edward was scared of his own shadow. Over the past year or so he'd been so badly treated by someone, probably the Sheridan couple, that he'd become frightened of his own voice. The boy had nightmares, and he looked nervously around him when he spoke, and avoided the dark corners. There was caution in him where Zachariah would have expected to see his father's brashness.

Of one thing Zachariah was certain: Gabe would not have allowed his children to travel with a couple who would treat them badly, since he'd doted on the boy.

It was by luck rather than design that Zachariah had found the key to unlock Edward's tongue. When Clementine had congratulated him over using the dog he'd accepted the praise as his due.

He spoke her name softly, tasting it on his tongue and allowing it to drift away on the soft breeze. 'Clementine . . .'

He smiled. She was no respecter of his feelings or his position in life, and although she made him uncomfortable at times, there was nothing false about her. He liked her; perhaps liked her too much – in fact he was acquiring a strong affection for her, which was an unexpected and not altogether pleasing development.

The week before had been a case in point. He'd gone up to the nursery on a whim when Polly had been eating her evening meal. Iris had been already asleep. Edward was leaning against Clementine's shoulder as she sang him a lullaby, her fingers gently caressing his scalp.

Zachariah had backed away without being noticed when she'd lowered the boy to the pillow and kissed his cheek. Warmth, longing and envy had churned inside him for something he'd never experienced.

He remembered those same beds, occupied by two boys. He remembered the goodnight kisses . . . but not for him. His shyness had been interpreted as sullenness, and he'd become brash to attract the attention he coveted. All Zachariah had wanted was to be as loved as his older brother – a brother he'd worshipped.

His immaturity had not allowed him to see the shallowness of his sibling hero, or the manipulation Gabe employed – not until later. His father had been a braggart, and had barely noticed him. His mother had called him a graceless lout. His father had barely been cold in his grave when Zachariah had been sent away from home. It had been the ultimate betrayal.

His mind snapped back to the present. His mother would never have held him in comfort against her like Clementine held Edward. He knew then that he'd made the right choice by employing her, relative or not, though it had been instinct at the time.

He headed up the incline towards the house. There was a task he must undertake before he left. He must inspect the contents of Gabe and Alice's trunks, and store anything of value in a secure place for the children to have when they were older.

He handed his horse over to the stable hand, then went in to see Stephen. 'We'll be leaving for London in a week. Evan can take the stage a day or so earlier. I'll leave Ben here with the carriage and the grey for the use of Miss Morris and the children. We'll saddle up the carriage horses.'

'Yes, sir.'

He went up to the master bedroom. It was clean and tidy. The cupboards were empty and impersonal. It was a splendid room with woven red and gold hangings and a painted ceiling. The bed could have accommodated six people and the room had a view over the fields. He'd never been able to bring himself to move in there.

When he opened the trunks his nostrils were assailed by a musty stale smell. There was a jumble of clothing, mostly dirty. He recognized one of Alice's gowns, almost rags now. She'd been such a clean and dainty woman. It had been too bad of Gabe to bring her down this low with his excesses. There was a gold-set brooch pinned to the bodice in the shape of a posy of flowers, and fashioned from red stones with pearl centres and enamelled leaves.

He removed it and set it on the dressing table. That would be kept for Iris to wear when she was a little older, along with any other feminine trinkets. He must remember to look in every pocket for valuables, but if Gabe had been impoverished he would have gambled away anything of value, or sold them. The smaller trunk contained some books, letters and writing implements.

He felt furtive going through his brother's belongings, and rather grubby. These trunks contained the sum of his brother's life. They contained very little of value to bequeath to the family he'd begotten. In fact, they reeked of failure.

He sensed someone was watching him, and the long mirror offered him a reflection of Edward peering around the door. Zachariah smiled and said, 'Come in and join me, Edward. Is anyone looking after Iris?'

He nodded. 'Polly is. Wolf wandered off and Miss Clemmie and I went to look for him. She went down to the kitchen to see if he was there. She said the cook feeds him too many scraps and he'll get fat and won't be able to chase the rabbits away from the vegetable garden.'

'She's right.'

'I heard a noise and thought . . .'

'That I was your father?' Zachariah smiled at him. 'It's all right for you to think that, and to talk about him. Sometimes I wish I were him.'

Edward opened his mouth then shut it again when Zachariah patted the bed. 'Some of his personal things are in this small trunk. Climb up on the bed. You can sort it out if you like. Put aside anything you want to keep for yourself and for Iris when you grow up, but not clothing because it's dirty and old and I'm going to burn it.'

Edward scrambled on to the feather mattress. 'Papa was going to buy our mother a new gown when he got some money. He said it would be made of silk and he'd build us a big house with a ballroom, and the governor would dance with her and she'd look so pretty that he'd be the proudest man in the world.'

Zachariah's throat constricted and he pulled the boy to his side in a quick hug. He was well aware of Gabe's love for his wife, and for that alone he envied him. Gabe's superficial charm and his hopes and dreams would have amounted to nothing though, and in the end he would have disillusioned his son. 'Your mother was a lovely lady.'

'Iris climbed on a chair and scribbled whiskers on their picture, then she fell off the chair and bumped her head. Polly is trying to wash the scribble off.'

'What about Iris, is she hurt?'

'Miss Clemmie kissed her better.'

It sounded like a good deal to Zachariah.

'Why did Iris scribble on the picture? We must look after that painting because it's the only image we have of your parents.'

'Iris was upset. She said the picture doesn't look like them.'

'And what do you think about that, Edward?'

He shrugged. 'I don't think so too, but sometimes it does. Miss Clemmie says it's because I'm trying to forget what happened, and that's all right.'

'Would you like me to move the portrait? There's a space in the dining room.'

He nodded. 'I don't like looking at it. Sometimes I think Miss Clemmie is our mother, especially when she hugs me. Miss Clemmie's eyes are brown and shiny . . . like Wolf's eyes when he sees his dinner. Hers are pretty, but Wolf looks fiercer.'

Zachariah tried not to laugh. As compliments went, it was well observed. 'Her eyes certainly are pretty,' he said and then he changed the subject. He didn't want to think about Clementine with her shiny eyes, else he'd think about her all day.

'Here's a ring with the family crest on that used to belong to your great-grandfather. It won't fit you until you are older so we'll put it in that box on the dressing chest. You can come and look at it any time you want to. There are a few small pieces of jewellery that belonged to your mother, as well. Iris can have them when she grows into a young lady.'

Edward dipped into the trunk. 'Here's a spyglass. It's got my papa's name on it.' He pulled it from the case.

'He'd want you to have it now, not wait until you're grown up. It looks as though it needs a good clean because the leather case is going mouldy. I imagine Ben will help you with it. He knows how to clean brass and leather.'

Edward looked down at the telescope in his hands. 'You can see a long way into the distance with it. Papa and me used to watch the kangaroos.'

'I've never seen a kangaroo. What does it look like?'

'A big rabbit, bigger than Papa even. It has a long tail and short front legs. Papa said it uses its tail to stop itself from falling over . . . it has a pouch at the front where the baby kangaroos sleep.' He moved to the window and placed the telescope against his eye, screwing the other one up. 'There's Miss Clemmie. The wind is blowing her hair about.'

Zachariah joined the boy and physically stopped himself from snatching the instrument from Edward's hands so he could get a closer look. He smiled when he saw her in the meadow. Clementine had no right to look so charming when her hair was flying about like a tail on a horse in a gale. When she picked Wolf up he stretched up to lick her face and she screwed up her mouth and her eyes and shuddered.

Both he and Edward laughed, though Zachariah couldn't help but wonder what she tasted like.

'Edward, I've found him,' she called out softly as she came up the stairs a few moments later. 'Where are you?'

Zachariah gave Edward time to scramble back on to the bed before he answered for the boy. 'We're in here.'

She appeared in the doorway and Wolf began to yelp when he saw Edward.

Zachariah smiled. If she'd been his wife she'd have a maid to take care of such matters as wind-blown hair, so as to delight him with her appearance. *If she'd been his wife!* He scotched that thought. He liked her as she was, completely natural, lacking in artifice and . . . unmarried! 'The wind has unravelled you.'

Her free hand went to her head and she laughed, unconcerned. 'So it has. Is Edward being of help?'

He took a moment to imagine that length of hair in his hands, flowing through his fingers like a river of amber silk . . . to imagine her face turned up to his, her eyes wide, her expression a cross between expectation and alarm at what the outcome might be. He felt the strength of his manliness in his reaction to her presence . . . but whether it was strength or weakness he couldn't afford to indulge it . . . not here. And he couldn't even betray what he was thinking. She'd walked away from other employers for lesser reasons.

'These are his father and mother's trunks.'

Edward gazed up at her, his eyes bright and pleading. His features were lean, like those of a miniature greyhound, for his body had only just begun to display a small amount of childhood plumpness. Both he and Iris had regained energy quickly as their illness came to a conclusion, but Clementine made them rest every afternoon so they didn't tire themselves out.

'May I stay with Uncle Zachariah?'

'If he doesn't mind, though he looks to be busy.'

Zachariah smiled at the boy, not wanting to disappoint him. 'Edward is no trouble. Besides, I've nearly finished. It's a task I should have done earlier. I'll bring him back to the nursery in time for tea, I promise.'

'Perhaps you'd care to join us, Zachariah? I can ask the cook to send up some extra muffins.'

'Thank you, Miss Clemmie, I promise to be on my best behaviour.'

A smile winged his way before she left, taking the dog with her. Picking up some crumpled and smudged pages with writing on he left the small trunk for Edward to explore by himself, while he went to the window to examine the papers.

There was a letter addressed to him in Gabe's handwriting, dated six months before.

> *My esteemed brother, Zachariah*
> *My life is in ruins. I am up to my ears in debt.*
> *I have arranged for my beloved children to return to England at the end of the spring. They will be supervised on the journey by a married couple called George and Sarah Sheridan, who we met when we were prospecting for gold.*
> *George is a lawyer. Although I haven't known them very long,*

I'm convinced they are trustworthy. You will recognize Sarah by the colour of her hair, which is russet. I have assured them you will cover my IOUs and process several expenses on my behalf. This, I know you will do. You are the only person I've ever been able to trust, Zach, and you don't have it in you to leave my children in need.

They set sail in two weeks' time. I have already sent an account of my debts to your lawyer and friend John Beck. I beg that you honour them on my behalf. As always, Alice stands by me. Until we have made enough money to return home and run Martingale as it should be run. I've discovered a small amount of gold and am hopeful that more will be forthcoming. I'm determined to turn over a new leaf.

There were no new leaves for Gabe to turn over. Gabe had forgotten that the estate no longer belonged to him by right. Did he really think Zachariah would have paid his debts once more, and then hand the estate back to him to bankrupt all over again? Anger flickered through him, and then he grimaced. It didn't really matter now, since Alice and Gabe must have died not long after he'd written this letter, and certainly before he'd had time to post it.

I implore you to care for my children as you would if they were your own, my dear brother, since nothing is their fault. Love them if you can, though I know your nature is dispassionate. At the very least treat them kindly until Alice and I can hold them in our arms once again.

  Your brother,
  Sir Gabriel Fleet Bt.

The addition of the formal title was a reminder to Zachariah that Gabe took precedence, and at the time he wrote the letter he expected the estate to be returned to him, as part of the family property attached to the title. Gabe's intentions were always thwarted by his inability to carry them out, since he was inherently lazy. But Zachariah's brother had always been a master of manipulation.

Zachariah's glance fell on Edward and he experienced warmth

in the region of his heart. He hoped Edward didn't take after Gabe in that way. As for himself, Zachariah considered, was he as dispassionate as Gabe had suggested? He thought not. He just seemed to lack the ability to allow his emotions to express themselves fully.

Self-controlled, Clementine had called him, which wasn't a bad thing to be. He smiled, thinking she knew damned little about men, and that any control they might possess depended entirely on the circumstances. He did know he was thinking about Clementine more and more. She was an attractive creature, even if she did have a sharp edge to her tongue, and he was a healthy man who appreciated the flirt of her skirt and the whisper of female fragrance she left in her wake. And thereupon lay the danger. Laughter huffed from him. He was loath to label such appreciations as love. It was simply a bodily reaction.

Edward looked up at his laughter. The box was almost empty and he was surrounded by a heap of bits and pieces. Here was Gabe's pocket watch, stopped at four-thirty, the silver case with its crest tarnished. He ran his thumb over the face. Was that the time Gabe had entered the water to rescue Alice?

Because their meeting with the Sheridans was acrimonious he hadn't asked them where Gabe and Alice had been interred. It must have been quite a flood to sweep him away, because Gabe had been a strong swimmer when they'd been boys. Zachariah wondered where his brother's pistols were. In a pawnbroker's establishment along with any jewels Alice had owned, he imagined, as they had been on several occasions.

Perhaps he should ask another male's advice about love. 'Can you remember what love feels like, Edward?'

The boy thought for a moment and nodded. 'It makes you laugh as though somebody is tickling your stomach. And it feels like being thrown in the air and being caught by my papa. Sometimes it feels like Miss Clemmie when she strokes my head and kisses my cheek and I pretend to be asleep.'

Now Edward had found his voice he was growing increasingly eloquent. Despite his young age he was obviously a typical male, one who would instinctively feign an action to court a woman's favour. The thought of tickling Clementine's stomach was highly appealing, but throwing her up in the air wouldn't be at all dignified, especially if he dropped her. As for pretending to sleep with his head against her breast and waiting for a kiss . . . 'You like Miss Clemmie, don't you?'

Edward smiled and nodded.

'So do I. We'd better go and get our tea before she comes looking for us.' As he pulled the boy up he tossed him in the air. Edward screamed with laughter as he landed safely back in Zachariah's arms, then he began to giggle. Hoisting him on to his back, Zachariah set off at a slow gallop for the nursery with Edward clinging precariously to his back.

'Giddy-up, horse,' Edward shouted.

'Hang on tight,' Zachariah warned as they headed along a corridor and up two flights of stairs.

An alarmed Clementine came to the door with Iris clinging to her skirt and her hand to her heart. 'I heard Edward call out.'

He lowered the giggling boy to the floor. 'We were indulging in a little horseplay.'

'Horses is it? No wonder you're both late.' She pursed her lips and sighed with a faked exasperation that didn't fool either of them. Iris followed suit, the action of such a diminutive female making him grin. Obviously children learned by copying their elders. He reminded himself not to cuss when he was around them.

Lord . . . if Gabe and Alice knew that their daughter was going to be raised by such an independently minded female as Clementine, they would turn in their graves. Although the pair of them had been scatterbrains, they'd given every indication of being more conventional in their ways than Zachariah had ever been.

'Don't forget to wash your front hooves before you eat,' Clementine said. 'The horse trough is behind the curtain.'

Zachariah sent her an apologetic look when Edward whinnied, loathing to abandon the game. 'Yes, Miss Clemmie. I'm not usually so childish, you know.'

'Why not?'

Her eyes were definitely as shiny as Wolf's, but with a hardly repressed amusement rather than doggy greed.

Taken aback he stuttered, 'I have no answer to that, except to remind you that I'm not a child.'

She smiled. 'I suspect you never have been a child, and the

game with Edward has done you both good. You should be childish more often.'

'It's not in my nature to be childish.'

'Until, or unless, we are confronted by it, do we ever know what our natures consist of?'

'You're right; we don't.' He smiled. 'One day you might surprise yourself, Miss Clementine.'

Caution shimmered around her like a dusty cloud as she appeared to consider the possibilities of his meaning, and then she shrugged. 'I'd rather not.'

'Don't you trust yourself?'

'Sometimes I do. At other times I'm not so sure. It rather depends on the situation at the time. What has this got to do with you behaving like a child?'

'Nothing . . . it was just a diversion. I'll be going back to London at the end of the week.'

'Oh . . . I see.'

'Was that dismay in your eyes? Will you miss me?'

She rallied fast. 'You're my employer. It wouldn't be seemly for me to miss you. The children will, and Edward in particular since he's still insecure. You've stepped into his father's shoes and he's attached himself to you. When you leave he might feel abandoned.'

As Zachariah had felt abandoned on many occasions. He'd survived the parting from his parents and so would Edward. He would have to. But while he understood her concerns, he resented being pressured by the guilt that this snippet of a woman was layering on to him.

'What would you suggest, that I take you all with me? That would make the drawing-room tongues flap.'

'Ah yes . . . we can't have that.'

Was that sarcasm? He mentally stamped on the flicker of ire he experienced. He would not allow her to rile him. Yet the next moment he found himself explaining, when he really had no need to.

'I'm doing the best I can for the children. I can't promise to be perfect but I will never abandon them. Edward needs to grow up in the home he'll eventually inherit and learn how the estate is managed.'

'He's an awfully small boy to take the weight of the estate on his shoulders.'

'It will give him a sense of pride to understand what's expected of him in the future, and work towards it. He also has to get used to me coming and going. My business doesn't run itself.'

'Yes, of course. I hadn't taken that into consideration. I'm sorry, I wasn't judging you . . . I just feel sorry for Iris and Edward.'

'You will all have to cope without me, and since you've made it clear that missing me is an unseemly trait for a woman to have, it will make it that much easier for you to console the children until I return.'

'You sound awfully pompous at times.'

Did he?

He glanced at the portrait. His brother was several shades lighter now Polly had effectively used her scrubbing arm on his face. 'The last time I saw Gabe that pale colour was when he downed a glass of brandy our father had left on the table. I'll take the portrait down with me when I go, and see if Mrs Ogden has any ideas. Could be that the canvas just needs a good all-over wash. Perhaps we should arrange some drawing lessons for the girl if she's going to scribble moustaches on all the ancestors.'

'I'll talk to her and warn her against such action. They are such a handsome bunch, and it would be a shame to spoil them.'

He heard her trying to stifle a giggle as her eyes met his. They had a devil of mischief dancing in them. He could have kicked himself for allowing her to get the upper hand, yet he chuckled. 'If I show signs of becoming an old windbag I'm certain you'll tell me. Come now, Clementine, let's join the children at the table before the muffins get cold. I'll tell them I'm going away while we have tea, so they can get used to the notion, and I'll caution Iris myself on Gabe's behalf.'

The children took the news without too much distress, though Edward said with consternation, 'Will we have to leave here and go to the orphanage?'

'No . . . this is your home now. I thought I'd made that clear.'

'For always?'

'For always, Edward, I promise.'

'Even if we'd done something bad?'

'Of course . . . You're children. I don't expect you to be perfectly behaved all of the time.'

Zachariah exchanged a quizzical glance with Clementine when Edward heaved a sigh of relief and smiled at Iris. He must have been more worried about his sister's embellishment of the portrait than he'd let on.

'Mr Bolton and Ben will sleep in the male servants' quarters while I'm away, in case they're needed,' he told Clementine.

'It's so peaceful here; I can't imagine there being any trouble.'

'I'm not expecting any, but sometimes we have an occasional vagrant knocking at the door who might be the worse for drink. You should feel safer knowing the men are within shouting distance.'

'I'll shoot them,' Edward said, suddenly finding some empty courage and a mythical pistol to settle the imagined threat with.

Zachariah said firmly, 'You'll do no such thing, Edward. You're much too young to handle a firearm. Besides which, you haven't got a pistol. Mr Bolton and Ben will handle it.' Fleetingly he wondered again what had happened to Gabe's firearms.

Edward opened his mouth and then shut it again before looking down at his hands and saying fiercely, 'You'll come back, won't you, Uncle Zachariah?'

How transparent the child was in his desperation to have someone to love him – someone constant in his life who he could look up to. Zachariah remembered the feeling so well. But although Zachariah could sympathize, Edward had to toughen up, despite what he'd been through. He remembered the power of bribery. 'I'll be back halfway through December, all being well, and I'll stay until spring. I'll buy you a pony and when you've learned to look after it, then I'll teach you to ride it.'

Edward's eyes began to gleam.

'In the meantime I expect you to train Wolf. He's your dog and you're responsible for him, but you mustn't allow him to think he's the master. Ben will show you how to go about training him; he's good with animals. Allow Iris to join in with Happy.'

'Happy is too daft to learn anything. He just rolls on his back and waves his legs in the air when you speak to him.'

'Happy will learn from Wolf's example, you'll see.' Zachariah drizzled some honey on to a muffin and gazed at the pups while he held it ready to eat. 'You'll soon learn, won't you, Wolf? Happy will learn from you?'

Taking Zachariah's attention as an invitation, Wolf gave an ungainly leap and snatched the muffin from his hand.

'God's truth!' Edward's piping curse was buried under a deeper one from Zachariah, but which was similar in sentiment.

Wolf dropped his prize when he stopped to lick the honey from his snout. The morsel was snatched up by Happy, who darted under the table with it and swallowed it in one gulp.

A moment later the dogs were seated side by side, their wagging tails sweeping the floor, and gazing up at the table through eyes shining with expectation.

Iris dissolved into loud giggles.

Clementine pointed a finger at the door. 'Out!'

The dogs slunk into the next room where they gazed soulfully at them from under the bed with their eyebrows twitching.

Clementine laughed. 'What did you say about teaching dogs manners, Zachariah Fleet?'

It was a low punch, but there was very little he could retaliate with. 'Allow me to beg your pardon for my bad language, Miss Clemmie.' He noted the beginnings of her smile. She'd expect him to set a good example, so he gazed at the boy. 'Edward?'

'Sorry, Miss Clemmie. It just slipped out of my mouth.'

'Well, next time catch it on your tongue before it does.' She gazed from one to the other. 'Apology accepted, gentlemen. Now . . . let's get on with tea.'

Six

Zachariah intended to leave before dawn. In order to avoid a lengthy, and possibly tearful goodbye from the children, he'd said his farewells to them the night before.

Iris had been sleepy against his shoulder. Circled by Clementine's arm, Edward's head lay against her breast as Zachariah told them a story.

Edward was in just the place Zachariah wouldn't have minded

occupying. He remembered the boy telling him he liked being cuddled and sometimes pretended to be asleep when really he was still awake. He envied him.

A couple of candles provided light. He was pleased with his choice of staff for the nursery. Polly was competent and pleasant-natured. Clementine came up to his expectations in every way . . . well, almost. When he finished his story she tucked the children in bed and began to sing them a lullaby.

The scene filled him with warmth: the low, tuneful voice, the shadows dancing in the firelight and the children's faces, so innocent and sweet as she kissed them goodnight – it brought a lump to his throat and a feeling that he didn't want to leave Martingale House and his newly acquired family behind. But leave them he must.

Polly hadn't returned from her dinner yet, and Zachariah moved to the window to gaze out into the star-sprinkled darkness. 'The sky's pretty, isn't it? There's a full moon tonight and it's just beginning to rise behind the trees. Come and watch it with me,' he called out.

Clementine joined him and they watched the glow increase as the moon floated up into the sky, orange at first, then yellow, then bursting with white light that chased away the shadows.

'We should have allowed the children to stay up and watch it.'

'There will be many more for them. I'll be sorry to leave.' He took her hand in his. It was a small hand; the palm softer than it had been when they'd first met. He'd expected her to jerk it away, but she didn't. Clementine Morris surprised him at every turn.

'It won't be long before you return.'

The warmth from their bodies filled the space between them, and the gentle curve of her breast was half-hidden now by a sensible country shawl, one that Mrs Ogden had fashioned for her out of a blanket. 'Is there anything you need bringing from London when I return?'

'I have nothing in London to bring.'

'Except me.'

She ignored that. 'I'm contented with what I have.'

He gently intertwined her fingers with his. It was a sneaky move, and he smiled when she didn't seem to notice – or if she did, he met with no resistance, which was encouraging.

Zachariah had never seriously considered the plight of people who didn't have family to turn to in times of trouble, probably because he'd always been competent at managing for himself, by fair means or foul. But there was a world of difference between men and women, especially if children were involved.

Though he supported charity, he'd never given the recipients of it much thought except to feel pleasure that he was in a position of being able to provide the needy with a bowl of broth and a roof over their heads. Pleasure? Smug might be a better word. He'd survived worse attacks on his conscience, and sometimes he was too critical. 'Has this become your home?'

'I've always had to make my home where I can. This is the best one so far, but I can't get too attached to it, for one day it will no longer be mine.'

'Why won't it?'

'Children grow into adults. The time will come when they don't need me.'

'Ah . . . yes. At which time you'll be firmly settled into spinsterhood.'

'The thought of being a spinster doesn't bother me since I've been one from the day I was born . . . But the thought of being a spinster without means of support does bother me.'

'I could do something about that, I expect.'

He couldn't tell her there might be a legacy from her grandmother, when they weren't even sure they had the right person. He hoped John had made some progress on that front.

He could read practically every thought that went through her mind from her expressions. Hope was followed by uncertainty. Did she think he was offering to set her up in a little country house? Would she consider it if he suggested it? It would be the one commodity she had to sell.

A brief light flickered in her eyes as she seemed to consider the options open to her. Then they narrowed. 'I daresay you could.'

Obviously she wasn't thinking he might wed her. She was thinking the worst. Was *he* thinking he might wed her? He ran the ball of his thumb gently across her palm, admitting to himself that it had crossed his mind. Would it be so bad to be married to such a lovely woman?

'What are you doing, Zachariah?' She sounded reproachful rather than angry and a gentle tug parted their hands.

'Good Lord, I was tickling your palm.' He managed an expression of surprise, one that didn't fool her for a second, since she pressed her lips together in that way women did when they were exasperated.

'Your pardon, Clementine, my thoughts were elsewhere. I was thinking I could invest some of your salary. You will be earning forty pounds a year, roughly double the average wage. If I invested half of that, in ten years there could be enough to give you the means to buy modest accommodation, and provide you with a small annuity for life. You would be young enough to use it as a dowry should you wish to wed and have children of your own.'

'I don't see any reason to pay a man to marry me. Let him pay me to marry him.'

They both laughed at the outrageous suggestion.

'May I think it over?'

'You can. Stephen and I will be leaving early in the morning, so let me know when I return. Will you kiss the children goodbye for me?'

When she nodded he took her face between his hands and kissed her as tenderly as he knew how. Her mouth was as soft and pliable as a peach, and it positively invited this sort of attention. He was taking a risk, he knew, but it was something he'd longed to do. She might hit him, or she might run away. No matter, he'd simply go after her and bring her back. He looked into her eyes afterwards, shining in the moonlight, and he ran his finger down her nose and smiled.

She didn't return the smile, but took in a deep breath. 'Don't tell me that was a goodbye kiss for the children,' she said, sounding underwhelmed by his attention.

'No . . . it was one for you. You gave every indication of enjoying it.'

'What I felt is immaterial. You took a liberty that was certainly uninvited, and I've never been kissed like that before.'

'Like what?'

'So . . . yet so . . . Oh, I don't know.'

'Intimately personal?' he suggested, feeling the need to rumple her up a bit.

'Yes . . . it was unexpected. I should never have allowed it.'

'Have you been kissed before at all?'

'No . . . yes . . . no . . . not willingly, but yes . . .'

'That's very clear. I'm sorry . . . did you not enjoy it then? I could have sworn you liked being kissed. If we tried it again I might be able to improve on it?'

'You're impossible, Zachariah Fleet,' she hissed, and to his amusement she stamped her foot. 'You should be ashamed of yourself.'

'For being a man? Oh, I am. I'm totally ashamed. I'd much rather be a woman.'

She giggled. 'You're a liar!'

'Yes . . . it's something I'm good at.'

Edward made a noise that sounded suspiciously like laughter, and he turned over in his bed.

Polly signalled her advancement up the stairs with the wavering light of a candle and a heavy tread.

Clementine turned and walked away from him with a rapid step that made her buttocks twitch.

Spinster or not, one day he'd kiss every inch of her naked body, including that provocative rear, until she was helpless and quivered from head to toe.

By bedtime he regretted his action when an obverse thought slapped him on the head and flattened his erotic ramblings. What if Clementine ran away because of his attention?

Doubt was an impossible bedmate so he tossed the thought aside with a dollop of bravado. What if she did? He could soon get someone else.

But would that someone else be as perfect as Clementine?

He lay in the darkness in his day clothes, covered by the quilt to save time in the morning. All he'd have to do then was pull on his boots and his outdoor wear. His ears were pricked, his mind pondering on Clementine's perfections and listening for any sounds of her departure.

In the distance a fox barked, its mind on mating . . . another answered with several yips.

He chuckled. If he had a mating call it would be a long, drawn-out howl of frustration at the moment.

Midnight chimed and he began to relax. Clementine wouldn't

run away at this time of night, and she wouldn't sneak off after he'd gone, leaving the children with only Polly to console them. By the time he returned from London she'd have forgotten his kiss. And he wouldn't allow it to happen again.

Though she had such a soft, shapely mouth . . .

The next morning Zachariah was surprised to find Clementine in the warmth of the kitchen, her apron almost swamping her as she juggled the heavy skillet to cook their breakfast. At least he and Stephen would have something warm in their stomachs for the journey.

Her hair was in a long, slick braid that gleamed as the candlelight played on it, for it was still dark beyond the window glass.

'What miracle is this?' he said. 'My cook seems to have lost several years and has shrunk overnight.'

She gave him a cool look that would have withered most men.

'I do hope we're going to part as friends. Don't send me away with a frown, Clementine.'

A tiny little crease appeared at the corner of her mouth as she pursed her lips, and then she gave a peal of laughter. He wanted to pursue the train of thought that had led to it but there wasn't time.

'How many sausages would you like?'

How mundane the ordinary sausage was when a man's mind was occupied with satisfying a more carnal appetite. Still, there was enough breakfast to feed an army. 'Two, and some ham and a couple of eggs, please.'

Stephen appeared at the door. He was a calm, muscular man of about fifty, with a wife, grown-up children and grandchildren in London.

'The horses are ready when we are, sir. They've got a bit of ginger in them this morning. They sense the journey I reckon, and they know they won't have a carriage to pull. Ben's walking them around.'

'Pull up a chair and eat some breakfast, Stephen. What's the weather going to be like?'

'Hard to say with the mist hiding the sky, and darkness still upon it.'

Clementine set a plate of food in front of Stephen and filled their cups with steaming tea.

'I'll wrap what's left of the breakfast between two chunks of bread in a muslin cloth, in case you and Stephen get hungry later on.' Deftly, she made two parcels that would fit easily into their saddlebags.

Then they were ready and outside, swamped in long coats and country hats that were more suited for the road than the smarter tall ones.

Stephen touched the brim of his hat before he mounted the fretting horse. 'Thank you for the breakfast, Miss Clemmie, it was much appreciated.'

So, the casual name he'd given her had reached the staff quarters, Zachariah thought. 'Kiss the children for me,' he said, and a fiery blush flooded her cheeks. He laughed, pleased to be having the last word – and even more pleased with the thought that she'd be waiting for him when he returned.

Then they were on their way. He looked back to where she stood in the mist. It clutched her with long wraith-like tendrils and closed around her like a thorny briar, as though she belonged to the house and it intended to keep her captive.

Cold against his face, the mist formed into icy unwelcoming droplets on his coat.

He'd looked back into a world of grey swirling shapes. The house, the children and Clementine had all disappeared, like characters from a fairy tale. Perhaps they'd never really existed in the first place. There came a moment of panic. Had he imagined it? Were the dead trapped in a layer of other lost souls who were trying to find their way out of limbo and into the light?

He grinned reluctantly. Who would have thought he had such childish imaginings still hidden inside? The thought that he did have them clung to his mind for a few moments. He could understand why Edward had bad dreams now. He pinched his thigh until it hurt, something he used to do as a child to remind himself he was alive, and breathing.

The horse under him squealed when a bird exploded from the undergrowth. It bucked a couple of times, its powerful rump bunched as though it was on springs. Zachariah only just managed to get it back under his control. Stephen came up beside him and spoke soothingly to the horse. The animal was used to his voice and after a short time he settled down.

'The mist has spooked them. Best we ride side by side until it lifts, sir. They're used to each other's company in the shafts.'

Zachariah was pleased he had Stephen as a companion on the journey. The coachman didn't talk unless he was called on to answer a question or had something worth saying. Nevertheless his reticence was companionable, and he didn't complain like Evan did.

When they turned on to the road, Zachariah had the oddest feeling that Martingale House had cast him out now the heir to the title had moved back in.

The town of Poole was just beginning to stir. Luggage carts trundled by, pushed by muscular men, and were loaded up with provisions in baskets. Barrels stood in queues on the quayside waiting to board, and there were sacks of flour, crates of clucking chickens and squealing pigs, a small keg of rum.

It occurred to Zachariah that if he were to visit the children on a regular basis, he might be more comfortable travelling in one of the small sailing boats that ferried passengers round the coast.

When they reached Christchurch the weather began to lift. It was going to be a fair day. They stopped at an inn for a second breakfast and a tankard of scalding tea. Keeping Clementine's package for a midday repast, they pushed on, making good time until they and the horses showed signs of fatigue. Slowing down they made it to the next inn just as night fell.

The ostler took the horses from them and ran a practised hand over their quivering flanks. 'This is as good a pair of carriage horses as I've ever seen. Nice lines and well muscled. Have you come far today?'

'The other side of Poole.'

'Dorset, aye? There's some nice countryside down there. I reckon these lads need a good rub down and a feed. Are you staying the night, sir? You'll have to share.'

Zachariah nodded.

'Good, tell my wife when you go in, if you would.' He held out a hand. 'I'm Joe Makin.'

'I'm Zachariah Fleet, and this is Stephen Harbin, my head coachman and groom. The condition of my horses is down to him.'

The three of them shook hands and then Makin nodded. 'You go inside, sirs. My good wife has a side of mutton on the spit and potatoes roasting in the tray underneath. It should be ready to serve in half an hour or so. My son will fix you up with a tankard of ale and a room, in the meantime.' He led the horses off towards the stable block, talking to them all the way.

The children would be sleepy-eyed and ready for bed now, Zachariah thought. Clementine would be reading them a story. She might make one up, or read something from Grimm's fairy tales, unless she thought it was too frightening.

'I wonder if the children are all right,' he said to Stephen, throwing his saddle bag on to one of the beds.

'Reckon so. They were poor little scraps frightened of their own shadows when they arrived. If I may say so, Mr Fleet, you seem to be doing right nicely by them.'

'Miss Clemmie does most of the work.'

'Aye. Miss Clemmie has got the mother instinct strong in her. She should marry and have a couple of little 'uns of her own.'

Alarm jolted through him at the thought of losing a perfectly good substitute mother for his wards. 'Most of the single men in the district are too old to father a child.'

'Age doesn't mean they can't perform when the need arises. I had an uncle who fathered a child when he was eighty-two.'

Zachariah stared at him. 'How old was his wife?'

'He didn't have any wife to start with. He got the itch with a servant girl and fathered the child on her. She was only young, about sixteen, but a sly young cub. He married her when her stomach began to swell. She kept him at it, wore him out, and when he died six months later she got everything he owned.'

'What about the child?'

'Turned out there wasn't one. Like I said, she was a sly young cub.'

'He died happy, and there must be worse fates.'

Stephen grinned. 'Miss Clemmie wouldn't need to do such a thing – not with her looks. One day a handsome young man on a fine horse will come riding by and will sweep her right off her feet.'

Zachariah threw Stephen a dark look. 'He had better not unless he wants his arse peppered with buckshot. That young woman is employed to provide motherly services for my two wards. She has signed a contract to that intent. If anyone wants to court her they'll have me to get past first. Now, wipe that smirk off your face and let's go down and sample the ale. My throat feels as though it's coated with sawdust.'

Without the carriage and a female to cater for they made good time. The nearer they got to the more populated areas of London the worse the smell became and the more debris littered the streets.

'Has the Thames always stunk this badly?'

Stephen grinned. 'Sometimes it's worse. We've been breathing in clean country air for the past few weeks so we're bound to notice the difference.'

They turned into Russell Square about seven in the evening, where Zachariah's home was discreetly situated behind a façade of pale brick and stone, and wrought-iron balconies. It was in the middle of a row of identical buildings – one of which belonged to John and Julia Beck.

Leaving the horses with Stephen to take to the stable block where they'd be tended to, he said, 'Take a week off to spend with your family, Stephen.'

A few minutes later and Zachariah stood inside the hall listening to the clock tick. The house was well furnished and neat, big enough for him, but not too big. The few servants needed to maintain him and the house knew their jobs, and mostly went silently about them.

He entertained now and again, usually with his peers. He didn't have anyone he'd consider a close friend, apart from John and Julia, and he looked on them as his mentors. He loved them both, as far as he knew how to love.

Inside him a small knot of loneliness appeared.

He dismissed it and sent a messenger to John and Julia to inform them of his return and to tell them he'd call on them tomorrow after he'd rested. While a fire was lit in his room and a hip bath was being prepared, Evan tutted over the dust in his hair and the state of his clothes as he set a tray with a brandy decanter, a jug of water and a couple of glasses on the table.

'Stop fussing, Evan. What do you expect when I've just spent two days on the road? My hair can wait to be washed until the morning. In the meantime I just want a thorough wash, followed by a bowl of broth and a good sleep.'

Zachariah had enjoyed his shallow bath, especially when Clementine slid into an empty space in his brain and bathed with him. He imagined her sitting at the shallow end, naked to all glory, her calves over his thighs. He imagined more – taking her legs in his hands and sliding her gently towards him.

It occurred to him that he was thinking of her too much for his own good. Leaning forward he plucked the jug of cold water from the table and poured it where it would do the most good, nearly yelping from the cold medicinal dowsing.

Afterwards, with his robe tucked cozily around him and his stomach full, he stretched his legs out towards the fire in an attitude of complete relaxation and thought of Clementine some more. He wondered if he had the energy to get into bed. But the need to sleep was not yet forthcoming, and besides, he heard voices.

A few moments later Evan poked his head round the door, disapproval written on his face. 'Mr Beck is here to see you. I told him you were about to retire and he said he'd only keep you a few minutes.'

Zachariah had too much respect for John Beck to turn him from his door, however inconvenient the time.

'Thanks, Evan. Send him up.'

John looked agitated. 'I'm glad you're home, Zachariah, and I'm sorry to burst in on you like this, but there's something you should know. In fact, I was just about to send a messenger to Dorset and ask you to return. An unexpected problem of quite a serious nature has arisen.'

'And I think I know what it is.' Zachariah dismissed the hovering Evan, saying, 'Do that in the morning, Evan. You can wait downstairs to see Mr Beck out.'

After the door had closed behind the servant, Zachariah turned to his mentor. 'I've been half-expecting you. Take a seat, John.

As you have always told me, two heads are better than one on a problem.'

Folding himself into a chair, John gazed at him. 'How did you get to hear of it?'

'It's merely suspicion on my part, nothing else, though I think Clementine suspects that all is not as it should be. The children are not what I expected, they are too cautious . . . Edward in particular. They did not recognize the portrait of their parents, and if there's a family resemblance it's so vague as to be almost non-existent. I'm beginning to suspect they're not my brother's children at all, but imposters.'

John gazed at him in astonishment. 'They're not your brother's children? What nonsense is this? Of course they are; the likeness is unmistakeable. I don't understand, Zachariah, we seem to be talking at cross-purposes with one another.'

'Cross-purposes? If there's another problem I can't think what else it can be. I hope it's nothing to do with Clementine. I don't know what I'd do without her now.'

John drew in a sharp breath. 'Be that as it may, Zachariah. Another young woman who calls herself Alexandra Tate has turned up, one who professes to be Howard Morris's daughter. As such she is claiming the legacy . . .'

Seven

Zachariah didn't know what he'd expected, but it certainly wasn't this – not when life had just settled into a relatively calm flow, where everything was falling nicely into place.

He eyed his comfortable bed, the covers turned back on the soft feather-filled mattress and quilt that waited to embrace his tired and aching body. He wished John had waited until morning because there was nothing he could do tonight, except stay awake and worry about it. But then, if John didn't tell him he'd only worry about what the problem was . . .

He didn't know whether to laugh or cry. Long ago he'd learned that every problem has a solution if patience is applied to the discovery of it, and he appreciated the counsel John offered on occasion, as his way of life dictated.

'You'd better tell me about it.'

'While you were away I was approached by an elderly gentleman who introduced himself as Samuel Tate. He said that he and his late wife had raised a foster daughter from birth, and he thinks she may be the heiress we are seeking.'

'Could she be an imposter?'

'That's what I thought at first . . . one of the young women most probably is.'

Zachariah frowned. 'Did you tell Samuel Tate about Clementine or the children?'

John raised an eyebrow at that. 'I didn't consider they needed to be informed, since the children have nothing to do with the legacy claim, and we are still investigating Clementine's background. The strange thing is she's got a similar background story. Her father is Howard Morris, who died at the battle of Waterloo, though she has always used the name of Tate.'

'Her mother is . . . no . . . don't tell me. It's Hannah Cleaver, yes? The same mother as Clementine.'

'I wish it were that easy. Samuel Tate said her mother was one of his distant relatives, a young girl called Alicia Bishop, who was taken advantage of by the soldier.'

Zachariah frowned as he tried to recall a face to fit the name. 'The name's slightly familiar but I can't quite place it.'

John's smile had an ironic curve to it. 'Then you'd better brace yourself, Zachariah.'

Brace himself? Good grief, hadn't there been enough shocks?

Obviously not, for John now informed him, 'Alicia Bishop is the maiden name of your late sister-in-law . . . Gabriel's wife.'

Zachariah stared at him, wondering if his comprehension had deserted him altogether. 'Ah . . . of course it is. Gabe had always referred to her as Alice, and so did everyone else.' As it sank in, he felt as though his stomach had been punched into holes. He cleared his throat. 'Surely Alice wouldn't have been old enough . . .'

'According to Samuel Tate, Alicia was considered precocious at a young age, and promiscuous when it was obvious she was with child. She was hurriedly married off to Howard Morris, who died a few weeks later.

'When the infant was born it was arranged that she be left with the great-uncle and aunt in Portsmouth when he died. They were a couple whose youth had been left behind and who had no children of their own, so they were eager to care for the baby. Alexandra's foster mother died three years ago and her foster father wants to see her settled before he dies. She didn't know of her parentage until recently . . . except she thought she was a Tate. To learn that she was otherwise upset her.

'The thing is, Zachariah, money has changed hands in the form of a small annual stipend, arranged by the church where Samuel Tate did some clerical work and lay preaching. I've spoken to church officials but they will not reveal where the money came from. They regarded me with suspicion, as the officials of most conventional and established religions do. You might have more success.'

'I doubt it. I'm looked on with disapproval by those in the establishment.'

'Who are envious of your success. Unfortunately the reputation of your family always precedes you.'

'The Bishop and Fleet families were efficient at the distribution and disposal of unwanted children. Unfortunately they dig them up again when the smell of money is in the air.'

'I'd prefer it if you'd wait before you pass judgement on this, Zachariah. Samuel Tate wants nothing of her Morris grand-mother's legacy unless the girl is entitled to have it. His honesty impressed me. I wondered if Alicia told your brother about her previous marriage and the daughter she gave birth to.'

Zachariah was beginning to see Alice in a different light. Having his flirtatious sister-in-law's past uncovered made him uneasy. She was dead, and although gossip wouldn't bother her or Gabe now, to all intents and purposes they'd left two children behind who needed to remember their parents with respect.

Had he respected his own parents? He shrugged. That was a different matter altogether since he'd hardly ever had any until John had taken him in hand. He could think of no reason to cast him out of the family except for the Bishop family to have complete control of Gabe, for he would never have harmed his brother in any way. The fact was, his disposition had been such that they hadn't liked him.

But John was right . . . he was being judgemental. Alice and Gabe had loved each other dearly, and people were entitled to make mistakes in their youth. 'I doubt if Gabe knew, though love is very forgiving, they say.'

'What about Clementine; where does she fit in?'

'For Clementine to be awarded the inheritance she'll have to prove that Howard Morris was already married to her mother when he wed Alicia and sailed off on his final journey. He was a bigamist, yet he catered for both his daughters as best he could on his small salary. What does that say about him?'

'Either that he cared what happened to his children, or he was a fool. Where did you say that legacy came from?'

'Howard Morris's mother. It was an annuity she'd initially put aside for her son. The money is bequeathed to her granddaughter, the daughter of Howard Morris. But which one? Alexandra or Clementine? Obviously the grandmother knew about one of her granddaughters, but not about the other.'

Complications like this, Zachariah didn't need. He wondered if Clementine knew a paternal grandmother had even existed. A feeling of hurt nearly crushed him at the thought she might have deceived him. He should never have allowed her to get through his guard.

No . . . she wouldn't have known. How could she know? 'I must think about this, John. Perhaps we should ask the court to decide.'

'The wheels of the law grind slowly, and the process is too expensive. By the time the courts deliberated on it the sum would be swallowed up in legal fees. As a legacy it's little enough as it is.'

'Couldn't it be shared between them?'

'It would take a judge to decide.'

'Not if the two women agreed to the arrangement.'

John laughed. 'Given the circumstance would you expect two women to act that reasonably?'

An image of Clementine stamping her foot came into his mind and he grinned at the thought of the two of them doing the same thing, like a pair of sprightly ponies poled to a rig. Another thought dangled provocatively under his nose and he almost laughed. 'There's something you seem to have overlooked.'

'Which is?'

'By blood, Clementine and Alexandra are half-sisters fathered by Howard Morris. Alexandra is also a half-sister to Edward and Iris, through their mother, Alicia – if they are genuine claims.'

John stared at him. 'Good Lord! I'd never given that a thought.' He rose and walked to the small table, where a decanter of brandy stood. I think I need a drink. 'One for you, Zachariah?'

He nodded. 'Why do these problems land on my desk, when I was disowned by the family years ago? All I want is a quiet life.' Zachariah's grin widened. 'Did I ever thank you for those unpalatable truths you forced me to swallow from time to time, John?'

'In more ways than one.' John shrugged. 'You were wasting your life and along with it that fine brain you were born with. Julia and I merely diverted you from the path you were pursuing.'

'I parted company with religion when my father's razor strop first beat the dust from my britches. I was a prickly fool, and you left me with nowhere to turn.'

'You were defensive, and had no trust in anyone but yourself. I tell you now, Zachariah. You trusted the right person in that. Your instincts have served you well.'

'It didn't take me long to figure out I was the fool, not you. You treated me like an equal.'

'Which is the basis of our way of life. In return we expect you to live a good life and help those more unfortunate when you can. A man earns his own fortune from what he gives to others.'

'Gabe doesn't fit into that little homily. And if earning a fortune with one female in the form of Clementine – a young woman too intelligent for her own good – isn't enough, I'm now having a second female foisted on to me. Tell me, what have I done to deserve these poor spinsters?'

'Perhaps there are more of them, since Howard Morris seems to have been a busy fellow with the young ladies.'

When Zachariah darted John a horrified look, he laughed. 'Alexandra Tate may be a hoax,' John said in a manner that alerted Zachariah to the fact that he had his doubts.

'As long as Clementine isn't, because the children adore her and so do . . . so do the dogs I bought for the children. They are quite taken with her, or so they tell me.'

John's voice was as smooth as silk. 'Your dogs act as advisors and offer you a considered opinion? How very clever of them.'

'You know very well I was referring to the children.'

How astute of John to pick up his slip of the tongue! That was all he'd get from him tonight. Zachariah responded to Clementine as any red-blooded man might. She'd slipped under his guard, but that didn't mean he was going to marry the girl. Now there was a safe distance between them he'd soon forget her. He sipped slowly at his drink. It was smooth and warming and gradually relaxed him. With a small amount of adjustment things would work out for the best; they always did. 'Have you seen Alexandra Tate yet?'

'No, she was out visiting friends. Samuel Tate wanted to tell her himself, and I wanted to talk to you about it first. Besides, you have a better instinct for a lie.'

'I was born into a house of liars.'

'The girl lives in Portsmouth with her foster father, who is slightly infirm due to age. It isn't too far away.'

'I'll need a day or so to come up with a plan of approach.'

'You do realize that you don't have any legal liability, don't you? Under the circumstances, the grandmother's legacy should go to the legitimate daughter . . . that is, the issue from the first of the two women who married Howard Morris.'

Zachariah laughed. 'That advice is superfluous, John. You're planting seeds in my head in the hope they'll grow into roses if you shovel enough dung on them. This particular bush seems to have several thorns on it. It has more answers than questions. How did Samuel Tate hear of the legacy? What coincidence led Alexandra to have an almost identical story to Clementine? We must find out.'

'And we shall.'

Zachariah was finding it hard to keep his eyes open. 'After that I must find a way to satisfy myself about the identity of the children. But not now. I'm too weary to think straight.'

'I know someone who can make enquiries on our behalf . . . something that should have been done earlier.'

The brandy had gone to work on Zachariah and he couldn't

stifle his yawns any longer. 'I'm sorry if I appear inhospitable, John, but I'm throwing you out now. I'll call on you both tomorrow, when I have enough energy to think straight.'

John rose and drained his glass. 'Of course, I mustn't keep you from your rest after your tiring journey. I'll see myself out. Goodnight, Zachariah.'

When the door closed in John's wake, Zachariah threw off his robe, blew out the candle and got into bed, shivering as his naked body slid between the cool linen sheets.

Outside a cart clattered over the cobbles, there was the sound of the front door being bolted, and footsteps as John walked off to his home on the other side of the square. It was early yet. A dog barked, another took up the challenge and a couple of cats growled menacingly before exploding into spits and squeals. The city sounds were so different from the quiet of the countryside.

Despite his weariness, for a time Zachariah couldn't sleep. The moon appeared in his window, big and bright. It moved on. Laughter flirted from the mouth of an unknown woman in the street . . . low and husky with promise.

The romance of his thoughts was spoiled by the foul smell drifting from the River Thames, which seemed to be worsening. The tide was on the ebb, uncovering the decomposing detritus trapped in the bowels of the river mud.

After a while fog wrapped itself around the house and clung with a muffled intensity. It pressed against the window, and the noise of no noise at all hummed inside his ears, as though the blood rushing through his veins and the booming beat of his heart were the only living things in the silence.

His mind went around in circles without solution. He needed a woman . . . but not any woman.

He certainly didn't need a Miss Alexandra Tate in his life.

Perhaps he would seek a suitable wife when this was all over. Perhaps he'd marry Clementine. Did it matter where she'd come from or who she was, when his own background would give rise for concern to anyone who cared to resurrect it?

Now there was a debatable – and very controversial – thought to go to sleep on.

Except it kept him awake . . .

Eight

Alexandra

The house was situated in Garden Street, in a long row of narrow houses. It was north facing, which made the interior, with its dark green wallpaper and narrow windows, feel cold and damp, and appear gloomy. Even the fire in the grate offered no warmth or cheer.

The front room pressed in on Zachariah, so he wanted to rush outside and suck in a deep breath of air. It was clean though, extremely so. The windows shone and the surfaces were free of dust. A piano took pride of place in front of the windows. A passage ran through the house from the front door to the back. The clock gave measured, muffled tocks.

Zachariah had never seen anyone quite so elegant as the young woman who sat opposite John Beck. She was a beauty. Her hair resembled spun silk and her eyes were bluer than blue. Alexandra was taller than most women he was acquainted with. Seating herself on a chair, she arranged her skirts in a sideways sweep and proceeded to pour them tea from a china pot covered in pink flowers.

Her gown was a pale shade of green taffeta and a little shabby. A lacy cream shawl collar covered her shoulders. Her neck was a length of pale, translucent skin. She seemed uncomfortable and her smile had the tightness of artifice about it.

He compared them with a poetic eloquence that surprised him. Alexandra was a crisp and delicate bloom of winter into spring, for he detected very little warmth of manner in her. Clementine reminded him of a fiery drift and tumble of late summer into autumn. He compared them to each other. Both young women had exceptional looks but he saw no likeness between them. Much to his dismay Alexandra Tate showed a marked resemblance to his late sister-in-law . . . at least, as he remembered her. He'd not seen Alice for several years.

Alexandra Tate was less spontaneous than the woman who'd given birth to her. She had a more studied air, as if she'd spent most of her life being trained for this important incident in her life. Samuel Tate gazed at her with pride.

Zachariah knew he was clutching at straws. He didn't want Alexandra to be Alice's child . . . didn't want Alice to be less than perfect in his eyes, even though her family had been peppered with usurers who had loaned his brother gambling money at extortionate rates of interest. They had acted like a pack of hunting dogs and had brought the family down. Then they'd picked the bones clean and moved on, taking no hostages.

Except for the less than immaculate condition of her gown, Alexandra was a study of perfection. But then, he was looking for faults in her.

As he had with the interview of Clementine, Zachariah took the role of observer rather than inquisitor. He felt at a disadvantage in the girl's home, and would rather that the meeting had taken place in John's office. But the old man had been too frail to travel, while the girl had refused to attend it without him.

She nibbled on her lower lip for a moment as her glance took him in. 'My papa has not introduced us. May I ask who you are, sir, and what you have to do with this business?'

'My name is Zachariah Fleet. It's possible we might be related by marriage.'

She gave a faint smile. 'Not to each other, surely.'

Zachariah was not in the mood to flirt with the girl. 'One would hope not.'

Colour tinted her cheeks and her lips tightened. Yet her eyes were wide and filled with an artful sort of innocence. Her eyelashes dipped and trembled for a second, and then opened with the lashes glazed in tears. She gazed down at her hands again and murmured. 'My pardon, that was in poor taste. In what way are we related?'

'Through the woman you claim as your mother.'

He would have expected her to say her mother's name. Instead, she waited for him to continue.

'You do know the name of the woman I'm talking about, don't you?'

'Oh yes. Her name was Alicia Morris when I was born. It says so on the marriage licence.'

He exchanged a glance with John, who smiled and cleared his throat.

The girl called Alexandra Tate seemed to take it as a cue for she looked up at John and smiled. 'What is it you want to know about me, sir?'

'Anything you wish to tell me that will help your case.'

Her voice was light and pleasing. 'Ah yes . . . my case. My foster father's case actually. I haven't had the time to really study it properly. Papa told me there was a legacy from a grandmother, whose existence was unknown to me until then, and I would be entitled to claim it when I was of age. So here I am, claiming it as he has bidden me.'

'When did you learn of the legacy?'

'Two weeks ago.'

So this girl who had been born Alexandra Morris was about the same age as Clementine. It was an interesting coincidence – too much of one perhaps.

She took some papers from a box on the sideboard. 'These will provide proof of my identity.'

John scrutinized the papers before handing them over. Zachariah ran a glance over them. The date on the death notice of Howard Morris was different to the one on the papers he had in his possession.

'What do you know about your immediate family, Miss Tate?'

'I have recently learned that my father was an officer who died at the battle of Waterloo. After he died my mother married a baron. Both of them are dead.'

'Is that all?'

'Yes, sir. I've never been given reason to have an interest in others or believed that my foster father and his wife were anything less than my blood parents.'

'How did you learn of your mother's death?'

Zachariah leaned forward. He'd be interested in hearing the answer to that too.

She afforded a glance to Samuel Tate, who looked grey and tired, and he nodded. 'Someone who knew them told Papa several weeks ago. The event was recorded in a news sheet and they gave him a cutting, I understand . . . Papa?'

'Which news sheet?' John said.

'Goodness, does it matter?' the man said, raising a handkerchief to his mouth when he coughed. 'The report is amongst the papers.'

'We have to make sure we have the right person. Can you leave the papers for us to check up on?'

'Most certainly. They are copies. The originals are in the possession of . . . another party.'

'Eventually we will need to examine the original documents, since the matter might need to go before the court. Can you contact this other party?'

'I have an address somewhere. They gave me a card and I put it on the dresser, but I seem to have mislaid it. I'll look for it.'

Zachariah's ears pricked up. 'Are you aware of the amount of the legacy, Miss Tate?'

She hesitated and gazed at her grandfather again. 'We believe it to be quite a large sum; eight hundred pounds . . . or so the lawyer who visited us said. The copy of the will doesn't name an amount.'

'You have a copy of the will? Where did you obtain it from?'

'It was offered to me for a small charge. The lawyer knew Alexandra's mother well and he approached me with the information and proof.'

'They charged a fee for the consultation? May I enquire how much?'

The man said gruffly, 'Fifty pounds. A tutor doesn't earn much and we no longer had the stipend. It was my life savings. I'd saved it for Alexandra. We were living on a small allowance from her mother, but it abruptly stopped about four years ago. From what you are saying I can only surmise that we've been duped. I don't know what we're going to do now. I have no property to sell.'

The girl placed her hand over his. 'We'll manage, Papa. So there's no legacy. I thought it was too good to be true. Don't worry. I'll think of something. Find another job. Perhaps I could find work in a boarding house, or sew seams in the evenings.'

John said quietly, 'Is this whole story built on lies?'

The girl drew herself up. I believe my papa. He would have no reason to lie about it.'

'Except for the legacy.'

'We discussed it . . .' She shrugged, saying defiantly, 'Papa said if there was a legacy, then there would be no shame in claiming it if I was entitled to have it.'

Zachariah couldn't fault that type of reasoning. 'Can you tell me the name of this lawyer?'

'He called himself George Sheridan.'

He exchanged a glance with John. 'We've heard of him, and believe him to be a fraudster.' He remembered the money he'd paid to the man, and the long list of expenses they'd supposedly expended on behalf of his brother and the children, and felt angry at allowing himself to be so stupid. He could only blame himself for that. He'd been so eager to meet his wards that he'd thrown caution to the wind.

She was close to tears now, her careful poise relaxed. Her shoulders drooped with the despair she felt, though she tried to maintain her dignity. 'I'm sorry you were involved in this. Let me see you out. We won't bother you again.'

She stood, holding out her hand to her foster father and trying to disguise the desperation in her eyes when she said, 'I'm afraid we've been duped, Papa.'

Wearily he said, 'I'm too old to have fallen for that trick. I wonder how they knew so much about us.'

'They were acquainted with my sister-in-law's family. She must have confided in Mrs Sheridan.'

There was something about the old man that touched Zachariah, a droop to his shoulders that spelled out disappointment, but more than that – utter dejection. Zachariah felt sorry for him, for his eyes were more desperate than those of the girl now.

'May we stay a little longer, Miss Tate? There is a legacy, and it needs to be discussed, otherwise we wouldn't be here.'

Her eyes widened. 'But you just said—'

'Hear me out, Miss Tate. There's also a problem. There are two possible claimants for the legacy. As it stands now, your father appears to have been a bigamist. In other words he was married to two women, and both at the same time. His wives were each left with a daughter to raise when he died, and they were born within a week or so of each other.'

Her composure crumbled slightly and there was no artifice in her now. After a moment or two of thought a faint but cautious smile flitted across her face. 'You mean I have a sister . . . may I meet her?'

'At the moment her claim is being assessed, the same as yours will be. The only difference is that she doesn't know about it yet. I will enlighten her about that and tell her about you the next time I see her. If that's her wish there's no reason why you shouldn't meet. Obviously, only one of you is eligible for the legacy – and that's not necessarily the eldest of you, but the daughter from the first legitimate marriage Howard Morris embarked on.

'Perhaps you would relate your details to Mr Beck. Any information you may have as to the whereabouts of the Sheridan couple will be useful if we swear a complaint out against them, though I imagine those fraudsters will be long gone. In the meantime I'll supply you with an amount of money to temporarily support you, if you will accept it.'

Alexandra's reserve fled and she began to weep softly. 'Of course we'll accept it; you are too kind, sir.' She took her foster-father's hand in hers. 'Everything will be all right now, Papa.'

He was *much* too kind. Zachariah decided it wasn't a good time to tell her about the existence of Edward and Iris . . . not until he was sure. He sighed as he offered her his handkerchief. His life was getting more complicated by the minute and he was in danger of running out of handkerchiefs if he met many more weeping women. In that event he would probably weep himself and need them too.

Not that Alexandra had many tears, just enough to dampen her long lashes for effect as she gazed at him over the linen. She was dainty and had managed to turn tears into an asset instead of resembling an embarrassment, as some women did.

It was later, just as they were leaving when Alexandra drew him aside and said, 'Papa is a good man, but he's ill. This gown was bought from a stall so I'd make a good impression on any suitors that might wish to present themselves. He has spent a great deal of money on dancing and music lessons, in the hope I might attract a naval officer. He thinks that having the legacy can only heighten my desirability in that regard. However, to men like you, the amount would be insignificant, no doubt.'

'Indeed it is not, Miss Tate. Were it my money I'd put it to work and find some way of increasing it.' Which was exactly what she hoped to do by attracting a worthwhile husband, he supposed.

He hoped she didn't have him in his sights. A woman with her looks and accomplishments would be hard to resist, and the legacy, though small, would be further enticement. He was thankful he hadn't gone to sea, so didn't qualify as a suitor – though he'd observed that some women weren't fussy about the health, age or occupation of a prospect, when wealth was involved. He conceded, though, that having the right wife could prove to be an asset.

He gave her the benefit of his advice. 'You're a lovely young woman whose desirability needs no enhancement. You should not be in too much of a hurry to wed – not until you've made the right social connections. The Sheridans have already relieved your father of his savings and me of a considerable amount of money.'

She gave an arch little smile. 'I understand you are not a married man, sir?'

He sighed, and said shortly, 'Indeed I'm not, and neither do I wish to be.'

'I'm not telling you this to encourage a proposal, sir. I do not lack for admirers. There's one man who expresses a desire to wed me. He is a good and worthy man and talented with artistic leanings. I've made it clear to him that I would rather marry a man with more status.'

'Please address me as Mr Fleet.'

'My papa will not live much longer and he wants to see me advantageously settled. I want you to think well of him, Mr Fleet. Although they were not wealthy, he and my foster mother always treated me with the utmost love and kindness, and I was happy with them. It was a blow to discover I was not of their blood. Worse was the fact that I'd been abandoned by my mother, as though I was not fit to be part of the family. After all, she'd been married to my father, and was a widow thereafter, so there can be no stain on my character.'

Zachariah knew how that felt. He also knew when he was being manipulated. 'Allow me to make this very clear, Miss Tate. I'm not in the market for a wife.'

She coloured slightly. 'I wish Papa had never heard of this

legacy, for better to be left in ignorance and with your self-esteem intact.'

Zachariah doubted it. 'Unfortunately one can't gain any physical sustenance from self-esteem.'

'Papa has nothing left except your charity – not even his pride.'

Ah . . . his charity . . . and to think he'd imagined her to be after securing a ball and chain on his ankle. That was pride at its worst. How kind of her to remind him she was simply after money. She didn't miss an opportunity.

'Your foster father has you, Miss Tate, and I have the greatest respect for him. You can contact John Beck when the need arises. In the meantime, if we have any further news I'll send a message.'

'You're scheming, Zach,' John said on the way home. 'How did you find them?'

'The man was genuine and the girl too plausible. Alexandra attempted to manage me, and she was good at it.'

'Not like the lock-horns approach of Clementine, then?'

'No, nothing like Miss Clemmie.'

He tried not to grin when John raised an eyebrow and said, 'I do believe you're getting fond of that young woman.'

'Nonsense. I barely think of her at all. When I do it's because she's a thorn in my side. In comparison, Alexandra is twice the lady, and twice as accomplished.'

'But a trifle calculating and self-absorbed.'

'I can't blame her for trying when poverty is knocking on her door. She favours my sister-in-law in looks, I fancy, but she's a little too studied for my taste. She told me she's on the market for a worthy husband, and that's a role she'd been trained for.'

'Ah . . . it made you feel vulnerable, did it not?'

'No it did not. Besides, this little cuckoo has set her sights a bit higher than previously from what I gather. Now she knows her mother was married to a baron. That combined with the legacy will help her achieve her goal. She called me Sir Zachariah a couple of times. I told her to call me Mr Fleet.'

'Did you tell her the title wasn't yours?'

'No, I didn't think it wise when the children weren't mentioned. It struck me as odd that the Sheridans didn't mention them to the old man. Alexandra is aiming high, and they may have traded on that.'

'There is very little in life higher than your fortune and your ability to earn it and manage it. There are also rumours you might be due an honour for your work amongst the poor. Also, as things stand, the title might be yours by right if there's any doubt about Edward's paternity,' John said. 'You'd do well to remember that.'

'A title can be a liability, and I doubt if Alexandra knows the extent of my fortune. I think I could help her in her marriage quest though.'

'By offering to be her groom?'

'Perish the thought. She is personable though, and I could put her in the position of being noticed. I could hold a social evening to introduce her.'

'Miss Tate seems like a polite, but determined young woman.' John gave a soft laugh. 'You do realize she's as badly off as Clementine was . . . though her social graces are an improvement.'

'As with Clementine, Alexandra's appearance can be improved with the right wardrobe. It will be worth outfitting her, you'll see. When her foster father has passed on – something that appears imminent – I will see what can be arranged for her. Perhaps I can find her something useful to do – like Clementine, who is not afraid of getting her hands dirty and enjoys the little she has in life.'

'Clementine was raised in a situation where physical effort was a requirement. There's no shame in that. You know, Zachariah . . . I think we should arrange to speak to Clementine again. Give me a short time to compare the papers.'

'I've promised the children I'll visit Martingale House halfway through December. As with Clementine, I'd welcome Julia's opinion on Alexandra Tate if you could spare her for ladies' matters and wardrobe duties.'

'I'm sure Julia would be delighted to spend more of your money, but she will only look for the good in the girl, so ultimately you'll have to trust your own judgement.'

Zachariah nodded. 'Did you notice the discrepancy in the recording of Howard Morris's death? They were a week apart.'

'He died at the height of battle . . . it would have been difficult
to be entirely accurate amongst such chaos, and his name may
have been entered on two lists. I will get someone else to look
through his records and double check my findings, since I may
have missed something.'

'Personally, I'm looking forward to seeing the interaction
between the two young women when they meet each other.'

'On your own head be it then, friend Zachariah, for they are
chalk and cheese. Alexandra is much more the lady.'

'And Miss Clemmie more the woman.'

To which John raised an eyebrow.

'Don't read anything into that. More pressing is the problem
of the children. If your friends in Australia can discover the
whereabouts of my brother's family, and whether there were any
children who survived, I would be grateful. Edward mentioned
an orphanage, but he clams up when you push him.'

'Ah yes . . . the children. What will you do if you discover
them to be imposters?'

Unease flooded though Zachariah. 'I don't know, John, I really
don't know.'

'Then I'll pray you have the wisdom to deal with the problem
in a fair and compassionate manner.' Giving his horse a gentle
nudge, John forged ahead, leaving Zachariah to follow.

Nine

Alexandra was grateful for the money Zachariah had left. It had
been a generous act, though from what she'd heard he wouldn't
miss such a small sum – the equivalent of her papa's life savings.
She gave a wry smile.

Zachariah Fleet seemed to be a cautious man, one who gave
very little of his thoughts away. She didn't know whether she
liked him or not, but she liked what she'd already learned – that
he was a wealthy self-made man with a shady past, one of considerable wealth. She wondered if he'd made his fortune honestly,
though he had a reputation of fair dealing; this she'd learned from

her papa's acquaintances when they'd gossiped over their chess games every Wednesday.

She smoothed his handkerchief on her knee. The square of fine white linen had one initial embroidered in the corner. Z. There was no second letter, as though he'd discarded it.

They said he gave a portion of his income to charity every year. She'd put that down as unlikely until she'd met him. The man with him, John Beck, had the look and the manner of a Quaker. Zachariah Fleet did not. She recalled a tale that he'd been plucked from the streets by a Quaker family. Some of their ways would probably have rubbed off on him. He was civil, but barely, and appeared indifferent to her looks. She'd been praised often, and to the point of vanity over her looks. Being ignored smarted a bit.

Zachariah Fleet was a man of few words – one who didn't suffer fools. His appearance was elegant rather than showy; his coat was cut from the finest of materials, his boots were fashioned from supple leather and he wore his clothes well.

She stood, balling the handkerchief in her palm as she watched him ride away. She'd considered he hadn't been particularly friendly. He would be a man who found it hard to trust people, and those he did would probably have to earn that trust. That she intended to do. He might not trust or like her now, but she hoped he would eventually.

Taxed by the meeting, her papa was almost asleep in his chair. She examined his face, still finding it hard to believe that this man she'd always loved, and who'd given her his all for her future, was not her father. The recent severing of the ties had been too quick, too unexpected for her fully to grasp. She felt twice abandoned, and angry that he hadn't told her before. Yet she kissed his forehead, saying quietly, 'I'm going to the market for some provisions.'

His eyes opened a little as he whispered, 'I wish I was strong enough to accompany you. Be careful, and don't encourage any strangers.'

'No, Papa. I might visit Mrs Elliot. I've heard that she hasn't been well.'

'Ask her to give my regards to Roland, and tell him I'm pleased to hear the boy is doing so well.'

★   ★   ★

Roland Elliot had been her father's student and was hardly a boy now. Alexandra had always found him to be a bit forward. He'd always gazed at her a certain way, his admiration clear on his face. She'd teased him now and again, allowing him the liberty of a kiss or a secretive touch. She smiled. It was satisfying, and exciting to know he was in love with her.

When she was outside, her basket over her arm and a little velvet jacket over her bodice for the sparse amount of warmth it provided, she experienced a moment of freedom. She had drawn a shabby cloak over the top for warmth.

What was her half-sister like, she wondered – if indeed there was one? Zachariah Fleet had smiled when he'd mentioned her, as if the thought of her had amused him.

Or perhaps it was the thought of Howard Morris being married to two women at the same time. She hoped it didn't get out and stain her character, which would spoil her chances of making a good marriage. She wondered about her own character. There was a recklessness inside her that drove her to visit Roland despite her resolve. Sometimes it was hard to control and she couldn't hide her smile. So was Roland sometimes.

When she arrived Roland was in the back room of the shop. He had his own business, selling china for one of the potteries – and indeed, he designed patterns to transfer on to most of them. Samples of the patterns were displayed on shelves. The delicacy of the designs, when coming from such large hands, never failed to delight her.

He pulled on his jacket when he came through, summoned by the tinkle of the bell. A pair of wintery grey eyes examined her. 'Miss Tate, what a pleasant surprise.'

His shirt was open and unbuttoned at the neck, where the hint of a curl was on display. She wanted to reach out and wrap it around her finger. 'Hello Roland. I've come to visit your mother.'

He tugged his sleeves down over strong, muscled wrists. 'Of course you have, but you've forgotten this is her afternoon for playing cards.'

'Yes . . . I had. I'm sorry I disturbed you.' She gazed around her, pleased by what she saw. 'Your shop is so pretty.'

He smiled. 'So are you. I was just about to relax and

take some tea before I started work on a new design. Will you join me?'

Alexandra hesitated. Roland was a handsome man with an attractive roguishness to him. She'd never been entertained by him without his mother present before. There was a sense of danger about it.

'I have some gingerbread we can share. It's your favourite, as I recall.'

She supposed it wouldn't hurt, just this once. After all, nobody but themselves would know.

She jumped when he reached past her to turn the key in the lock. 'That will prevent us from being disturbed. There's nothing worse than being interrupted when you're entertaining a lady.'

Her heartbeat picked up speed. 'Is that what you're doing?'

'Unless you intend to buy a dinner set painted to one of my designs, it seems so. How is your father?'

'Unwell. The doctor says he won't survive much longer. He sends you his fondest regards.'

Roland nodded. 'I'm sorry. He's a good man. What will you do then?'

Zachariah Fleet came into her mind. 'Oh . . . I've made some plans. It's possible I might marry.'

'So you've found yourself a naval officer who would make you a worthy husband.'

'Stop teasing. I'm beginning to change my mind about that since naval officers are always away at sea. Besides, it's possible that I'm entitled to claim a legacy, though I shouldn't really talk about it because there is another claimant. It will serve as a dowry . . . make me more attractive.' She wasn't going to tell anyone about her sister until she'd met the woman, since they were rivals for the money.

'Perhaps you should put me on that husband list of yours. You know I love you, Lexie. I find you attractive, even without the addition of a dowry. I always have. In fact, I recall that you accepted my proposal of marriage years ago.'

She couldn't help but smile at the thought. 'We were children. I was eleven and you were sixteen, and just about to be apprenticed to your uncle.'

'And you allowed me to touch your breasts when nobody was there to watch. You laughed and said it tickled.'

Something she'd never forgotten, though she felt flustered at such an intimate memory he held of her. 'A gentleman wouldn't recall such a thing.'

He chuckled. 'I'm no gentleman, just a hardworking tradesman. You were young, and they were too small to register . . . a disappointment really.'

She would not disappoint him now.

He held aside the curtain to the back room and as she passed he kissed her ear. She gave a little shiver and pretended not to notice as she went through into his workshop, where paints, pencils, inks and other instruments of his profession littered a bench. Her relieved her of her cloak and threw it on a chair.

In front of the far window there was an easel with a blank canvas on it.

'I didn't know you painted pictures.'

'It's a commission. I'm working on a design for a gentleman.'

'Can I see it?'

He hesitated for a moment. 'It would probably shock you.'

'Why would it?'

'It's a naked woman.'

She shrugged, successfully hiding the thrill of shock she did feel. She didn't want him to think she was unsophisticated. 'I have seen myself unclothed.'

'Not in this pose, you haven't.'

He took a role of paper from a shelf and slowly unwrapped it, smoothing his hands over it to prevent it from creasing. A pair of feet appeared, and then legs. One leg had a stocking wrinkled around the ankle. The other stocking was tied around a plump thigh with ribbons.

He stopped, grinning at her. 'You're blushing. Are you sure you want to see more?'

She was longing to see more. 'I'm not a child, Roland.'

'So I've noticed.' He unrolled it further, revealing a wisp of sheer cloth kept in place by a ringed hand. One finger divided the shadowy darkness of the loin beneath. The very same spot on her own body began to tingle so she wanted to stroke it.

She couldn't hold back the tiny gasp she gave. Sometimes being a woman was unbearably frustrating. It must be easier for a man who could indulge himself in matters of the flesh without restriction, while an unmarried woman could only imagine the delights of union, and was obliged to find relief in a private exercise that was never talked of. But then, perhaps other women didn't suffer from such afflictions as she did.

'I've seen paintings of naked ladies before – in books.'

'So, you're an expert. Would you like to see the rest of her?'

'I told you. It doesn't worry me.'

He unrolled the rest. The model was young, her hair was dishevelled and her eyes had a sleepy warmth to them. He became matter-of-fact. 'I haven't got her breasts right. Perhaps you could advise me.'

'You mean that some hussy posed for it . . . and without clothing on?'

'It was the lady friend of the gentleman who commissioned it. He chaperoned her. She was sulky because she was cold, and she whined until he took her home, and before I'd captured her breasts properly.'

What an odd way of putting it. Captured her breasts? As though they were running away from him, like a couple of energetic puppies.

'You're a woman, Alexandra. Tell me . . . where have I gone wrong?'

She tried to be as dispassionate as he was, though her heart was racing as she imagined her breasts being cupped by Roland's hands. 'The tips are only tight like that when it's cold. When it's warm they are smoother when they reach . . . well . . . the peak.'

'Ah . . . yes, the peak.' His glance went to her breasts, which unaccountably surged against her body. 'Perhaps you should pose for me.'

'I'd hate to disappoint you again, Roland,' she said drily.

'I doubt if you would . . . Your body is craving love and I know exactly how to love you.'

'Do you, Roland?'

He reached out and placed his hands against the velvet bodice. His thumbs found her nipples and gently caressed. 'You're so exquisite that I can't help loving you. Marry me, Lexie.'

Alexandra didn't know what to do, so she whispered half-heartedly, 'Stop it, Roland.'

He gave a regretful sigh, took her hands in his and carried

them to his groin, where she encountered the result of her teasing. 'See what you've done to me, my love.'

Reluctantly, she drew her hands away, but slowly, because she was curious. He pushed against her hands and she removed them.

'Allow me to kiss your breasts, just once.'

She didn't answer, but closed her eyes, expecting him to kiss her through her clothing. Instead, he unbuttoned her jacket. Her breasts fitted comfortably into his palms as he lifted them from her bodice like precious pearls from an oyster, and she didn't have the will to protest. He inclined his head so his mouth closed around them. Sucking her gently into his mouth his tongue curled warmly around them one at a time so they swelled into his mouth.

She groaned, and then sucked in a breath. *Oh goodness.* The core of her dampened and tingled. Was there anything more delicious? She couldn't wait to be married and have her husband bestow such intimate attentions on her, without her having to reap the harvest of guilt she gathered at the thought of such encounters with him. She pushed him away. 'No, Roland, it isn't decent.'

'Neither is what you've just allowed. You are longing to be indecent, and I'm just the man to be indecent with.'

'I know.' Her face glowed. 'I'm sorry. I promised my mother I'd keep myself . . . innocent for when I wed.'

'Marry me then, Alexandra, you know I love you,' he said. 'You can play the innocent with me.'

'I can't. My father wants me to marry a man of means, so I'll never want for anything.'

'I'll be a man of means eventually. I'm being offered so much work that I can hardly keep pace with it and am thinking of moving to London and taking on an apprentice.'

'But not soon enough. I want to enjoy myself while I'm young.'

'Doesn't it matter that you'd spend a lifetime with a man you disliked just to achieve wealth for its own sake? I've got money put aside, and I'm earning more and more from my artistic endeavours.'

'Yes it matters. I've just learned that my parents fostered me. My real mother wasn't an ordinary woman, you see, but a baroness. There is a legacy and I've been poor for a long time. I want good clothes and to be respected and welcome at social gatherings.

That's what I was brought up to do by my foster parents. I often wondered why, and now I know.'

'I see, so I'm not good enough for you now. Think on, my dear. Was your mother a baroness when you were born, or were you the result of some by-blow she opened her legs for? Why else would she have farmed you out?'

Near to tears, she choked out, 'I came here to visit your mother and you have been totally disrespectful. You disgust me, Roland Elliot.'

'No I don't. You know perfectly well which day my mother goes out. You came here to see me – to flaunt yourself to a man who loves you because you can, and it makes you feel powerful. And far from being disgusted, you're excited and aroused. That I can tell from the feel and the smell of you.'

He slid her breasts back into their cups and buttoned up her jacket. His fingertips caressed the velvet for a moment and then he took her face in his hands and gazed into her eyes. 'You're a trollop at heart, Lexie. You long for a man to teach you how, while you simper and torture the poor sod just for the fun of it in the meantime.'

If he touched her again like he just had she wouldn't be able to stop herself. 'Then I mustn't visit you alone again.'

'As to that, please yourself, but do this to me again and I won't be responsible for the outcome. As for your delightful breasts . . . they're perfect and I'd like to spend more time playing with them, but I have work to do.'

A thrill shafted through her body at the thought of such promiscuous excitement. 'That's disgusting. I was going to allow you to draw them, but now I won't.' She straightened up her bodice and secured it.

'You've already allowed me to. They are sketched indelibly on my mind and my palms. I know every inch of them now, from the golden freckles on the orbs to the pert turned-up nubs. I know exactly how they feel and look, and will add them to the portrait. I might even paint another portrait with your face on it.'

He laughed when she gazed at him in horror. 'Oh, don't worry, I'm not that vindictive. Nobody will know the breasts on that harlot are Alexandra Tate's gilded treasures – nobody but me. I'll derive satisfaction from knowing that some rich old man is drooling over them with lust in his eyes after having paid me a fortune for the image of them.'

'You don't mean that.'

'No . . . I don't mean it, because I love you and I'd rather nobody but me did the drooling. But take heed of the young woman in the sketch. That's what's likely to happen to you if you discard your friends and go chasing the elusive pot of gold. Most men are far from being fools where women are concerned.'

She placed her hand gently on his arm. 'I'm sorry, Roland. I want to leave this life behind and take up the new one that's being offered me . . . the one I was born to. I'll come and say goodbye when the time comes for me to leave.'

'As far as I'm concerned we've just said it.' He reached out to pluck a trio of porcelain figurines from a showcase and placed them in her basket. 'Here's something to remember me by – Harlequin, Pierrot and Columbine. It's a farce. Both men were fools who fell in love with the beautiful but treacherous Columbine.'

'I'll remember you anyway, Roland.'

'You know where I am if you need me. I'll show you out.' Taking her by the elbow he steered her through the workshop and showroom, where he helped her into her cloak. Unlocking the door he propelled her gently through it into the street.

The door closed with a brassy tinkle behind her.

Three weeks later Alexandra watched as Samuel Tate was buried next to his wife in a modest funeral he'd provided for through payments to a funeral club.

Many people came to pay their respects at the graveside, including Roland Elliot and his mother. Alexandra felt relief, because although she'd loved the man who'd raised her, caring for him had become a chore. However, she didn't show it, and accepted the condolences with grace, as a good daughter should. And she dabbed away her tears with the linen handkerchief with the Z embroidered in the corner, her thumbs tracing over the letter.

Roland nodded his head to her but said nothing, just stood next to his mother while she prattled on about how wonderful

Samuel Tate had been. Resentment niggled in her. They should have told her she was someone else's child. Her real mother had arranged payment, so she must have cared. And now the woman was dead and neither of them would have the opportunity to meet each other.

Alexandra had unknowingly earned her board by being a good and obedient daughter, even though she rebelled against it at times. There was a sense of freedom in her now and she was ready to break out.

But that didn't mean she wasn't sad, because Samuel had been both kind and loving in his treatment of her, as though she was his real daughter. She would miss him.

'I'll write to you,' she said to Roland.

'Please yourself.' He grinned suddenly. 'Don't forget me.'

Despite her sadness and her reluctance to lose Roland's regard, within a week Alexandra had sold most of their household goods to the incoming tenant. She booked a seat on the London stage-coach and packed her bag, wrapping the gift from Roland in her stockings.

She sent him a note asking him to meet her at the coach station to say goodbye. He hadn't answered and neither had she seen him amongst the milling crowd. So much for true love, she thought.

It was a cold December day when the coach set off and her heart nearly burst with excitement at doing something so daring and new. At the same time it was breaking at the thought she might never see Roland again.

Ten

Zachariah was preparing for his trip to Dorset, and he wasn't looking forward to the journey, especially in December, when the weather was uncertain.

Not long ago he'd nearly convinced himself to sell Martingale House. He held no fondness for the place. He wasn't a farmer and had no family – no wife or children. Besides, he owned a comfortable house in London where he conducted his business. The Dorset estate was too far away to visit often.

The only thing that had stopped him before was the fact that the estate was now making a profit under Mr Bolton's management, and if he'd sold it Gabe would have turned up, waved the title over him and demand the place back. That wouldn't happen now, but he had a different set of responsibilities to shoulder.

There was no room in his bag for the Noah's Ark he'd bought as a gift for the children, so he had to carry it by hand. Clemmie would like the toy. No doubt she would fill their heads full of nonsense, telling them a story of the biblical flood. There was also a dissection of the map of the world. It could be fitted together so they could learn about the geographic values of the world they lived in.

The stage was fully booked, but he managed to get seats for himself and Evan on the mail coach. It was uncomfortable because it ran during the hours of darkness as well as daylight, and with frequent stops, and it bounced through the potholes, making sleep impossible. But it also made him less vulnerable to the predators that prowled the highways, usually in pairs and looking for easy victims, for it carried an armed man on the back to guard the mail.

Long ago he'd heard that plans were on the drawing board for the railway to be pushed through from London to Southampton. He and John had spent an evening poring over a map and they plotted out the details of the route, then speculated by investing in a wide stretch of land. That had recently sold for a handsome profit.

The mathematics of that exercise had also given them a travelling time of three hours to cover the seventy-seven-mile journey.

'Incredible,' Zachariah had said. 'The railway has done wonders for commerce in the north, and will do the same for the south. Imagine getting all the farm produce off to the London market while it's still fresh.'

'You're beginning to sound like a farmer.'

'I suppose I am one really . . . though an absent one. I still have to know what's going on in the marketplace. However, I'm not thinking of farming now so much as transport. Imagine getting to Southampton in such a short time. Keep your eyes on the situation, would you, John?' he had said. 'I'm of a mind to buy some shares in the railway – as many as I can get.'

He picked up a parcel wrapped in brown paper. It was heavier than he'd thought. He'd take it inside the coach if there were enough room.

There was.

The other two passengers were men, and would be armed to the teeth, as he was himself. They preferred to sit behind the driver. Collectively, they would represent a formidable force to engage with.

Half-frozen to death the passengers huddled in their cloaks and swore a lot as the vehicle tore through the darkness. The guard blew the horn loudly when they reached the stops, and with lamps blazing in case something was coming in the other direction. Evan huddled in a corner looking a picture of misery. He was not a good traveller.

'Cheer up, Evan, the journey won't last forever, and at least we are on the inside,' he said.

'I won't be able to stand up when we get there.'

'You will, I assure you. In fact your backside will be so sore that you'll never want to sit on it again.'

Evan had saved his bacon in the past, when Zachariah had first embarked on his life of crime. He'd been caught with his hand in Evan's pocket.

Evan had been about twenty, and had grabbed him by the collar. 'What do you think you're up to, you thieving little bugger?'

'I'm hungry.'

'Well, you won't find the price of a meal in my pocket. I've just lost my bleedin' job as it is.'

'Doing what?'

'I'm a fetch-and-carry in the theatre. I wanted to be an actor, but I got up the skirt of the manager's wife. What do you want to be when you grow up?'

'The wealthiest man in the world, so I can tell everyone else what to do, even the king.'

Evan had laughed. 'Well, I reckon that's a good enough occupation to aim for. You won't achieve that by stealing from another pauper, but by going to school, learning your lessons and having respect for other people. When you achieve your aim I'll be your man. In the meantime we'll join up, since we've got to eat. Tell you what, lad, you come with me to the Quakers' kitchen. They'll give us a bowl of soup and they'll listen to your troubles and help you if they can. You sound like a bit of a toff to me. Where you from, lad?'

'The country. My pa was a baron.'

'I reckon he might have been at that. So what are you doing picking pockets in London?'

'The family didn't like me, so they sent me to be raised by a relative.'

'Who beat you half to death so you ran away. Or were you kidnapped and held to ransom? If so I might as well hand you in and collect it.'

Zachariah still remembered his surprise – first, that any of his family would pay a ransom to get him back, or that Evan had known his story – until he said drily, 'I think I've read both those play scripts before somewhere.'

'No . . . honestly. That's what happened,' Zachariah had insisted.

After that Julia had rescued him. John hadn't turned a hair when she'd taken him home. They'd found Evan a job and they'd remained in touch, and when Zachariah had realized his ambition, Evan had indeed become his man.

The passengers dashed into the bushes to quickly relieve themselves while the lathered horses were swapped for fresh ones. Zachariah hoped the drivers would delay long enough for them to buy a chunk of pork pie and a tankard of ale before setting off in a mad chase on the next leg.

They reached Poole the following day, early in the evening. They left the dusty red and black mail coach to take on its load and a new driver.

After a bit of a search they found a cab that would take them the rest of the way.

'Martingale House is it? You must be the squire, then, I reckon.'

Zachariah neither confirmed nor opposed the assumption. The fewer people who knew his business the better he liked it. Still, the man was pleasant enough, and accommodating.

'I'm Travis Jones and my horse here is Sally-Ann. I live in Briary Brook, not far from 'ee. I reckon you got here just in time, sir, since I was about to go home. That sky is full of snow, and most people will want to be indoors before it keeps them from going about their business, or catches them unawares on the road.'

A little while later snowflakes began to fall like downy goose feathers from the sky and settled softly on the landscape. Soon, they could hardly see the road ahead.

Zachariah banged on the roof when they got to the village. 'You can drop us off here, Mr Jones. Sally-Ann looks as though she needs a feed and a warm stable. I know exactly where we are and it will only take us fifteen minutes or so to get home on foot.'

'Well, make sure thee stays on the road.'

Evan collected their luggage from the cab while Zachariah thanked the driver and paid the man.

'You take care now, sir,' he called out.

'I will. Thank you, Mr Jones. Come on, Evan, follow me,' he said to his reluctant manservant. 'We'll soon have you warmed up. I know a short cut across a field.'

Except he misjudged his direction as the sky darkened. Half an hour later he said, 'I think we're lost.'

'There's a light beyond the trees.'

'Remind me to give you a raise, Evan. I thought we'd be stumbling around all night. We'll cut across the field.'

Ten minutes later, after pushing through a couple of prickly hedges, they discovered the road that led to Martingale House. The snowfall had increased and their immediate surrounds shone with the pristine white wall of it, one that seemed impenetrable, for it also blotted out the house lights.

They came to a fork. 'Left, right or straight ahead?' he muttered, his teeth beginning to chatter in competition with Evan's.

Evan gave a muffled huff, as though the wind had been knocked out of him. 'I beg your pardon, sir, but I hate the soddin' country,' he said nasally, and then, 'Martingale House is straight ahead.'

'You have a remarkable sense of direction, Evan. How can you be so certain in this weather? Was your father a bloodhound?'

'There is no need for sarcasm, sir. There's a brick gatepost with a sign on the wall next to it that clearly states Martingale House. I've just flattened my nose on it.'

Two steps forward and Zachariah walked into the same gatepost. 'Ah yes, I know exactly where we are now. At the road end of the carriageway, exactly where I'd planned to be.' His relief was so profound that he laughed.

'Are there any willing women in the area . . . buxom milkmaids and shepherdesses with milky white skin or the like?'

'Not unless you want to walk around with a pitchfork stuck in your backside. The servants are verging on elderly, and the ladies in my household are off limits. We'll have to act like priests.'

'Just as well, since my manly bits are frozen solid,' Evan said gloomily. 'I don't like the country much.'

'Now who's being sarcastic?'

'I am, sir. I'd resign from my position this minute if I had somewhere warm to go.'

'I'd be lost without you, Evan.'

'Yes sir . . . very amusing.'

Clementine gazed out of the window into the swirling snow. It had been dark for a handful of hours, if dark could possibly consist of the swirling whiteness beyond the cold glass surface of the windowpanes. The children were bedded down for the night, snuggled cozily under their blankets while the shadows from the firelight leapt and danced together on the wall.

They were tired after spending the early afternoon cutting holly to decorate the hall. When it began to snow Ben told them he'd found a sleigh in the coach house. He'd sharpened the runners and renewed the leather rein. If the snow settled, Ben promised he would take them for a ride.

The children were much more relaxed now. The routine they were in had made them feel secure and she'd increased their learning schedule. Edward was confident with arithmetic and his recognition of words had increased. He could write short sentences that made sense. Iris was still working on her letters, and she was fond of listening to stories.

Between them they had started writing stories and poetry to

paste in their own books. Mostly, Iris drew pictures and was proud to show them off. Edward was more secretive, but he'd given her a picture of a kangaroo, a funny-looking creature with a big tail.

The dogs joined her, standing on their hind legs with their paws on the windowsill and bodies thrusting against her to be fondled.

She was about to turn away from the window when a gap in the snow opened up and she saw two men on foot. Happy gave a yip and headed for the stairs. Wolf gave a deeper bark. Just as quickly, the sight of the men was obliterated, so she wasn't sure whether she'd seen them or not. It might have been a shrub moving under the weight of the snow. She recalled there was a lilac bush halfway along the carriageway.

'I think I saw someone in the garden, Polly. We'd better check, so I'm going down to tell Mr Bolton.'

'It's probably some poor soul lost in the snow and looking for directions. Sir Gabriel used to give them a bowl of broth and put them up in the servant's rooms, unless they were gentry, then they got a guest room.'

Lighting a second candle Clementine went downstairs and called Mr Bolton from the kitchen, where he was comfortably seated in front of the stove. It was warm in the kitchen, much warmer than the drawing room.

Mr Bolton rose to his feet and buttoned his coat. He was a young man, and strong, the younger son of a Somerset farmer and handsome in a rugged, country sort of way.

'I think I saw two men coming up the carriageway, Mr Bolton.'

'Thank you, Miss Clemmie. I imagine they've lost their way in the snow.'

The words had hardly left his mouth when the bell servicing the front entrance jingled urgently on its spring.

Clementine followed Bolton from the kitchen to the hall, picking up a small bronze statue on the way in case he needed help. There, he bawled at the blurred outline of a face peering through the painted-glass panel, 'State your business.'

'It's Zachariah Fleet with my manservant. Allow us entrance if you would, before we freeze to death.'

There came the sound of feet stamping as an attempt was made to leave the snow that covered them on the doorstep. The two men brought an aura of cold into the hall with them. Teeth chattered as they tried to smile a greeting. They threw off their damp topcoats and slapped their arms around their chests.

The dogs leapt at them, offering yelps of delight for Zachariah and menacing growls and sniffs for his manservant, who gazed sternly at them. 'Sit, you unruly creatures. Sit!'

The dogs sat and gazed up at him, panting.

'That's better.'

Mrs Ogden bore their damp top clothes off to the kitchen to dry. Mr Bolton followed, clicking his fingers to call the dogs to heel.

'Look after Evan, Mrs Ogden,' Zachariah called out as the small cavalcade of servants and household dogs trooped off.

As if he'd bared a window in his soul, Zachariah was infused with a sense of loneliness as he watched them move out of sight.

His servants would be warm in the kitchen, laughing and gossiping, while he, their master, would have to satisfy convention and eat his supper by himself at the long table. That would distance him even more – by profession and wealth.

Clementine was the only one left in the hall. She eyed him up and down as though she didn't quite know what to do with him. 'Come into the drawing room, where it's warm. I'll give the fire a stir with the poker.'

She placed the statue back on the table.

His smile was almost a grimace. 'What did you intend to do with that?'

'I thought it might be useful as a weapon if you were strangers and meant us harm.'

'Allow me to do that.' He took the poker from her and stirred what remained of the ashes around the log until it burst into flame. 'I hadn't realized you were so bloodthirsty.'

She refused to be drawn. 'Hadn't you?'

He stood in front of the fireplace, thawing himself out. Steam rose from his soaked trouser legs. She poured him a large measure of brandy. 'Here, this might help.'

He sipped it slowly, eyes closed as he savoured it. Each fiery golden drop that passed his lips and curled over the surface of his tongue served to relax him. His teeth chattered on the rim of the glass once or twice then he shivered and downed the rest in one smooth swallow.

There was blood on his hands, long scratches. 'You're bleeding.'

'We had to push through a couple of hedges.' His eyes opened and he smiled at her. 'It was the most uncomfortable of journeys on the mail coach. Then we got lost . . . to be more precise, I got us lost.'

She took the glass from his fingers. 'Another . . .'

'Thank you but that one was more than sufficient. It's warmed my bones. Now I need some food in my belly.'

His stomach rattled in agreement.

'I'll tell the cook to heat up some broth.'

He gestured to the chair. 'Mrs Ogden knows her job. Tell me . . . how are the children?'

'They're well . . . it was getting near Christmas and I thought . . . we all thought . . .'

'That I wasn't coming? I'm sorry, I was held up with some rather urgent business. Did you miss me?'

'Certainly not; I've been much too busy.'

'So have I, but I managed to miss you several times. Didn't you think of me even once?'

'I might have; I can't really remember.'

'How have *you* been, Miss Clemmie?'

'Well . . . and you?'

A smile spread across his face. 'Well enough, I suppose. How formal we're being.'

For no reason he could think of, she laughed. 'Don't go away; I'm going to get something to clean those wounds up, and some salve to soothe them, otherwise they might fester.'

When she came back with a basin of warm water he was leaning back in the chair. He didn't make a noise when she placed his hands on a folded towel and bathed the scratches, though he winced when she dug to remove the tip of a thorn. Gently applying salve, she secured some linen bandages around them. 'There.'

His hand closed over hers before she could remove it and he bore it to his mouth and kissed it. 'They're better already. You're an angel.'

He was watching her through his eyelashes. 'I have things I must tell you tomorrow,' he said.

'Will I like what you have to say?'

'I don't know, but it's something you must learn about sooner or later. I should have told you before tomorrow, and for that I apologize.'

'If you told me today that would be before tomorrow and you wouldn't feel the need to apologize.'

Her words brought a wry smile to his lips. 'You talk nonsense sometimes.'

'Sometimes I can't think of anything sensible to say. I just talk for the sake of it. You make me feel . . .'

Exactly what was it he made her feel? That she was a woman of grace and intelligence? That she was his equal? 'Feel what?'

'Nothing in particular . . . just a vague awareness that I'm someone important to myself.'

He laughed. 'Did you regard yourself as unimportant then? What would the children do without you? What would I do?'

'You're talking about being needed for a specific task.'

'And you are trying to capture an emotional connection. That's a concept I'm uncomfortable with. One thing I'm aware of is that you bring out the worst in me.'

If that were the worst, the best would be irresistible. 'I was trying to say that you treat me as an equal and I appreciate it.'

He appeared to be surprised. 'I don't regard you as anything other than my equal.'

There was a knock at the door and Mrs Ogden entered. Zachariah still had hold of her hand. She pulled it away before the housekeeper noticed.

'Your supper is ready, sir. Would you like to eat it in the dining room? I'll light the fire in your bedchamber in the meanwhile, and prepare the adjoining room for Evan's use.' Her glance fell on the bowl of water. 'I'll take those if you've finished with them, Miss Clemmie.'

When Mrs Ogden left they stood up together and Clementine said, 'Would you like some company while you have your supper?'

'You're a nice young woman, but there's no need. I'm used to my own company and will be retiring shortly after I've eaten. Evan will be ready for me then.' He kissed her gently on the forehead. 'Sleep soundly, Clemmie.'

'Goodnight, Zachariah. I'll see you at breakfast. It will be a pleasant surprise for the children. They've been keeping a look-out for you.'

'For me?'

'If they didn't have their uncle coming on a promised visit, what else would they have to look forward to?'

He shrugged, saying bleakly, 'Very little.'

And Clementine knew exactly how he meant it. The children had nobody else left to love.

Eleven

The snow had stopped falling, but the sky was still heavy and low. The horizon melded into the sky with only the occasional dark twig poking through the whiteness to indicate the path of a hedgerow.

The children stared out of the window, their eyes rounded with wonder.

'Are we inside a cloud?' Iris asked, her voice an awed whisper and quivering with excitement.

Clementine pulled a red velvet smock over the girl's warm petticoat, then brushed her hair and tied a ribbon in it before turning to Edward, who was seated on a low stool, and grunting as he tugged at his boot.

'Edward, you're putting that boot on back to front.' She turned it around. 'There . . . try that.'

The boy gave it an extra-hard tug and toppled backwards off the stool, his leg in the air and the boot dangling from it. Iris began to giggle.

Clementine hauled the child upright. 'You have to slide your toes around the heel and into the foot, Edward. Try it again.'

Edward's next attempt was more successful.

'Well done, Edward.'

The voice came from the doorway and they all turned towards it.

Iris gave a delighted little squeal when she saw Zachariah and rushed to give him a hug.

Edward held back a little, as he usually did, then edged forward, as cautious as a fox and with a certain amount of uncertainty in his eyes – but hardly able to contain his smile. He held out his hand. 'Welcome home, Uncle Zachariah.'

As Zachariah took it Clementine noticed his hands had been doctored by a much more proficient nurse than herself.

'Thank you, Edward. I've come to escort you all down to breakfast.'

'Edward can slide down the banister,' Iris said when they reached the landing at the top of the stairs.

Clementine turned her glance on the boy, trying to hide her alarm. 'Can he now? That's a surprise.'

'You weren't supposed to tell anyone, Iris.'

'That's what sisters are for, stopping a chap from scaring everyone witless.'

'Would it scare you if I did it?'

Zachariah laughed. 'It's your head. If you want to bounce off it at the bottom, go ahead.'

Iris turned to grin at her. 'Edward was scared you'd make a fuss if I told you, Miss Clemmie. You won't, will you?'

'I would have. But it's too late to do that now you have your uncle's seal of approval.'

Edward gave a little shrug. 'I only wanted to surprise Uncle Zachariah.'

'Of course you did.' She gazed down the long shiny slide of the handrail, her heart in her mouth. It would be irresistible to a boy, and she wouldn't mind sliding down it herself if she wasn't hampered by her skirts and didn't have an audience. 'Go on then. Be sure of this. I'll only make a fuss if you fall off and hurt yourself, and that will be a big one.'

Edward grinned. 'I won't fall off, I promise. It's easy if you don't go too fast.'

'How do you stop yourself from going too fast?'

'By holding on tight.'

'You'd better get on with it then.'

Edward hopped astride the rail, and with his rear pointing towards the hall he began to slide backwards. He managed to slow himself towards the bottom, and then dismounted to grin up at them.

'It's perfectly safe,' Zachariah said, and followed him down in exactly the same manner, only faster and with more confidence.

He stood at the bottom looking up at them. 'You next, Iris, then Miss Clemmie. I'll catch you.'

Iris grabbed her hand and clung to it. 'I don't want to, Miss Clemmie. I'm scared.'

'Then you don't have to, and neither will I.' She and Iris descended the stairs and walked past the grinning males, Clementine murmuring, 'You're becoming a convenient excuse for causing mischief in this house, Uncle Zachariah.'

'Is that a good thing or a bad thing?'

'Good for them, since it tells me they feel secure with you, even when they're being less than perfect.'

He laughed. 'It's not so exciting when you know you're not going to get into trouble when you're caught. The last time I slid down that banister I got a strap across my rear and I couldn't sit down for a day or two.'

'Now you can slide down it any time you feel like, an action that would be of more use if you could slide back up again.'

When they were seated Zachariah placed a small dollop of oatmeal in each bowl for the children and drizzled honey over it. 'I want you to eat well during this cold weather. It will help keep you warm.'

Edward wrinkled his nose. 'May I have some bacon instead?'

'After you've eaten the oatmeal. It's only a small amount.'

Mrs Ogden interrupted breakfast. 'Ben said it would be better if the children go out in the sleigh this morning, because it's going to snow again in the afternoon.'

'They have their lessons to do.'

Zachariah's laughter rang out. 'You're a hard taskmaster, Miss Clemmie. I think we can dispense with them for one morning. A ride in the sleigh is something that mustn't be missed, and this snow might melt as quickly as it came.' He turned to Mrs Ogden. 'Tell Ben I'll take the reins and he can stand on the back to balance the weight. That grey can get a bit sprightly at times. I just hope he doesn't get the urge to jump over a hedge.'

'What about your hands?'

'I'll be wearing gloves. Stop worrying, it's only a few scratches.'

* * *

The beast high-stepped along the drive, then under Zachariah's expert handling they picked up speed and went into a fast trot. Ben had found some bells attached to a leather strap and had hung it on the sleigh. They jingled along the lanes, their breath turning to vapour and their cheeks glowing from the cold.

When they returned to the house, Zachariah sent the children up to the nursery with Polly. 'You'll find a couple of gifts waiting there for you.' He turned to Clementine. 'Come to the drawing room when you're ready, Clementine. We need to talk.'

Changing her cloak for a warm shawl, she tidied her hair and went down in time to open the door for Mrs Ogden, who was carrying in a tray with coffee.

'I've brought you some muffins straight out of the oven, sir, and I'll send Annie up to the children with some hot chocolate to drink with their muffin, if that's all right with you, Miss Clemmie?'

She nodded. 'The muffins look delicious. Leave the tray on the table, Mrs Ogden. I'll see to it.'

'I'd prefer it if we were left undisturbed for the next hour,' Zachariah told the housekeeper. 'I'll ring if we need anything.'

'Yes, sir.' Giving a little bob and studiously avoiding a glance at either of them the housekeeper left.

Zachariah smiled as he turned to her. 'She'll jump to conclusions, I'm afraid.'

'Yes, I daresay she will. Would you like me to pour the coffee?'

'Please.'

She handed him a muffin, thick with a crunchy sugar crusting and with butter melting from its steaming innards, and placed his coffee on the table next to him. When he reached out for it she noticed some blood had seeped through the bandage. 'How are your hands after the sleigh ride?'

'A little sore . . . and don't tell me I should have listened to you, because I already know it.'

She made her eyes as round and as innocent as she could, but couldn't resist a response. 'As if I'd claim such a satisfying victory at the expense of my employer.'

Zachariah laughed. 'Stop smirking and eat your muffin. I have something to tell you.'

'What is it?'

'I have no intention of discussing it with a mouthful of crumbs, so eat.'

Perhaps he was going to dismiss her. No, he wouldn't have offered her refreshment. He would have sat behind his desk and been distantly correct. *Miss Morris. I've decided to terminate your services . . .*

She bit into her muffin and it burst into her mouth with a buttery soft explosion. *Not when there's food like this around,* Zachariah Fleet, she thought, and closed her eyes. 'Mmmm!'

She washed it down with the coffee then dabbed her mouth with a white starched table napkin and gazed at him. 'That was delicious. What did you want to tell me?'

'I don't know how to say it, so have been tossing it around in my mind.'

'Goodness . . . is it something so bad then, Zachariah?'

'It depends how you feel about it.'

'I won't know that until you tell me.'

He took a sip of his coffee. 'I brought you here under false pretences, Clemmie. You see, my dear, there was a legacy involved. John tracked the likely recipient down, and that was you. But we needed to check if you were the right person.'

'Probably not, because I don't know anyone who would leave me anything.'

'The legacy came through your father's family.'

'Howard Morris? But he'd already paid for my education.'

'The legacy originated from his mother.'

'If I'd had a living grandmother my mother would have taken me to her, surely.'

'Perhaps she did, and you've forgotten. Remember, you were only a child when you and she parted company.'

'I'd have remembered a grandmother. It's possible she disapproved of my mother and disowned her. But I think my mother would have told me.'

'John has to deal with facts, not supposition born of sentiment.'

'Yes, I realize that. Why is this legacy such a problem?'

'Recently, another young woman stepped forward with a claim to it. Her father was also Howard Morris, who died at the battle of Waterloo.'

'Oh . . . I see.' She frowned as her mind sifted through the possibilities. 'Yes . . . I really think I do see. I have a half-sister. What's her name?'

'Alexandra. She didn't know she was a foundling until a few weeks ago when John and I went to see her. She was raised by foster parents.'

'Poor Alexandra.'

'You needn't feel sorry for her. She loved her foster parents and they loved her. In fact, she would have had a better, and more secure upbringing than you had.'

'What does my half-sister look like? Are we alike?'

'Alexandra is exceedingly fair, and has many social graces. She's taller than you, with blue eyes. The resemblance between you isn't marked, but I haven't really tried to make any comparisons.'

But he'd noticed that Alexandra was exceedingly fair with blue eyes, and had been brimming with social graces. Had he looked past the surface? 'Is she unmarried?'

'Yes, she's unmarried, but I'm sure she'll make an advantageous marriage, since she's been brought up with that aim in life. I'm inviting her to Martingale House along with Julia and John Beck in the New Year, so you can meet her and get to know her. I hope you don't mind.'

'Why should I mind? This is your home and I'm just a servant in it. You can invite anyone you like to stay here.'

'You're put out. You know you're more than just a servant to me. I rely on you, and I've grown to trust you with all that is dear to me. You know more about me than anyone, except John and Julia Beck.'

She was acting like a sulky brat, she knew. She drew in a deep breath and forced a smile to her face. How could she feel so threatened by a complete stranger – someone she'd never met? 'It seems odd to suddenly discover I might have a half-sister. May I ask you something, which you might find a bit indelicate?'

He took her hands in his. 'I think I know what you're going to ask and we don't know which of you is his legitimate daughter yet. You see, it appears that Howard Morris was married to two different women at once, and you and Alexandra were born around the same time.'

'I see . . . at least, I think I do.'

'I imagine John Beck will soon sort it out. He's acquainted with someone in London who has access to the records. He's going to try and find out more, and will want to speak to you again when he's here. There are some aspects of this puzzle that don't quite add up. When he's sure, one of you will be entitled to the legacy. 'Would you like to know the amount involved?'

'I don't want to have high expectations of something that might come to nothing. Do you think Alexandra will like me?'

His expression was one of dubiety. 'As to that, we can only wait and see. Is it important to you that she does?'

'If I'm to acquire a sister, it would be pleasant if we got on well.'

And that, thought Zachariah, might not be possible. Alexandra knew what she wanted, and despite her assumed airs and graces she would always put herself first.

He'd come to realize that Clementine was a tender flower. She wanted to please everyone, and was willing to allow herself to be taken advantage of in the quest to achieve that. She was argumentative, yes, but that fierceness hid her soft nature. It formed a barrier against hurt. She wanted to love and be loved, and that was easily transferred to the children, who'd reached out to her in their own need.

Goodness, what a house full of misfits they were – all waifs and strays, who, one way or another, had been abandoned by those who had given them life. He had it in him to make them all whole. He impaled a stray curl of gold-tinted hair on his finger and moved it from the back of her ear to the front so it lay against her cheek. Her skin was a pale, flawless covering over her fine bones. 'It belongs there.'

'It tickles my face when the wind blows.'

'Then I'll tell the wind to stop blowing. I like you a lot, Clemmie, and so do the children. Will that do for now?'

She nodded.

He'd not set out to make her cry, but a pair of identical tears rolled from the depth of her soft brown eyes and tracked down her cheeks. She wasn't being fair to him.

'Stop crying,' he said, his voice harsh as he fought the instinct to pull her into his arms. He didn't want to feel like this about her, so soft and guilty, and leaving himself open to hurt and disappointment.

She backed away from him. Dashing the tears away with a corner of her shawl she turned and walked away, stiff-backed.

She was almost at the door when he said, 'Come back. I haven't finished our discussion.'

She stopped. 'Then finish it. You have ten seconds.'

He waited, taking a couple of deep slow breaths to hold his anger in check, then said, when the tenth tick of the clock told him his time had expired, 'I apologize . . . I hate it when you cry, I never know what I've done or said to cause it.'

'You didn't say anything to cause it.'

'Then why the devil are you crying?'

She turned, her face almost tragic. 'You said you liked me.'

'Well, what's so wrong with that when I do like you?'

'Nothing's wrong with it. It made me feel happy and sad at the same time and I cried.'

'You cry over nothing?'

She came back to where he stood and gave him a watery smile. 'You cry too, you just don't shed tears. Sometimes you gaze into the distance and your eyes are far away and incredibly sad, as though you're gazing into your past and trying to find yourself. Saying you liked me was something precious because nobody has said that to me before. It meant a lot to me, like being given a gift. 'Thank you, Zachariah, may I cry now?'

'No, you may not . . . I'd rather see you smile.'

'You remembered a happy time from your early childhood when Edward went down the banister, didn't you?'

'There's very little of the boy I used to be in this house.' He spotted a grain of sugar on her delicious mouth. Lifting it with the tip of his finger he drew it into his own mouth. 'Sugar. I always thought you were sweet.'

She tried not to snort.

'And don't you start snivelling over that remark else I'll throw you out into the snow. You'd better go,' he said gruffly. 'I've got a meeting with Mr Bolton before dinner.'

'Perhaps you'll find a new you in this house if you look hard enough.'

'I'm not looking for one.'

'You haven't considered, though, that one might be looking for you.'

After she'd gone Zachariah chuckled. She was talking nonsense. What an intense little creature she was at times. If she'd had that reaction when he said he liked her, how would she react if he told her he loved her?

Where the hell had that word come from? He must watch his tongue when he was around her from now on, because she would probably believe such a lie. His life was complicated enough at the moment without adding matters of love to the list.

Love or need? Clementine lived in his home. She cared for his wards, ran his household and relied on him. He couldn't ruin her. Yet the more he saw of her the more he wanted to.

Were he to wed it might as well be her, and that might yet prove to be the case. What he'd said to her was true. He did like her, and she'd cried. But that wouldn't be enough for her. She would want all of him, his body, his heart and his soul. She'd give him the same in return, for she understood him.

So the question remained. Was it love or was it need?

After a couple of days the snow cleared, much to the children's disgust.

Zachariah went to the market and came back with a sturdy, but gentle-natured brown pony.

Quivering with excitement Edward was lifted into the saddle. His feet were firmly in the stirrups and his hands gripped a leather strap across the pony's back. Zachariah attached the animal and its burden to a leading rein.

Clementine and Iris watched from the window seat on the landing window and Zachariah led the pony up and down the carriageway, allowing Edward to get used to the motion.

'Will Uncle Zachariah teach me to ride?'

'One day, when you're older, I expect. Ladies have special saddles, I believe. They don't ride like men do, but sideways.'

'That's silly. How will they know what's in front of them?'

She grinned, imagining Zachariah trying to find a reason to explain that to a four-year-old girl. 'You might have to ask your uncle that.'

Twelve

Alexandra, who'd learned to twist her foster parents around her little finger, didn't take to instruction easily – despite her strict upbringing. Agreeing with them had usually resulted in her getting her own way.

Zachariah Fleet had left a certain amount of money to clothe her, and she intended to spend every farthing of it on garments of her own choice, despite Julia Beck's unwanted advice.

The fabrics Alexandra was presented with were sumptuous. The gowns she chose for herself were heavy with embroidery, their necklines low on the shoulder and showing a little of her breasts. Roland would like them; he'd be able to sit and stare all he liked.

But she had underestimated the determination of her hostess. Julia Beck was horrified by her choice and discarded them one by one. 'Come, come, Miss Tate, that type of neckline is unsuitable for day wear, especially in these cold months. You will need something practical and warm for every day.'

'I will purchase this little fur shoulder cape with the matching muff. And just look at that pretty embroidered bag. There are evening pumps to match. How sweet.'

Bustling with annoyance, Julia reminded her she was holding the purse strings. 'They are too expensive. I cannot allow you to take advantage of Mr Fleet's generous nature to that extent. We will buy gowns suitable for day-to-day wear, and a modest gown for entertaining.'

'Of course we will. But they are all so pretty and the neckline of this ball gown will enhance my shoulders.'

'There will be precious few balls at Martingale. Mr Fleet prefers a quiet life when he's in the country.'

'Don't be vexed with me, Mrs Beck. I'm only teasing you.'

To save arguments Alexandra allowed Julia Beck to choose the travelling gown. It was olive green, a hideous colour that made Alexandra's complexion look muddy. What was more, it was made of thick material. It was as if the woman had picked that gown deliberately and for that very reason.

These Quaker people were so dull in their choice of clothing, Alexandra thought, though she kept her counsel. The gowns she'd chosen for herself were no more shocking than any other normal woman wore. She didn't see why she shouldn't have something pretty. She intended to have her way in the matter of the ball gown and one of two other things, and had noticed that Mrs Beck kept all the invoices together in a small compartment in the bureau.

The day before they were due to leave for the country Alexandra feigned a headache when Julia and her husband went to bid farewell to their children.

'Oh, I do hope you're going to be all right for the journey.'

'I'll be perfectly all right in the morning, I promise.'

As soon as her hosts had gone, Alexandra packed the green travelling outfit and a burgundy taffeta gown she didn't particularly like, and she took them back to the dressmaker's premises, where the fawning proprietor was only too eager to change them for more expensive garments. She added the pumps and handbag, then the muff and cape.

'Place it on Mr Fleet's account, please.'

'I will need Mrs Beck's signature.'

'Oh . . . of course you do. Did I forget to tell you? Mrs Beck is suffering from a headache, and her instructions were to bring the invoice back with me. We're leaving for the country tomorrow, where we will join Mr Fleet.' She smiled. 'It's a secret, but I'm sure I can trust you with it. I wanted something special, you see.' She shrugged. 'It *is* for a celebratory occasion, but I promised not to tell anyone. You do understand, don't you? If you won't let me sign for it then I'll have to cancel the sale. I admired it the first time I saw it, and considered it to be a wonderful gown to be wed in. You're such a clever and artistic designer, Mrs Spencer, and I will recommend you to all my friends.'

A smile crossed the woman's face. 'I always think that my customers deserve the best I can do. Mrs Beck has always been a good client of mine and her recommendation has brought a new clientele to my door, so I'll trust her on this.'

Alexandra managed to get the clothing indoors before Julia

and John Beck came home. She went to the bureau first and placed the invoice in the middle of the bundle.

When she packed the gown in her trunk she stroked her hand gently over the lace-edged tiers of blue silk. No doubt there would be a stink when the deception was discovered, but she would handle that when it happened.

She was not looking forward to the journey, though it would be a little more comfortable by private carriage if the weather held out and there were only a few ruts to contend with.

There was a faintly awkward atmosphere inside the carriage, though the Becks were exceedingly polite. Julia chattered about nothing, until Alexandra felt like screaming. Couldn't the woman see she was shivering with the cold?

When she alighted from the coach at one of the inns and mud splashed on her skirt from a passing vehicle, Julia remarked rather caustically, as though she'd discovered her deceit, 'Oh, such a pity. You should have worn the travelling gown for the journey. It's more serviceable . . . and the mud would have brushed off. Also it would have been warmer. I'll see if I can find a thick shawl in my luggage for you to wear.'

Julia Beck might chatter, but both she and her husband had been evasive when it had come to answering questions about Mr Fleet. Nevertheless, Alexandra tried to strike up a conversation about him.

'Have you known Mr Fleet long?'

The two of them looked at each other and smiled before John said, 'We've known him for many years, and we're business partners. He's a good man.'

'Mr Fleet must have been a child when you first knew him then.'

'Yes, I suppose he must have been.'

She said outright, 'You seem very close; are you related to him?'

They would not be drawn. 'Zachariah is as dear to us as our own sons,' John said smoothly, and changed the subject. 'Have you been to the country before, Miss Tate?'

She gazed out at the stubbly brown fields that were enclosed within hedges of woven sticks. They had very little foliage. Then there were the stark outlines of leafless trees stabbing crooked fingers against a drab grey sky. Sinister black birds circled the copse like witches on broomsticks, and her heart dropped. She hadn't expected the country to be so sparse and unappealing.

It reminded her of her life so far: drab.

Eventually their destination came into view, a sizeable house topping a gentle rise, and wrapped in a copse of trees. The house seemed to be isolated in the middle of nowhere, if one was to ignore a small village they'd passed through. She'd learned that Zachariah Fleet owned property in London, too, so he was a man with considerable wealth.

How different it would have been had her mother kept her. She might have grown up in a house like this one and her step-father would have been a baron, not a simple tutor. Surely that would have given her a better advantage in life.

John Beck had asked her if she'd been to the country before. No, she'd never been to the country, and whatever happened, she doubted if she'd be staying long. Not that she had anywhere to go, but there was always Roland if her plans came to naught.

A housekeeper came from the front door, bobbed a curtsy and let them in. A couple of men came from the stables, unpacked the luggage and followed them inside while the carriage horses were turned about and led towards the stables.

The front door had barely closed around them when the tall figure of Zachariah Fleet came down the stairs, a smile on his face. 'John . . . Julia. How pleasant to see you again. I hope the journey wasn't too tedious.'

Julia kissed him on both cheeks. 'Isn't it always tedious? But it's worth the trial of the journey to see you at the end of it.'

His glance came her way, blue and impersonal. 'Miss Tate, welcome to Martingale House. We'll do our best to make you comfortable while you're here. Come into the drawing room, all of you. My housekeeper will be along shortly.'

Alexandra wondered where her half-sister was as she looked around the comfortable drawing room with its blue furnishings and darker blue and silver patterned wallpaper.

Inside the house was warm and welcoming, and there was the smell of freshly baked bread coming from the kitchen that made her stomach rumble. She pressed her hands against it.

Somewhere in the upper reaches of the house came the sound of a giggle and the patter of feet. A dog barked.

'Be quiet, Happy.'

There was a hushed, but loud whisper. 'Come back, Iris. We have to wait until we're called, then Miss Clemmie will take us down.'

'But Happy's gone downstairs.'

'I expect he's gone to the kitchen to see what he can scrounge.'

A woman's voice this time: 'Iris . . . come back up at once. Your hands and face need a wash and your hair is untidy.'

A faint smile touched her host's lips as he gazed at Julia. 'The children are excited at meeting you, but I'll allow you to settle in first. And you can meet them at breakfast tomorrow morning.'

So, Zachariah Fleet was a married man with children. Alexandra imagined he'd be a strict father, and his wife would be cowed.

'How can you be so cruel when you know I'm eager to see them?' Julia grumbled, and then gazed from one man to the other when they laughed. 'There, you rascally creatures, you were teasing me. I knew it.'

'They will be down soon and I will introduce you to them, Julia.'

A short time later a knock came at the door and a young woman entered, ushering two children in front of her. Her gaze went directly to Zachariah Fleet and her welcoming smile was reflected in her eyes. He went to her side as if drawn there. 'This is my nephew and niece, Edward and Iris, who are also my wards.'

They looked like a family posing for a portrait until Iris dipped into a wobbly curtsy and spoiled the illusion.

'You're not supposed to do that until the guests have been introduced,' Edward said as he manoeuvred himself into position against his uncle's leg and gazed up at him, the hero worship in his eyes plain for all to see.

When Zachariah Fleet ruffled the lad's hair he smiled at being the recipient of special attention, however small.

The young woman placed a hand to her mouth to stifle a giggle, and Zachariah Fleet grinned at her. 'It was a pretty curtsy all the same, don't you agree, Miss Clemmie?'

'Fit for royalty to receive.'

Alexandra revised her earlier opinion. She had not been told about the children, and disappointment settled inside her. It wasn't that she disliked children, but she didn't like them all that much either.

'Children . . . this is Mr and Mrs Beck, who are my dearest friends.'

Mrs Beck almost pounced on them, her smile full of affection. 'I've been so longing to meet the pair of you. How wonderful. We shall have some jolly times together while we are here.'

Edward bowed over his hand. 'I'm pleased to meet you, Mrs Beck . . . and you, sir. I've got a new pony that I'm learning to ride.'

'You must show me how well you ride tomorrow.'

Julia wrapped the young woman and the children in a hug. 'How well you look, my dear, the country air must suit you. Doesn't Clementine look well, John? And the children are so sweet. Such a pretty little girl with such nice manners, and young Edward is so polite. They are a credit to you, Clementine. Don't you think so, Zachariah?'

'I expected no less. The children like her, so they are always on their best behaviour for her.' Zachariah turned to them. 'Go upstairs to Polly now, while I get our guests settled.'

'Is Miss Clemmie coming?'

'In a little while.'

Clementine blew the children a kiss. 'I'll see you before too long.'

The children blew kisses back and headed for the door.

What a nauseating display, Alexandra thought. If they were her children to look after they wouldn't be allowed such liberty.

Their host turned to Julia. 'I've given you the usual bedchamber. I think it would be a good idea if we allowed the two young women some privacy.

'Miss Alexandra Tate, may I introduce you to Miss Clementine Morris, who may or may not be your relation, and who supervises the children. Clementine, Miss Tate has recently suffered bereavement with the death of her foster father. I'll be in the library with John if you need me.'

So, Clementine used their mutual father's name, as if she had the sole right to it.

A pair of brown eyes assessed her. 'I'm so sorry to hear of your loss.'

Alexandra inclined her head in as gracious a manner as she was able, because along with most of her spine, her neck ached from being thrown about in the carriage like a sack of potatoes. There was also a prolonged surge of envy in her when she gazed upon her rival, for that's what she was – a rival for the legacy. The girl was pleasant to look at, but Alexandra knew she was no match for her own looks.

She managed to swallow her ire, as years of learning how to control her emotions had taught her. 'Thank you, Miss Morris, my foster father's death was a great blow.'

Clementine's eyes closed in a moment where she seemed to be thinking. Then the lids opened on a puzzled expression. 'You remind me of someone.'

Alexandra decided to lodge her claim with this girl, right now. 'Our mutual father, Howard Morris, perhaps?'

'It couldn't be him, since I was born after he died.'

'I never even knew about Howard Morris until a few weeks ago. It's disconcerting to think you are one thing and then find out you are someone else.'

They gazed at each other while a maid brought them refreshment. The woman bustled around sending inquisitive looks her way. She would carry any information she gleaned back to the servants' quarters, no doubt. The fussing annoyed Alexandra. Already tired from the journey, she snapped, 'Leave us.'

The atmosphere tightened after Annie left, red-faced with the embarrassment of being dismissed so curtly.

'You didn't need to speak to her like that.'

'The staff are too familiar.'

'They've worked here a long time and deserve some consideration.'

Alexandra bristled. 'They are servants, and should know their place. So should you, Miss Morris. Whether you prove to be my sister or not, I understand you're employed by Mr Fleet. That makes you a servant in my eyes.'

'I know exactly what my position is in this house. You're a guest, Miss Tate. May I suggest that if you know so much about managing a household like this, you should be well aware of what *your* place is in it.' She stood. 'I'm answerable only to Mr Fleet. I think this conversation between us is now at an end. Enjoy your refreshment. I'll send a maid to take you to your room when one is available.'

Half an hour ticked by before a knock came at the door. 'It's about time,' Alexandra said when a maid appeared. 'I was beginning to think I'd been forgotten.'

'Sorry, Miss. I was unpacking your trunk and hanging your gowns in the wardrobe. The fire is alight and your chamber is nice and warm. I've put a jug of warm water and a bowl in your room and laid all the toilet things out in case you want to refresh yourself. Now, if you'd follow me please, Miss Tate.'

The maid's back bristled with affront as she went upstairs.

Five minutes later Alexandra tugged at the bell pull. It was ten minutes before the maid arrived, out of breath. 'Yes, Miss.'

'The water is lukewarm, and you've hung my gowns up without pressing the creases from them.'

'I have other duties to attend to, Miss.'

Dragging the gowns from the wardrobe, Alexandra threw them on the bed. 'Take them downstairs to press them else I'll report you to Mr Fleet. And take this with you.' Alexandra thrust the jug of water at her so violently that the contents slopped out the top and hit Annie in the face.

The maid cried out with the shock of it.

Sensing a movement in the hall outside, Alexandra said solicitously, 'I'm so sorry. I tripped over the rug.'

'What on earth is going on? You're soaking wet, Annie,' Julia Beck said, coming into the room uninvited.

Alexandra gazed at the girl and smiled. 'Well, go on, Annie, tell Mrs Beck what happened.'

'Miss Tate tripped over the rug and I was splashed.'

'I see.' The woman eyed the tangle of clothing on the bed. 'You go and get dry, Annie, I'll help Miss Tate hang her clothes up.'

'Thank you, Mrs Beck.'

'My gowns need pressing.'

Julia dismissed that. 'Oh, the creases will drop out in a day or two if they're shaken out and hung properly. How did you get on with Clementine? Such a dear girl.'

'I did my best to make friends, though I think Miss Morris is rather put out by me being here. She excused herself and left me waiting. She must have forgotten me because it was half an hour before a maid attended me.'

'Clementine did?'

'I've just been allocated this room, and as you can see it's nowhere near ready.'

'Mr Fleet doesn't come here much and the house is run by a reduced number of staff. It's not like being in London society. Where we are capable of managing for ourselves, we do. Mr Fleet relies heavily on Clementine. She has sole charge of his nephew and niece, and manages the day-to-day affairs of Martingale House in his absence. She is a capable young woman.'

'Oh, I can see that she is. I imagine it's because I was tired, and misinterpreted what was said and done.' Alexandra remembered the gown she'd bought, visible under the other garments. 'Don't worry about my wardrobe, Mrs Beck, of course I can hang it up by myself. Thank you for pointing out my shortcomings. I feel quite ashamed of myself.'

'There's a dear girl. We must all help each other where we can.'

'I'll also apologize to Miss Morris, and hope she'll forgive me.'

'If there has been a misunderstanding between you I'm sure she will.'

Alexandra apologized over dinner, aware that any dissent that might arise from it would make Clementine appear churlish.

'I'm sorry about the misunderstanding we had earlier, Miss Morris. I do hope you'll forgive me for mistaking you for a servant. I misinterpreted your position in the household.'

'It was partly my fault, I imagine. I never know what my exact position is in the house. I suppose it could appear that I was a maid to an outsider, so let us forget about it.'

An outsider, was she? 'I would rather clear the air now.'

'Discussion serves only to cloud it at this time. Any friction between us is a private matter. I do not intend to embarrass the present company with a trivial matter that is of no concern to anyone else.'

Clementine was quick-minded, and had deftly turned the tables on her. Alexandra drew in a slow breath. 'Then I hope you'll call me by my Christian name, and allow me to address you by yours, Clementine. It would be much friendlier.'

'I have no objection . . . Alexandra.'

'There,' Julia soothed. 'We're all friends again.'

Julia was mistaken, Alexandra thought, her glance going to Zachariah Fleet who was gazing at Clementine in mild contemplation, his thoughts safely guarded behind the calm surface of his eyes. He was a man completely in charge of himself.

Or was he?

Alexandra saw Clementine flick him a grin that was little more than a twitch of the lip and her host raised his eyebrow slightly.

There was something intangible between them . . . a frisson of tension that was felt rather than seen. They were certainly aware of each other.

Was Clementine his mistress; was that why she was paid? After all there was a nursery maid for the children, so why would they need someone like Clementine to have sole charge of them?

The thought that they might be lovers gave her pleasure as well as a sense of power. In such a situation it would be easy to ruin Clementine's reputation with a word here or a word there.

Thirteen

Clementine tried to like Alexandra, but despite the supposed connection between them she couldn't bring herself to adopt the role of long-lost sister. She suspected that Alexandra felt the same way towards her.

Alexandra seemed to have two faces. The public one was all elegance. She played the piano brilliantly, sang sweetly and was beautiful as well as clever. Every time she seated herself she was a study of grace and she hardly disturbed the air when she rose. When they were in the same room together, Clementine felt clumsy and awkward.

Alexandra's hair stayed in its ringlets, unlike her own, which had strands that detached from her braid to dance around her head with every puff of wind that blew. Clementine had never been good at enhancing her own looks, but then, she'd never felt she had to before.

In private, Alexandra was impatient and always found something to criticize. She was meticulous and demanding about the most unimportant of matters, which was annoying.

'Look at the dust on this glove. The banister must need cleaning and someone should speak to the housekeeper.' Though who she thought was the *someone* responsible for informing Mrs Ogden, wasn't quite clear. Or she would pick on the children. 'Go and ask your maid to wipe your noses . . . and please try and control those dogs. They came into my room when I was resting and were quite unruly. They knocked the cup off my table with their tails and leapt on the bed.'

Edward went so far as to poke his tongue out at her back, and Iris giggled. Clementine then had to reprimand them, and forbid them to have any cake for tea as a punishment. Lack of respect towards any guest could not be encouraged, even though Clementine had childishly felt as though she'd like to poke her own tongue out at her. She also suspected she was being under-mined by Alexandra, but couldn't understand why.

Worse, all the servants hopped to do Alexandra's bidding, lest they were reported to Mrs Ogden. Mrs Ogden had muttered one day, 'If she doesn't stop ringing that dashed bell and complaining I think I'll strangle her with the bell pull. "Do this! Do that!" Who does she think she is, the mistress of the house?'

To which Annie answered, 'I wouldn't be at all surprised if she fancied herself in the role. She's got her eye on the main chance, does that one. I see her simpering to Mr Fleet and making sheep's eyes at him. If he ain't careful he'll find himself standing at the altar with her . . . then God help us all.'

Mrs Ogden gave a derisive snort. 'Not Mr Fleet; he's too clever for the likes of a little gold-digger like her. Fleet by name, Fleet by nature – that's him.'

It all came to a head one day when Clementine couldn't find her nursery maid. Clementine discovered Polly in Alexandra's bedchamber, arranging the woman's hair. She waited until she came down the stairs then tackled her about it. 'That isn't your job, Polly. Where are the children?'

'Miss Tate wanted her hair done seeing as though you're going to that charity music performance. Mrs Beck said she'd look after the children for a while. I'll be finished in a few minutes. I just need to press her gown.'

'I see. Well, try not to be too long. She isn't the only one who needs to get ready.'

She found the children downstairs in the drawing room, where Julia was reading them a story.

'I'm so sorry, Julia. Polly will be available to look after them in a little while, and in the meantime I'll be here. So if you want to go elsewhere you don't have to worry about the children.'

'It's all right, dear. I enjoyed their company. They've been so good that I can only say they're a credit to you.'

'What's a credit?' Iris asked.

'It means that you've behaved yourself and I'm going to give you a piece of my Turkish Delight as a reward.'

Clementine could almost see Edward's ears prick up as he turned Julia's way with a big smile. 'I've been good too.'

'Of course you have, my dear boy. You will both have some.'

Her glance went to Clementine. 'You should treat children like dogs, my dear. Praise them often and feed them treats as a reward, then, apart from a woof or two, you should never get any trouble from them. That goes for men too. They like to feel appreciated and useful, even when they're being the opposite.'

The exchange made Clementine laugh.

Julia patted her hand. 'There, that's better. You've been looking a bit glum lately. Will you be doing something with your hair? You should be getting ready, you know.'

'I can never do my hair. I expect I'll just braid it.'

'You certainly will not. I'll ask Zachariah's man to fashion it for you. Evan used to work in the theatre when he was young so is a genius with hair and dress. What are you wearing?'

'I haven't given it much thought.'

'You should consider wearing that cream taffeta gown with the tiered skirt and collar. It's very becoming. And that embroidered shawl will match the rosebuds decorating the scalloped hems. Come, dear, we will give the children their treat and leave them with Polly while I help you dress. We don't want to keep Zachariah waiting. His patience is not infinite, and it's already stretched a little thin.'

Tears filled her eyes. 'I'm trying to keep everything under control, but the servants keep getting called on to do other than their normal tasks.'

Julia gave her a hug. 'The responsibility of running this house is not yours alone, my dear, and don't think that Zachariah hasn't noticed the effort you've been putting in. No doubt he will reward you in his own way. After today I will confer with Mrs Ogden and suggest to her that the servants be reminded of their assigned duties.

'Alexandra will complain if they don't attend her immediately.'

'Let her. She has far too much to say for herself.' She lowered her voice. 'Although I shouldn't say it, she's a disagreeable creature altogether. Further to that I will ask John to counsel Zachariah as to the benefits of seeing if he can hire a ladies' maid from the domestic agency for the duration of her visit. In fact, I will interview the candidates myself, and make sure she's suitable. Now, dry those tears, else your eyes will be all red and puffy, and most unattractive.'

Within ten minutes Evan was working on Clementine's hair. He was a dapper little man. Soon he had her hair parted in the middle and drawn into a knot at the crown, where a posy of creamy silk flowers was attached. Miraculously, the strands of hair that usually flew about her face were tamed into pretty ringlets.

'There, I told you Evan was a genius,' Julia said.

'He certainly is. Thank you so much, Evan, it was kind of you.'

He made a little bow. 'I'm at your service, Miss Morris. There's very little to do here in the country when compared to London, so you just have to ask.'

The children inspected her before she went downstairs to where the men waited with Julia.

Zachariah's eyes widened as she descended, and when he took her hand in his and kissed it, saying, 'You look lovely,' she felt the colour float gently into her cheeks like a soft pink cloud.

She might look lovely, Clementine thought, but Alexandra looked exquisite as she drifted down the stairs in a blue gown that displayed most of her shoulders – one that put Clementine firmly in the shade and widened Zachariah's eyes even further. She had a white fur collar over her arm, which she handed to Zachariah with a simper, presumably to place around her shoulders so he could view her charms up close. Did she think to make a servant out of him?

Clementine wished she had the courage to be so artful.

Evan descended the stair last, brush in hand to make sure his master and his gentleman friend were free of any last-minute lint to mar the perfection of their cutaway jackets.

Both wore freshly starched cravats. Zachariah's hair was parted in the middle and fell below his ears in a tumble of unruly waves. He was an exceedingly handsome and well-formed man. So was John Beck, though his hair was streaked with grey and his complexion was taking on that rough outdoors texture that came with age for most men.

Zachariah handed the cape to Evan. 'See to Miss Tate first. Mrs Beck tells me I need to hire a ladies' maid on a temporary basis, something I should have thought of myself. I know someone who runs an employment agency, and if he's there this afternoon I'll ask him to recommend someone for the position.'

'Yes, sir.'

Beside her, Julia sucked in a breath. 'I cannot remember you buying that gown, Alexandra. In fact, I distinctly remember us discussing it and coming to the conclusion that it was far too expensive.'

Alexandra smiled. 'I believe it was you who reached that conclusion. But I couldn't resist it so I changed my mind and I took the green travelling gown back and exchanged it.' She turned to Zachariah, her eyelids gently fluttering. 'I know I've presumed on your kindness, sir, and beg your indulgence. I do hope you'll forgive me.'

How prettily she said it. Clementine felt like sticking a dagger between her shoulder blades. No, not one dagger but a dozen! More than that, she'd like to slow cook her on a spit over a fire like a suckling pig.

The power of Clementine's imaginary revenge was so fierce that she almost smiled with the pleasure it offered her to just think it. Then she reprimanded herself as she recognized she was seething with jealousy, which was not a positive trait to encourage.

Zachariah shrugged, as offhand as his manners would allow. 'It's only a gown, Julia. As Miss Tate is very well aware, she needs no enhancement and would look just as enchanting in a gown made of sackcloth and ashes.'

Hah! she thought. Removing Alexandra from the spit, she impaled the immaculate Zachariah there instead.

When he smiled at her, however, she forgave him. Moving to her side when John went on ahead with Alexandra and his wife, he said, 'You'll be travelling in my carriage with Miss Tate. Come along, Clemmie, else we won't get there until it's time to return home.'

Alexandra had seated herself comfortably in the middle of the seat, her skirt arranged so it wouldn't crease.

Zachariah handed Clementine in and took the seat beside her. 'I hope you are comfortable, ladies. Considering you had no maid you both look very becoming. An oversight on my part, I'm afraid. I must hire one for the duration of your visit, Alexandra.'

'Evan offered to help me out,' Clementine ventured.

'How very droll to use a valet as a ladies' maid,' Alexandra cooed.

'Not at all. Evan used to work in a theatre and he has many skills. You should ask him to tell you about it. He can be very entertaining.'

'I used Polly as a maid for my hair. She's inexperienced, but fashions a reasonable style. After all, it doesn't need two servants to care for two small children. Oh, I forgot, Clementine . . . you're not a servant are you? But you said you received an allowance. If you don't mind me asking, what exactly is the description of your position here?'

This was going to evolve into a right royal argument if she wasn't careful, but still she said, 'I do mind you asking since I've already informed you of it.'

Zachariah leaned forward. 'Clementine is my guest. She also tutors my wards and provides a maternal presence for them. For that service alone she is worth her weight in gold. I would suggest that you desist from being too inquisitive, or jumping to wrongful conclusions, Miss Tate.'

'My pardon. I wasn't suggesting . . .' Alexandra turned to gaze out of the window, flags of colour burning her cheeks.

Clementine felt sorry for her and said to him, 'Between us we have made Alexandra uncomfortable. I'm sure she didn't intend to be inquisitive. Perhaps we should just drop this particular subject.'

Zachariah shot her an exasperated look.

Unexpectedly, Alexandra agreed with him, but her voice contained a faint nuance of hurt. 'Mr Fleet is right. I was being inquisitive, but I was trying to get to know you a little better.'

He sighed. 'My pardon if I upset you, Miss Tate.'

'I'm sure I deserved it.'

'No . . . Clemmie was right to take me to task.'

Zachariah was not a man who was naturally inclined to indulge in small talk. They made the short journey to Dorchester mostly in silence, a slight atmosphere making conversation awkward.

The carriage conveying the Becks followed on behind them.

When they reached their destination he alighted first and helped them down. Alexandra flowed down the carriage steps supported with the lightest of touches on his hand.

Clementine trod on the hem of her skirt and she stumbled. Zachariah spanned her waist with his hands and lifted her down, as if she weighed nothing at all. 'I have you safe, my little gadfly,' he said, his whisper designed for her ears alone. When their eyes met for a moment and he smiled, an indescribable awareness shivered through her.

From the moment they entered the room Alexandra became the focus of all eyes, which she took as her due.

Clementine was familiar with some of the people there – part of the congregation of the same church. They exchanged smiles and made small talk as Clementine introduced Alexandra to their host, Emma Cheeves, whose husband presided over a bank.

'How lovely to welcome yet another guest from Martingale House. My goodness, Mr Fleet does seem to collect an assortment of beautiful young ladies. You must be a relative because you remind me somewhat of the female side of the former baron's family. Don't you think so, Miss Morris?'

Clementine didn't see how two people could be described as an assortment, and the reference to the baron's family triggered an elusive vision of a face, one that left her mind immediately. Besides which, Zachariah wouldn't like his business to be discussed in public.

'Oh, as to that I couldn't really say. I've never met any of Mr Fleet's family except his nephew and niece.'

'Always so discreet, Miss Morris. One wonders what you really do at Martingale House. So mysterious . . . are you connected to the family?'

Clementine felt uncomfortable at being the centre of attention. Next to her Alexandra gave a light laugh. 'I've been given to understand that Clementine was resident in a workhouse, and she didn't even know Mr Fleet until a few months ago.'

The woman tossed her a look laced with scorn and her voice took on a ring of authority. 'What exactly *is* your position in the household then, Miss Morris?'

How smug Alexandra sounded when she murmured, 'I've asked her that myself. Miss Morris is paid for her services and she doesn't understand that accepting payment makes one a servant.'

Clementine could have pointed out to her that the fancy gown Alexandra wore had been paid for by Zachariah, but she didn't, for he'd be angry at the thought of being the object of such gossip.

'It wouldn't have happened in Sir Gabriel's day. Now there was a gentleman with charm – too much at times, but he always treated a lady as one should be treated, and the servants were reminded of their place from time to time.'

'The same servants still live at Martingale House, and are part of the family now. Mr Fleet said they know their jobs without him constantly reminding them,' Clementine told them.

One of the women asked in a more kindly manner, 'How are your young charges keeping, Miss Morris? They are such dear children . . . a tragedy that they lost their parents.'

The thought of the children made Clementine want to smile, but she didn't. She was upset, and felt like crying, so she choked out, 'They are recovering well from their grief at the loss of their mother and father. Like most children they respond well to love.'

Alexandra gave a tinkling laugh. 'I try to mother them a little when Miss Morris is attending to her other duties. The children can be naughty, but they get their own way too often, I fear, and that isn't wise. Were they my children they would be disciplined more often. And really, who has heard of children eating breakfast with the adults in the dining room?'

'How very bizarre. Spare the rod and spoil the child, I say.'
Mrs Cheeves nodded wisely.

Clementine's ears began to burn, but with anger rather than
anything else.

'Perhaps you'd like to walk the length of the room with me,
Miss Tate. You must meet my son. He is following in his father's
footsteps and will become a partner in his father's bank before
too long. Are you staying in the district for long?'

'Just until a family legacy has been proved, then I'll return to
Portsmouth, or London I imagine . . . Unless I meet someone
suitable and wed them in the meantime.'

'You have admirers then?'

'One or two.' The pair turned their backs on her and drifted
away, heading for Basil Cheeves, a pale-faced young man with a
long chin.

Julia joined her. 'I heard all of that exchange. Far be it for me
to think ill of anyone, but that young woman is extremely forward
and very conceited.' Julia placed a cup of warm, spiced wine in
her hands. 'Here, my dear, this will chase away the winter chills.'

'Thank you, Julia.'

'Zachariah will not like this.'

'Please don't tell him, Julia. He will only look on it as a petty
women's matter.'

'My dear . . . Zachariah may be reserved by nature, but very
little gets past him. He sees you here, alone and distressed, and
shivering like an abandoned kitten – as he poetically put it. He
sent me to rescue you. Soon the news will circulate; he'll see the
glances turn your way as people speculate over your relationship
with him.'

'And they will think the worst.'

'For himself he won't care what they think. He will care about
how it affects you though, and if the gossip continues he'll do
something about it.'

'What can he do? You can't stop people from gossiping.'

'I daresay he will think of something. He knows the power of
his position in the community here. If he walked out and took
his house guests with him it would cause Mrs Cheeves a great
deal of embarrassment. She might even be ostracized.'

'He must not . . . not over me. It would be too cruel, for

when he returns to London I will have nobody to be my champion.'

The small orchestra filed in and the guests moved towards the seats. Alexandra seated herself with Mrs Cheeves in the front row, the skirt of her gown a shining swathe of silk. Basil Cheeves was staring at her, an expression of admiration on his face, and something else. There was something reptilian in his slightly bulging eyes and the flickering tip of his tongue that he frequently used to dampen his lower lip. Clementine shuddered.

Relief washed over her when Zachariah and John gazed across the crowd of heads. Julia waved to them and they seated themselves either side, with John on her side and Zachariah on Julia's.

'Miss Tate is sitting with our hostess,' Julia informed them.

'So she is. Mrs Cheeves is always at the fore when welcoming a new arrival to the district, and just as quick to discard them if they don't measure up.' Zachariah leaned forward. 'You look flushed, Clemmie. Has something upset you?'

'No . . . it was the mulled wine. I drank it rather quickly and it brought the blood rushing to my face.'

He smiled at that. 'Are you warm enough now?'

She nodded, charmed by his smile and the infinite hyacinth blue of his eyes. The warmth she experienced had hidden depths and a repertoire of private sins that she wished she could experience with him, and without censure.

The orchestra tuned up with a multitude of uncoordinated squeaks and scrapes that sounded nothing like music. It made her wince. Then a thread of melody emerged from a violin to shimmer like a firefly in the air. Everyone fell quiet.

Clementine gazed at the programme. Schumann, Bach, Brahms and Strauss. She'd never heard music played by professional players, and had difficulty pronouncing the names of the composers in her mind, but the music turned out to be as exquisite as it was sensual, and it played upon her emotions, so sometimes she smiled and sometimes a tear rolled down her cheek.

When the concert was over, she asked Zachariah, 'Am I allowed to keep the programme?'

'I expect so. Why do you want it?'

'To place in my treasure box. I keep my memories in it.'

'Memories?'

'I've never been to a concert before and might never go to one again, so when I'm old I'll be able to look at the programme and remember this particular concert.'

'I should have thought of that. Every young lady should have a treasure box. I must give you a memento to keep in it.'

'You're teasing me.'

'I like teasing you.'

'I'm not likely to forget you, Zachariah.' As soon as the words left her mouth she realized she'd been too personal and wished she could recall them.

His glance met hers and the buzz in the room faded into the background when he said, 'Thank you, Clemmie. That's the nicest remark anyone's ever offered me.'

'I didn't mean it to sound so personal.'

'A pity.' He lifted her hand to his mouth and kissed it.

The noise resumed. Somebody laughed, glasses chinked.

Zachariah smiled at her. 'Shall I ask the musicians to sign the programme for you? I imagine our host has a pen and inkwell they can use for the occasion. Sit there and I'll go and ask him for it.'

People were gathering in little groups to talk. In the time he was away nobody approached her, though people kept looking her way, the women sometimes sniggering behind their fans, the men's eyes bold and speculative. She knew why, and tried not to mind.

Alexandra was in the centre of a group consisting mostly of younger people. She was talking animatedly and seemed to be the centre of attention. Basil Cheeves hung on her every word.

'It looks as though Miss Tate has attracted an admirer,' Julia said, coming up behind her. 'Have you enjoyed yourself, my dear?'

'Immensely. Zachariah has gone for an inkwell, so the musicians can sign my programme.'

'How very low class,' whispered a woman to her companion, within earshot of Clementine.

As the pair began to drift away her companion replied, 'She called him by his Christian name. Miss Tate told me in confidence that the children's governess was too forward, but Mr Fleet allows her to get away with it because the children like her. He will probably tire of her before too long, then we'll see where it gets her.'

'Mr Fleet is certainly handsome.'

'And a good match for any woman, since he is worth a fortune. I hear that Miss Tate is an heiress of some considerable endowment. The gown she's wearing is the latest fashion in London.'

'The young Mr Cheeves paid Miss Tate a lot of attention this evening. I saw Mr Fleet's eyes on them earlier, and he didn't look happy about them being together . . .'

Surely Zachariah hadn't fallen in love with Alexandra, Clementine thought. What if he married her? She would be miserable for the rest of her life. It was unthinkable!

Clementine pretended she hadn't heard the gossip, and then pretended not to mind that the slap down had wounded her. Neither worked, however, and tears glinted in her eyes.

Julia placed a hand on her arm. 'Take no notice. See, here comes Zachariah with the inkwell.'

The members of the orchestra were pleased to sign her programme, and Zachariah kept her by his side for the following half an hour and drew her into the conversation.

'You've met Reverend Cuthbert, haven't you, Miss Morris?'

The man smiled at her. 'Miss Morris comes to church regularly, and I'm pleased to see the young baron and his sister with her. A pity you don't set such a good example, Mr Fleet.'

'My life is mostly lived in London.'

'Then I'll have to make sure the spiritual education of the children is adhered to in your absence.'

'I think not, Reverend Cuthbert. At this early stage of their lives, Miss Morris is perfectly able to manage their spiritual education as well as she manages to tutor them in their letters and numbers.'

'And if she needs help in such matters?'

'Then I will know where to turn, Reverend,' said Clementine. 'I was, in fact, thinking of enrolling the children in the church school next year. Edward in particular needs the company of boys to interact with. However, I have yet to discuss the matter with Mr Fleet, who will no doubt be interested in the curriculum.'

*   *   *

They left just as darkness began to fall. Alexandra had obviously enjoyed herself, and she chattered incessantly about the people she'd met, and repeated the gossip she'd heard.

'I have promised to play the piano and sing for Mrs Cheeves and her friends. There will be a small professional fee.'

Zachariah said, 'Accepting a fee is out of the question, since you're my guest and they are my clients and business associates. You don't want them to think you're somebody I hired to entertain us, do you?'

His barb hit home and there was a sudden chill in the air. Alexandra turned to gaze out of the window, a mortified expression on her face. 'I didn't think my remarks would be passed on.'

'Yet they were, and at the expense of Miss Morris. I expected better from you.'

'I'm sorry.'

Distressed, Clementine placed her hand on his arm. 'Can we leave it at that, please, Zachariah? Alexandra has apologized. Despite everything, I enjoyed the concert and I thank you for that.' She nearly kissed his cheek but held herself back just in time.

She had a sudden longing to be seated before the nursery fire with the children either side of her, their eyes filled with sleep and dreams as she told them a story.

She loved Martingale House and the children, and she loved Zachariah Fleet. There, she'd admitted it to herself – she loved Zachariah Fleet.

What would she do if he fell in love with Alexandra?

She would be happy he'd found love and would wish them both every joy in life. She grinned. Damn it . . . no she wouldn't. She didn't have it in her to be that noble and self-sacrificing. She might poison Alexandra instead.

As if he'd read her thoughts, Zachariah slid his hand over hers and gently squeezed it.

Fourteen

Sunday came and Clementine readied the children for church.

Zachariah joined them in the hall, impeccable as always. She had a strong urge to reach up and ruffle his hair.

When she looked sideways at him he said, 'I'm coming with you.'

'You don't usually.'

'I thought I should set the children a good example.' He gazed around him and lowered his voice. 'Let's hurry before Miss Tate gets wind of it.'

'I'm sure the children will appreciate your sacrifice.'

Laughter rumbled from him and his voice purred against her ear like a satisfied cat. 'You have a wicked bite to your tongue this morning, my Clemmie.'

'At least it's not forked.'

She wrapped Edward's scarf around his neck. 'Make sure you sit still during the prayers, Edward, and don't misbehave.'

'I like the singing best. Can I sit next to you, Uncle Zachariah?'

'If you want to risk experiencing a bolt of hellfire.'

'And me,' Iris said, and then came a puzzled, 'What does misbehave mean?'

In the distance the church bells began to ring. 'Do Julia and John intend to join us as well?'

'They'll be attending the friends' meeting in Poole.'

'I hope you're not joining us just because you think the gossips will snub me?'

'They will snub you. Why else would I go to church, unless some miracle was to occur and the gossips were struck dumb? Can you imagine their mouths opening and shutting, with nothing coming out?'

She grinned at the thought.

'Your nature will make you walk past them as though you're deaf, or as though they don't exist. They will have you bottling up your tears while you try to show them that you don't care, and you will be upset for the rest of the day. I thought you'd like someone on your side, so with your permission I will be your knight in shining armour.'

'And if I don't give my permission?'

'I'll come anyway, if just to give the Reverend Cuthbert a shock.'

She gazed at him. 'You must know that your presence will make them gossip more. I imagine they'll save the worst venom for when you've returned to London. It was nice of you to think of me.'

'I think of you often.'

She turned to fiddle with Iris's bonnet while her blush came and went, and managed to say, 'Do you?'

'You know damned well I do.'

'I've got a wobbly tooth, Uncle Zachariah,' Edward said, bursting with self-importance. 'Miss Clemmie said that when it comes out I'll grow a new one in its place.'

'Well done,' he said. 'It's a sign that you're growing up.'

Iris scowled at Edward. 'I want a new one too.'

Zachariah stooped to kiss her cheek. 'You'll have to wait until you're older, little Iris. Let's go out to the carriage now. The church bells are ringing and we're going to be late.' He straightened and gazed at her, his eyes narrowing when the ringing stopped. 'Far be it from me to accuse you of duplicity, Clemmie, but was it your intention to cock a snoot by walking down the aisle after the service started, so they'd think their treatment of you had shamed you into hiding?'

A smile crossed her face. How well he read her. 'Would I admit to such provocation? Mr Cheeves always uses your family pew, by the way.'

'Does he . . . does he indeed? That's interesting.'

They arrived just as the first hymn had ended, and then entered the church on a blast of cold wind. Every head turned as they proceeded down the aisle, leaving Ben to join the servants at the back of the church. Zachariah, his hat held on his arm, nodded pleasantly to people of his acquaintance.

When they reached the family pew at the front, he said to the rector, 'My apology for being late and disrupting the service, Reverend Cuthbert.' Turning to Mr Cheeves he disrupted it further by informing him, 'I'm given to understand that this pew was donated by my great-grandfather for my family's use.'

'Usually the pew is empty.'

'How odd. Miss Morris assures me that she brings the children to church every Sunday. Is that not so, Reverend?'

He nodded. 'I believe Miss Morris usually seats herself further back, sir.'

'I will move, of course.' With a stiff little bow and a terse apology on his lips, Mr Cheeves ushered his family together and moved them to an empty pew. Basil Cheeves offered Zachariah a challenging look on the way past – something he ignored.

'Shall we pray?' the Reverend Cuthbert said, his sigh hovering on the fringes of exasperation.

Zachariah smiled. 'By all means.'

The sight of the Cheeves family had spun a small pebble of thought into Clementine's consciousness. As she bent her head and went through the motion of praying, it nagged at her. The concert programme came to the fore. Had there been some anomaly on it? Not one obvious enough to capture her attention completely. She would inspect the programme when they got home.

Her mind wandered off to her favourite subject – Zachariah. The children adored him, though he put no special effort in to make it so. He appeared to enjoy his time with them and listened to what they had to say, however childish. Considering that he'd been badly treated for most of his childhood his gentleness was surprising. But perhaps he was gentle because he knew only too well what the alternative was like.

A kiss touched her cheek and she smiled. Zachariah? *In church!* Her eyes flew open. She was almost disappointed when she saw Iris smiling at her. But what was she thinking? Of course it wouldn't have been Zachariah!

After the service a few people stopped to engage Zachariah in talk, while Clementine settled the children in the carriage.

'You were saying a long prayer,' Iris said. 'Was it about me and Edward?'

'I wasn't really praying, I was pretending to.'

Iris giggled. 'That's naughty.'

'I know it is. I was thinking how lovely it was to have such well-behaved children in my charge. Your mama and papa would be proud of you.'

'I can't remember them. I love you and Uncle Zachariah instead now, Miss Clemmie.'

'So do I,' Edward said fiercely. 'You're better than our parents.' He turned to stare out of the window, stiff with the outrage he felt at being orphaned. Even after all this time his resentment would probably stay with him through life.

Clementine stroked her fingers through his hair. 'Don't be angry with them, Edward. It wasn't their fault that they died.'

'What if they didn't die? What if they didn't want us, and pretended to die, but just ran away?'

Gently she asked, 'Is that what you think happened?'

He shrugged. 'I don't know.'

'I know how you feel, my dear. My father died before I was born, and my mother sent me away to school when I was just a bit older than you. I never saw her again.'

He turned, the anger being replaced by interest. 'Did she die?'

'Yes, she did, and I was sad for a long time.' She placed a hand against his chest. 'Sometimes the thought of her made me hurt inside here. It's called grief. It gets less painful after a while.'

Zachariah joined them in the carriage, tapping at the roof with his stick to signal to Ben that they were leaving.

Iris informed him, 'Edward's caught grief. I hope I don't catch it. I don't want to have itchy spots again.'

Clementine exchanged a smile with Zachariah when Edward sent a snort his sister's way.

'When they reached Martingale House, Zachariah passed the children over to Polly with the instructions, 'Bring them down to the hall in ten minutes, and they can eat breakfast with the guests. Best manners today, children.'

'What was that grief thing all about?' he asked after they'd gone.

'Edward remembered his parents and he was angry.'

'Come into my study, I'll ring for some tea and we can talk.'

'About what?'

'This and that; I rarely see you alone these days.'

'Because I have very little idle time on my hands, and neither do you.'

He took her by the hands and drew her into his domain, a shabby half-panelled but pleasantly warm room that was packed with gloomy furniture and books. Battle-scarred leather chairs faced each other on either side of the fireplace like a couple of sagging old warriors. A chess set with a chair either side of a wooden chess table was set up in mid-game.

'I'm sorry the room is so shabby. I meant to have the place refurnished and redecorated, but I'm hardly here.'

'It could be quite a pleasant room if it was refurbished.'

'It doesn't look like the home I would like to live in.' He stirred the fire up with an iron poker and added a log. The flames caught and the log began to spit sparks up the chimney. He placed a spark guard around it.

Mrs Ogden came into the room with the tea tray, smiled benevolently upon them, and then left with instructions to keep some breakfast for both them and the children.

Zachariah moved to the chess set, contemplated the board for a moment, then smiled. He moved the white knight before looking her way and saying, 'Have you noticed how Mrs Ogden smiles when she sees us together?'

'She's been here a long time and likes having a family to look after.'

He moved to the window and stared out. 'I daresay she does. Most of the house servants were loyal and stayed on after Gabe went abroad, even though he hadn't paid them for some time.'

'You said this doesn't look like the home you'd like to live in. What does your ideal home look like, Zachariah?'

He turned, appearing surprised by the question. 'I don't know . . . happier, I suppose.'

'Explain happier.'

'This room was where my father dished out his punishment. I can sense his presence here. I often wonder if it's haunted.'

Her blood ran cold. 'But you still come in here.'

'He's dead and I'm grown up so I'm no longer afraid of him.'

'But you sense him here and you don't like it.'

'I have no answer to that except to say he can no longer hurt me.' Crossing to the desk he picked up a book. '*Robinson Crusoe*. I read this as a child and thought it would do for Edward.' He put it down again and his eyes engaged hers. 'What do you think?'

'Edward will have to wait until he's a little older and can read fluently. You're changing the subject, Zachariah. You often do when the conversation gets more personal. I think you should stop prowling around the room like a caged lion and sit down. My head is swivelling like that of an owl.'

Seating himself in the opposite chair, he grinned. 'I don't like being subjected to a personal inquisition. Besides, I've told you all you need to know. I prefer to keep some in reserve in case I need to draw on it. So do you. Have you told me all about Clementine Morris?'

'You're the most difficult man to engage in small talk. You hide behind a façade of prickles. Can you think of anything that took place in this room that made you happy?'

Head to one side, he regarded her with a smile. 'I think I first kissed you in this room.'

'It was in the nursery.'

'What about the other kisses: didn't they make an impression on you?'

'Not at all.'

'Perhaps I should kiss you again.'

She tried not to smile. 'And perhaps you shouldn't.'

'Scared?'

Far from it; she would welcome his kiss if she thought it would mean anything to him. 'I can't afford to get involved. You've seen how it is for me here. The local people are already making my life almost intolerable.'

'As I recall, wasn't that kiss in the nursery meant for the children?'

'You'd be a fool to think I believed that, Zachariah. You're not a fool and neither am I. Didn't anyone ever kiss or hug you when you were a child?'

He shook his head. 'This house – and especially this room – didn't represent love or affection in any form.'

'You should change it. Look how dirty and smoked-stained the ceilings are. Painting them will brighten them and allow the detail to emerge. Get rid of the gloomy furniture, the saggy old chairs and the dark and dirty wallpaper. Make what you will of it and change it.'

'Is it that simple to get rid of a lifetime of neglect? No, don't answer that, Clemmie, else you'll put a twist on it and make it too personal again. You have my permission to refurbish this room to your liking after I go back to London. It will give you something useful to do and you might even paint over my unhappy youth. I'll tell Mr Bolton to get some pattern books and carpet samples. He will know where to employ the best tradesmen for the job.'

She gazed around her, knowing she would enjoy the task. 'Will you tell me what colours you prefer?'

'You choose.' His mouth twisted in a rueful smile. 'What did Edward have to say about his parents?'

'Ah . . . I wondered when you'd get around to that. When I told Edward his parents would be proud of him, he said that we were his parents now and he loved us better than his own parents. He was angry because they died, then wondered if they were still alive. He suggested that perhaps they hadn't wanted them, so had run away.'

'I see.'

'You have doubts about the children, don't you?'

He nodded.

Her heart reached out to the children. 'What will you do if . . .?'

'John asked me that and I told him I didn't know. I still don't, but I've been thinking about it.

'I promised Edward that he and Iris would always have a home here, but that was before the doubt had set in. In all conscience, I cannot go back on that promise. There's no reason why they couldn't live here under my care and be educated to earn a living, as long as they don't have unreasonable expectations as to their status. Besides, I'm getting used to the little tykes and I quite like them.'

'You seem to have an instinct for fathering.'

He grinned. 'I'm doing my best, but I think I know how *not* to bring them up rather than how to. Shall we go and eat some more breakfast? I didn't have time for anything but a spoonful of porridge before we went out.'

'You achieved quite a lot on that spoonful in church.'

He laughed.

They rose at the same time and gazed at each other. He reached out and curled a wisp of her hair around his finger. 'I do love that little curl.'

'Zachariah, no,' she said, but it was a half-hearted protest because he was as transparent as glass.

'I just want to know what a hug in this room feels like.' He drew her against him and held her there, her head resting on his shoulder. She breathed him in, her mouth resting lightly against his jaw. A minute later he turned her face up to his and kissed her. It was a gentle and loving caress.

Neither of them heard the knock at the door and they sprang apart when Edward said, 'What are you doing?'

'Miss Clemmie had some dust in her eye. I was kissing it better.'

'Mrs Ogden sent me to tell you that breakfast is ready.'

'Has your eye improved sufficiently, Miss Clemmie?'

He had tripped himself up and she giggled. 'I can see perfectly now.'

When they entered the dining room, Julia said, 'You look flushed, my dear. I hope you're not suffering from a fever.'

The children managed to slip into the seats on either side of Zachariah, who accepted from Mrs Ogden two plates with a small rasher of lean bacon, a coddled egg and fingers of bread fried to a crisp.

Tucking Iris's napkin under her chin, he gazed round at them all. 'Reverend Cuthbert's sermon must have whipped her into a ferment.'

John chuckled. 'That sounds promising. What was the sermon about?'

'I have no idea . . . Miss Clemmie?'

Iris said, 'Miss Clemmie pretended she was praying. But she was really thinking about Edward and me.'

'Aha!' John said, laughter in his voice. 'I hope they were good thoughts.'

'Yes, sir. Miss Clemmie tells us we must always think good thoughts.'

'How utterly boring of her,' Alexandra said with just enough laughter in her voice to render the remark inoffensive.

Zachariah chuckled. 'I'm inclined to agree with you, Alexandra, though sometimes I'd like to know what's going on in her head.'

So . . . he was using Alexandra's first name now. Well, why

shouldn't he? After all, her half-sister was Zachariah's guest. Not hers. Half-sister? She had tried to find some kinship in their relationship and had failed.

Alexandra sent him a smile. 'Nothing devious, I'd imagine. I'm sorry. I was late in rising. I missed going to church with you.'

'I thought the service was quite interesting today, didn't you, Miss Clemmie?'

'Totally absorbing.'

'What can I get you for breakfast?'

Zachariah Fleet. Where were these thoughts coming from? Clementine had never been interested in men before, and the jumble of shocking thoughts and physical reactions she experienced when she was in the presence of Zachariah Fleet was bewildering. What's more she had lost her appetite.

'Just some preserved fruit.'

Alexandra said, 'Goodness, is that all? You eat hardly anything.'

'I eat enough to satisfy my appetite. I've already had some oatmeal.'

Alexandra was sitting under the portrait of the late baron and his wife. The colours were brighter after the wash it had received from Mrs Ogden, and the scribble was gone.

John Beck was looking at it too. Then his gaze lowered to Alexandra and moved up again.

Clementine gazed at the picture in puzzlement. The resemblance between Alexandra and the woman on the portrait was marked.

Then Zachariah set the bowl of fruit in front of her and she could feel his breath warm against her scalp. His mouth on hers, so warm and tender, was a vivid and irresistible memory she could barely ignore.

She hadn't wanted her life to be complicated by falling in love with Zachariah. He was a man like any other, and with the same appetites. If she allowed him to, he would take her into his bed and use her, then leave, as had the men in her mother's life. If she stayed she'd be too weak to resist him, her only security being some man's mistress instead of being paid for by the hour by different men.

Oh yes, she knew what her mother had been involved in. She'd pretended not to know because she didn't want her judged by others. And while she'd loved her mother, that didn't mean she wanted to end up like her.

Perhaps it was time she moved on, like she had in her previous employment. She couldn't go back to the workhouse in London, because that would be the first place he'd look for her, if he bothered to look for her at all. She would wait and see what happened with the legacy. Now she'd noticed the resemblance between Alexandra and the woman in the portrait, she was almost certain who would be the beneficiary of the legacy.

Zachariah must know whose daughter Alexandra was, since his sharp eyes wouldn't have missed the significance of the resemblance, but did Alexandra know? Probably not, else she'd be even more insufferable than she was already.

Clementine decided not to think past that at the moment. Zachariah was being cautious. He would do nothing until he was sure of his ground.

Not for one moment could Clementine imagine that she and Alexandra were related. They were nothing alike. She was curious though, because she'd never known her father and couldn't picture him.

When she thought of leaving Zachariah she fell into a dark yawning place where there was no light or softness. And when she thought of leaving the children as well, her heart began to bleed and she was afraid for them.

His nearness brought the blood to her face again.

'Are you sure you're not coming down with a fever?' Julia said.

'Positive.'

'Miss Clemmie had dust in her eyes and Uncle Zachariah was ki—'

Zachariah scraped his chair back along the wooden floor and leapt to his feet. 'Those dogs are under the table. Come out of there, you scrounging hounds. You know you're not allowed to be there. Quickly, Edward! Grab Wolf's collar and we'll take them out.'

The pair of them dived under the table, where a kerfuffle of sounds, knocks and mild curses went on. The dogs escaped, scrabbling across the floor and shooting through the door. They nearly knocked Mrs Ogden off her feet when she came in.

'I'll be blessed,' she said and shouted after them, 'Don't you critters go and annoy Cook now.'

The scuffling under the table carried on after the dogs had departed.

Clementine tried not to laugh, but she couldn't help it when Julia exchanged a significant look with her.

Lifting the tablecloth Clementine said, 'Gentlemen, you can come out now; the dogs have made their escape.'

Zachariah and Edward took their seats, breathing heavily from the exercise – Edward's inappropriate conversation now diverted, but not overlooked by those who'd picked up the significance of his slip, for Julia and John were smiling at each other and Alexandra had a frown forked between her brow.

Fifteen

The day had been cold and crisp and the dogs stretched out in front of the nursery fire, their eyelids twitching open now and then in case they missed something, or their legs moving as if they were chasing rabbits in their dreams. They were almost fully grown now – at least, Clementine hoped so, but they were still bursting with the energy of their puppyhood.

As evening fell the frost became a thick white blanket that covered the furrows of ploughed earth. There, the seeds lay dormant, waiting for the warm stirring of spring to wake them.

The sky was filled with stars and the moon rode high, a glowing orb circled by a halo of light that pushed its rays out into the reaches of a velvety dark sky.

'Is the sky heaven, Miss Clemmie?'

'It looks like it might be, since the stars are so pretty.'

'Mr Bolton said that there's a rhyme that goes: "A ring around the moon is a sign of rain soon".'

Iris sighed as they gazed at it. 'It looks like fairyland and I don't want it to rain because then we have to stay indoors.'

A star shot across the sky and the children cried out with delight.

'Quickly, close your eyes and make a wish.'

'I wished the cook would make one of those apple cakes.'

Clementine grinned at the girl. That was a wish bound to come true.

'What about you, Edward?'

'I wished I could go up to heaven and say hello to my mama and papa.'

Not such an easy wish to fulfill. She scrambled for something he'd like to hear. 'If you remember them in your prayers, the angels will leave your message on a star, and they'll be happy.'

'I've made a book for Uncle Zachariah. It's a bogafree – the story of my life, and nobody else is allowed to read it so it's got SECRET written on the cover.'

She tried not to smile. It would be a short biography. 'That's thoughtful of you, Edward. Your uncle will like receiving a gift that you've made for him. You can give it to him when he comes up to say goodnight.'

'I've arrived,' Zachariah said from the doorway and her heart leapt so high that it nearly ended up amongst the stars.

'Aren't you chilly by that window?'

'We were looking at the sky and we saw a shooting star and made a wish. Iris wished for an apple cake and Edward remembered his parents and wished the angels would send them greetings. Come and see how pretty the moon is tonight.'

'It's always pretty. What did you wish for, Miss Clemmie?'

'I'm contented with everything I already have at the moment. It would be greedy of me to ask for more.'

He joined them on the window seat, huffed steamy breath on to the cold surface of the window then wrote their names with his fingers. 'In the morning the windows will be covered in frosty patterns.'

'Will we have frosty names?'

'We might. When I was small there was a telescope on a stand here,' he said. 'I'll look in the attics and see if I can find it.' He pulled the window hangings across. 'Say goodnight to the dogs and get into bed now, you two. I'll read you a story tonight.'

When Zachariah finished and stooped to kiss them goodnight, Edward said sleepily, 'Don't forget to take the book I made you.'

'I won't . . . and I'm sure I'll treasure it. It will have its own special place on the study bookshelf.'

Which wouldn't be hard because there were plenty of spaces where books were missing.

They moved into the other room, leaving a nightlight flickering in a saucer. He picked up Edward's book, a loose collection of pages tied together with a piece of string, then placed it down again. 'Are you coming down, Clemmie? Alexandra is going to play the piano and sing for us later.'

'She's talented . . . and beautiful.'

'Yes . . . she has a great deal of grace. Come to the library and read Edward's bogafree with me first.'

'It's private. He wrote it for you and it took him a long time. He's a sensitive child whose feelings are very deep. He's given you his trust with this, Zachariah. It seems as if the biography is important to him, and I won't encourage you to break that trust or make fun of his efforts.'

'I admit I have a lot to learn about children but I wouldn't laugh at him because he's a tender little soul.'

'A bit like you were, I imagine.'

Reaching out, he caressed her cheek and she didn't have the will to take a step backwards.

'How did you get to be so wise, my Clemmie?'

'I'm far from wise and I'm not yours.' She wished he wouldn't talk to her as though she was precious to him, and although it was too late to wish for something on the shooting star she did so anyway – she wished that she *was* precious to him.

'Can you dance?'

She laughed because the question was unexpected. 'I'm afraid I have no performance talents. I can't dance, sing or play a musical instrument. There wasn't much call for it in the school I was in, or the workhouse.'

'I'll teach you to dance the waltz.' He took her by the arms and pulled her closer.

'What are you doing?'

'Teaching you to dance. Put your hand at my back and I'll do the same. Good.' He picked up her other hand and, holding it, extended their arms. 'Now you take a series of steps . . . one two three . . . one two three. Circle . . . one two three . . .'

Clementine found it easy to dance the waltz and she relaxed and began to enjoy herself. He pulled her fractionally closer and began to hum a tune as they danced in time with it. Suddenly he swung her off her feet and she began to laugh. Her hair came undone and tumbled down her back.

He pulled her close and gazed down at her in the moonlight coming through the window. Her mouth dried up as he gazed at her.

He let his arms fall to his side when she backed away. 'That was fun.'

'It's about time we had some. As Alexandra pointed out to me, we are much too sober and should entertain each other in the evenings. After observing her at the social, it's obvious she needs more lively company. I think she finds the country dull.'

So they were all to perform, like monkeys jumping through hoops for Alexandra's entertainment. 'Do you find the country dull?'

'I'm fascinated by the seasons. I don't think I ever saw a seed of wheat planted and grow out of the earth before. Then it turns from green to gold, when it's harvested. A miller grinds it into dust and the cook makes a loaf of bread. It's a living work of art. Something I never gave much thought to before.'

'Zachariah, I've got to go and braid my hair if we are to be entertained and entertaining.'

'Allow me to braid it for you.'

It was much too intimate a task. She could imagine his finger-tips, a gentle caress against her scalp, and her hair bunched in his hands. The skin on the nape of her neck exploded. Goose bumps chased around her body – as countless as the stars they'd admired in the sky. A delicious little shiver chased after them. 'Polly is coming up the stairs; I think it would embarrass her to discover you arranging my hair.'

He nodded. 'The new ladies' maid starts tomorrow, I believe. I hope she suits.' He picked up Edward's book and turned away. 'I'll see you in the drawing room a little later, Miss Clemmie. Oh, hello Polly, I didn't hear you coming. Your charges are fast asleep; I think I bored them with my story.'

'I doubt it very much, sir. They look forward to being told stories, and young Edward has a lively imagination of his own.'

Clementine went down to her own room, where she braided her hair and secured it with a pink ribbon to match the gown.

She couldn't find her best shawl, one fashioned from the softest of cream wool and woven in a lacy pattern.

Her eyes fell on the Cheeves musical programme and she picked it up. Her gaze ran over the words and the signature. There was nothing odd about it; she must have been imagining it.

About to place it down again, she noticed some small printing along the bottom and took it closer to the candle flame. Her eyes widened as she wondered if it was a coincidence.

Downstairs she found the drawing room empty. Her knock at the study door brought a muffled, 'Come in.'

When she opened the door both Zachariah and John looked up from the chessboard, then smiled guiltily and rose to their feet.

'Is it that time already?' Zachariah said.

'I'm sorry. I didn't intend to disturb your game. I just wanted a minute of your time, Zachariah.'

John said, 'I'll leave you to it then.'

'Oh, you don't have to go, Mr Beck. It's nothing important. In fact, I'm probably being silly.' She handed Zachariah the programme. 'There's a name on the back that I noticed, and I wondered if it was the same George Sheridan who supervised the children.'

He gazed at it then murmured, 'The George Sheridan Charitable Trust. I've never heard of such a trust – have you, John? What do you think?'

'That it's worth checking on. We'll go and talk to Cheeves tomorrow. Find out where he heard about the Sheridan Trust. There were quite a few people at that concert, and at five pounds a head they would have collected quite a large amount for charity. Cheeves wouldn't be involved in anything criminal, would he?'

'I wouldn't have thought he'd do anything fraudulent since he has too much to lose. And again, as Clemmie said, the name might just be coincidental.' Zachariah's gaze came her way. 'That was well observed, Clemmie. We'll check it out tomorrow.'

It had never crossed her mind that George Sheridan might be a criminal, but the children hadn't liked him, and she trusted their instincts. 'Has he done something wrong?'

'Nothing that can be proved.'

'But you've just been questioning his honesty.'

'Yes, and I apologize for doing so in front of you. I'd forgotten that you were unaware of some of his dealings.' He took her hands in his. 'I'd be grateful if you'd ignore anything you just heard and not mention it to anyone.'

She nodded.

There was the sound of Alexandra playing the scales to warm her hands, going faster and faster to summon the audience, and prove her dexterity.

'We must arrange a recital and supper evening especially for her, and invite everyone in the district.'

'As long as it's just for her,' she said, feeling a bit put out, though she knew she'd hate to be the centre of attention, and wouldn't know what to say to anyone.

Ever astute, Zachariah said, 'I've hurt your feelings, haven't I? Please believe it's unintentional. Would you like to host a social evening?'

Panic rose in her. 'Good Lord, no! I'd hide under the bed. As for hurting my feelings, it was just a niggle.'

'You're not ready to carry off the role of a hostess just yet, my little house mouse. That's no reflection on your ability or a comparison to Alexandra, since you have an abundance of natural grace. It just means you have different skills.' He offered her his arm. 'Shall we go in?'

Alexandra was at her shining best in a gown of pale green, and with not a hair out of place. She wore Clementine's shawl.

Her hand fluttered over it. 'I hope you don't mind me borrowing your shawl. You rarely wear it yourself and I couldn't find you to ask. It suits this gown so well.'

Clementine rarely wore it because it wasn't a shawl that suited everyday wear. She was keeping it for best, though she couldn't remember wearing it since Mrs Cheeves' music social. Had Alexandra been through her clothing chest? Yes, she must have done.

'I would be willing to buy it from you . . . not that I have much.'

What else could she say but, 'Please accept it as a gift.'

'You're so generous, Clementine. It's lovely having a sister. Come and kiss my cheek.'

Sister or not, the last thing she wanted to do was kiss Alexandra's cheek, but thus summoned, Clementine found herself obliged to pay homage to the woman. The urge to bite her was nearly overwhelming. Goodness, she was turning into a cannibal.

'What are you contributing to our little concert tonight, dear?' Alexandra said, oozing sweetness.

Mostly, she'd be playing the ugly sister to Alexandra's Cinderella, she suspected. 'Oh . . . I don't have your talent, Alexandra.'

'No . . . I don't suppose you do, having spent most of your life in a charitable institution.'

'My father . . . Howard Morris paid for my education.'

'Ah yes . . . our mutual father. Not a man to boast about. What did you do before you were left at the school; did your mother have a profession?'

Clementine felt uncomfortable. 'My mother could sing, so she was employed to entertain.'

'Did she sing well?'

'To me she had the best voice in the world, but I was young and she was my mother and I loved her, so I was biased. I'm glad I knew her, even for a short time.'

'Perhaps it's better not to delve too deeply into one's background. Wouldn't it be awful if we'd been born to a felon, or worse.'

She couldn't help but say, 'One of us was, I believe.'

A huff of laughter came from Zachariah.

Hastily, Alexandra said, 'Well, never mind, it's not really a suitable subject for the drawing room.'

'I'm glad you've reminded us,' Julia said drily, her voice barely audible when Alexandra ran her fingers up and down the keys.

'I was going to ask you to turn the music sheets for me for this first piece, Clementine, but obviously you can't read music. What a shame. My foster mother and father said it was an essential part of a young woman's social education.'

'Along with good manners, I presume.'

Alexandra ignored Julia's barbed comment and her eyes alighted on Zachariah, who held up his hands in a defensive pushing motion. 'I'm afraid I don't have many social niceties either. I can dance a little, though I broke a few of Julia's toes in the process of learning.'

Alexandra dipped her eyelashes at him, to no effect. There was a satisfaction in the fact that Zachariah didn't respond to Alexandra's witchery.

His eyes engaged hers and with a twitch of the eyebrow he said, 'Should Alexandra decide to play a waltz I shall expect you to partner me, Clemmie. We'll dance around the room and pretend we're at a ball.'

Lord, he certainly knew how to make a woman feel alive . . . well, it was more hot and bothered and itchy than alive, she supposed, like a dog with fleas. Was this what drawing-room conversation was all about – flirting with each other? She wondered what he'd do if she joined in. Experimentally she tried to flutter her eyelashes like Alexandra did . . . a series of fast blinks really. But hers were less than subtle.

Zachariah laughed, and said, 'Do you have dust in your eyes again, Clemmie?'

A petulant voice broke in. 'I don't think I know any waltzes.'

'Then we'll waltz to a marching tune, or to no tune at all – since we are both beginners.'

Julia rose and crossed to the piano. 'I'll turn the sheets for you. Shall we get on with it, Alexandra, else it will soon be time to waltz off to bed? Zachariah's man, Evan, has offered to do a reading from *The Merchant of Venice* by William Shakespeare, with some card tricks to follow. I'm so looking forward to it. He used to be in the theatre, you know.'

The door slowly opened and a man stood framed in the doorway. He had a stooped back, a shock of red hair and a hooked nose.

'Oh, my goodness,' Julia shrieked and threw the piano music at him.

The noise woke the dogs, who decided to be heroes and barked ferociously at each other. Then Happy grabbed the man by one of his trouser legs and Wolf's teeth closed around the other one. Sorted out, they began to worry the man's ankles, making snarling noises.

'So much for Shylock,' Zachariah said, doubling up with laughter. 'A memorable performance indeed, Evan.'

'Call off the hounds, would you? They're insane. Still, they would be useful if you trained them.'

'Why . . . if it isn't Evan,' Julia said, sounding genuinely surprised. 'What an absolutely terrifying disguise; you're lucky someone didn't shoot you.'

Clementine giggled. 'It's not All Hallows Eve by any chance, is it?' She called the dogs off. Panting heavily they looked up at her as if waiting for a reward.

'Good dogs,' she said and patted them both. When Happy rolled on his back with his legs in the air, they began laughing all over again.

Alexandra tutted and, picking up the music, she began to play.

Sixteen

Cheeves look flustered when Zachariah and John appeared on his doorstep.

'My pardon for calling at such an early hour; I need to speak to you on a matter of some urgency.'

'Come in out of the cold, sirs. The fire is burning in my study, so we can talk there . . . though I am expecting an acquaintance to call within the hour.'

Mrs Cheeves was hovering in the background. 'May I offer you refreshment . . . some coffee perhaps?'

Zachariah shook his head. 'Thank you, Mrs Cheeves; we've already breakfasted, and this is a business matter rather than a social one.'

Cheeves dismissed his wife with a flick of his hand and opened his study door, saying expansively, 'Come in, come in, gentlemen.'

When they were settled, Cheeves leaned back in the chair behind his desk and smiled from one to another. 'I don't usually conduct business at home, but will stretch a point on this occasion.'

John spoke. 'I think you'll be thankful you did. How well do you know George Sheridan?'

His smile faded. 'It would be bad for the bank if I discussed a client's business.'

'It may be worse for your business and your character if you don't, Mr Cheeves.'

'Oh?' Cheeves picked up a paperknife, fiddling with it for a moment as he considered it. Then he looked up at them. 'Very well; I will take it without saying that what's discussed in here will remain private.'

Zachariah took over. 'We have reason to believe the man who calls himself George Sheridan is obtaining money by fraudulent means.'

Cheeves paled. 'Surely not, sir. He was introduced to me by my own son.'

'We cannot be certain, so we're here to caution you on the matter. Let me relate certain circumstances to you. A Mr Sheridan and a woman claiming to be his wife arrived from Australia with my brother's two children. They claimed to be the children's godparents. The children were ill, and they were frightened of their own shadows. However, that's by the by. I'm indebted to Miss Morris for her excellent care of the children.'

'Quite . . . goes without saying, a charming young lady,' George mumbled, slightly red-faced.

'Believe me when I tell you that Miss Morris is very highly valued by my household. As for George Sheridan, I believe him to be a skilled confidence trickster. He certainly had me fooled to begin with, but he overplayed his hand when the matter of the legacy came to light. I would not be surprised if your son found him plausible, and as a matter of courtesy young Mr Cheeves' name need not be mentioned as being involved.'

Having pushed his point home, Zachariah nodded to John. 'Perhaps you'd be kind enough to finish.'

'George Sheridan spent an outrageous amount of money conveying Mr Fleet's nephew and niece from Australia, with nothing except the children themselves to account for it. They also presented several large amounts in the form of IOUs signed by the late baron, which may or may not have been fraudulent. Sheridan claimed to have paid for the couple to be interred after they met with a fatal accident. In short, he claimed a large amount of money without receipt – money Mr Fleet paid on trust because he knew his brother to be a gambler and unreliable where money was concerned.'

'I understand, Mr Beck. I was quite familiar with Sir Gabriel's habits and foibles. He certainly lived life to the full with little care for the future, if you'll pardon me for saying so. I have yet to see what this has to do with me though.'

'Hear me out and we will come to that, sir. We had, and still have, no reason or proof to believe the Sheridans are anything other than what they presented. What we do believe is that the couple befriended the late baron and his wife and extracted information from them that could be used to their own advantage.'

'Such as?'

'A little while ago they contacted Mr Fleet's guest, Miss Tate, with regards to a legacy that might have been left to her in her grandmother's will. That information could only have come from the mouth of my brother, or more likely, from Alice, his wife, since the legacy concerns the female side of the family.

'Or it could have come from the man who prepared the will in the first place, using his knowledge of my brother's family and their friends. George Sheridan parted a sick old man from his life savings. The man died a pauper, leaving Miss Tate in straitened circumstances.'

'But Miss Tate has the grandmother's legacy to look forward to. Eight thousand pounds, we're given to understand.'

Zachariah and John gazed at each other, then John said, 'Such an amount is a gross exaggeration of the facts. It seems that Miss Tate has been fostered with expectations beyond her station or means. The existence of a possible legacy has gone to her head if she imagines it is anything near that sum.'

Cheeves gazed his way. 'I see. I don't suppose you'd tell me what the girl is worth. My son has shown an interest there so I must caution him not to be rash. If it's worthwhile he'll do the right thing, of course, and ask your permission.'

'In the first place you suppose right. In the second, I'd like to point out that my responsibility for Miss Tate only goes as far as it would for any other guest in my home. Miss Tate is not my ward and can only claim a slight family connection, and certainly not one of blood with the male line. We don't even know if Miss Tate is the true beneficiary of the will yet . . . another with an equally legitimate claim is waiting to be proven.'

'Do you have solid grounds to think the George Sheridan of the charitable trust is the same trickster?'

'All we're saying is that it's someone with the same name. It was only by chance that the name was seen on your music programme by someone who'd met him before. Then again, he might not be the same George Sheridan. I would have to see him to be sure.'

'Then I would be obliged if you would remain. He is coming to collect the money shortly, since he wishes to catch the stage-coach from Dorchester. In view of what has been said here, would you be interested in staying and identifying him if necessary? We can then see what eventuates.'

'I'd consider it my duty. My friend and business partner John Beck isn't known to him and can be by your side offering you support while I seat myself in the shadows in that wing chair and observe him.

'In the meantime I would suggest that you select two or three local charities where the collected money can be donated. I will double the amount if you will agree to forgo your commission for the event. It will be good for your business for you to be seen as a generous benefactor in the district, and will redeem your reputation if need be. We will see what comes of it.'

Cheeves nodded and rose to his feet, looking agitated. 'I must instruct my wife not to answer the door herself, and tell the housekeeper to bring George Sheridan straight in. And I'll have your coachman take your carriage round to the back in case he recognizes it. Will he be armed, do you think?'

'I doubt it, since he won't be expecting trouble.'

'I hope Cheeves has the wit to carry this off,' John murmured when the banker left the room.

'Oh, I imagine so. He's got much more than money to lose if he doesn't . . . namely his reputation.'

Sheridan was not long in coming. His wife was with him, but remained in the cab. She gazed towards the house, her bonneted head with its ringlets of bright hair framed by the window, and her presence lending Sheridan an appearance of respectability. This was not the same woman who had come ashore with him.

Gazing at Cheeves, Zachariah nodded. 'It's the same man, and his wife is with him. He's left her waiting in the cab, so he doesn't intend to stay here long.'

Zachariah slid into his wing chair where he was partially concealed, while John took up a stance on the other side of Cheeves to draw the man's gaze away from him.

George Sheridan was in a hurry. His sharp gaze dusted over John, then went back to Cheeves. 'We'd agreed not to involve anyone else.'

'I thought better of it. This is my legal advisor, John Beck, and he has instructed me not to hand over the proceeds from the social evening.'

Since Cheeves was shaking like a jellyfish and his voice had taken on a noticeable vibrato, Zachariah could only admire the small amount of courage he'd dredged up to speak at all. If he'd had any doubts about the man's honesty before in this matter he now discarded them. Cheeves didn't have the guts to involve himself in a fraud such as this.

'Why the devil not?' Sheridan said, anger to the foremost. 'We agreed that you should take your commission and I would distribute what was left through my charity trust. Where are the proceeds?'

John took over. 'Ah yes . . . the charity trust. I'm given to understand no trust actually exists − at least, not locally.'

'I haven't opened the trust account yet. I was about to use the donations Mr Cheeves collected from his musical afternoon to create the trust with.'

'And who will be your signatories to the account? Is Mr Cheeves to know who they are and who will benefit from the exercise?'

'I have business partners in London.'

'I very much doubt it, since it's only a few months since you stepped ashore after a voyage from Australia. I've advised Mr Cheeves to distribute the money he collected to charities in the district − and to pass the money through his bank so there is a clear record of its passage.'

'To that end Mr Cheeves has generously donated his commission,' Zachariah said.

Mr Cheeves looked surprised and opened his mouth as if to speak. Then he closed it again in a resigned manner.

At the sound of Zachariah's voice Sheridan had spun around. His face turned blotchy and he blustered, 'Oh . . . it's you, Mr Fleet. I haven't done anything wrong, you know.'

'It's not through lack of trying though, is it? I would suggest you leave now, Mr Sheridan. Your lady will be getting cold.'

Sheridan's voice strengthened. 'How are the children . . . no nasty little accidents, I hope? You have always been after the baronetcy, I believe. Now there's only the boy to stand in your way.'

Fury was a quick, dark fire consuming Zachariah's finer feelings. He drew in a deep, slow breath. 'Edward has nothing to do with this. Gabe trusted me, and he knew I'd look after the children. He wrote to me.'

'Yes . . . I read it. How pathetic of him. Your brother and his wife doted on those children, but they weren't good parents. Gabe and Alice were a pair of leeches sucking on society and had more airs and graces than King William himself. They didn't have friends, just hangers-on.'

'Of which you were the biggest, I imagine. His letter said he didn't quite trust you.'

'The children were nasty, sly little liars, especially Edward, who had his father's arrogance. They needed to be trained, and a good slap now and again brought them into line. We must drop in and visit them one day.'

'You will not be allowed admittance to my home. The children are none of your business now.'

'May I point out that your brother appointed my wife and I as the children's godparents. It's our duty to visit them from time to time, to make sure they're benefiting from a good spiritual education.'

'And may I point out that Gabe is no longer here, so he has no say in the matter of the children's education or anything else. In short, he has failed them in every way. And in the matter of his friends, any good sense he may have been born with deserted him if you're an example. Personally, I wouldn't appoint you to offer spiritual guidance to the occupants of a chicken pen trying to cross the road.'

Zachariah took a pistol out of the holster under his coat and laid it across the velvet cuff on his jacket, his thumb lightly resting on the priming pin. 'Keep out of my life, the lives of my friends and acquaintances . . . and especially my wards. If I see you in the district again I'll find an excuse to shoot you.'

'Don't be surprised if I swear out a complaint against you over the slur you've placed on my character.'

John smiled. 'I'll be quite happy to defend my clients, either before a magistrate at the assizes or at the old Bailey.'

A sneer crossed Sheridan's face as he turned away. 'Watch your back, Mr Fleet. Gabe had more enemies than he had friends.'

Friends who were so swollen up with hot air at being cheated out of their money that Zachariah had deflated them by promptly settling his brother's debts. But Sheridan didn't know that.

When the door slammed behind Sheridan there was a moment or two of silence, then John chuckled. 'You're formidable when you're riled up, Zach. I thought you were going to shoot him out of hand.'

Zachariah grinned at him. 'Who said I was riled up? The gun wasn't loaded.' He turned to Cheeves. 'Has that convinced you of the man's unreliable character, Mr Cheeves?'

The banker nodded, and his hands shook as he picked up the brandy decanter. He mopped his brow with a handkerchief. 'I'm afraid I'm not as brave as you two gentlemen. Would you like to join me in a brandy while I sort the donations out? You could act as witness.'

Zachariah shook his head and placed a purse on the desk. 'If I did my head count at the social accurately, this should cover my donation. The rest we will leave up to you. I would suggest that you ask your son, Basil, to witness it. It will act as a deterrent if he's ever faced with such temptation from a plausible confidence trickster.'

'When I think of what could have happened, and what it would have cost me and my family in goodwill, I am forever in your debt, sir.'

'Now, we must go, John.'

When they were on the road, John said, 'Do you think Sheridan might get it into his head to pay a visit to Martingale House on his way out of town? We have left the ladies without protection.'

'I expect Sheridan to take the stagecoach, but I don't think he's finished with us entirely. Mr Bolton is aware of the situation. Sheridan wouldn't be foolish enough to enter my house and go after the women and children, since he has nothing to gain from it. If he's wise he'll leave town, as he intended to.'

'You must be careful, Zach. There's a sense of purpose about that man, and he seems to be holding a grudge against you.'

'I can't think why. I'd never set eyes on him before he stepped off the ship.' He changed the subject. 'What should we do about Miss Tate? She's taking her quest to find a wealthy husband a little too far. My God! How did she come up with such an amount of money for a legacy? If that circulates, men will soon be queuing up at your door.'

'It could be her intention that by the time they learn the truth they are incurably in love with her. Alexandra is exceedingly fair.'

'And she knows it. She can't pass a mirror without inspecting herself from all angles. And she's an accomplished but obvious flirt. She knows how to use her femininity to her advantage.'

Zachariah sighed. 'I caught Clementine copying her . . . she fluttered her eyelashes at me.'

'To any effect?'

'Coming from Clementine the gesture was a complete disaster. I teased her and she became flustered.'

The thought brought a smile to John's lips. 'Clementine is a sweet young woman but she can't compete with Alexandra, who, apart from her conceit, seems to be an accomplished liar, wouldn't you say? Her gossip is having an effect, and Clemmie is forced to bear the backlash from it.

'Would you like me – or Julia perhaps – to talk to her about her behaviour?'

'No, John, I won't inflict her on you, since she's my guest. Besides, it would embarrass her. I'll talk to her myself.'

'You're not getting fond of her, are you?'

'I have no more than the normal thoughts in passing that any man would have towards a beautiful woman, and I can control that. Alexandra is not the type of woman I admire.'

'What is your type?'

He thought for a moment. 'I like a woman who can laugh at both me and themselves and isn't afraid to argue, even though her argument may not be logical.' He made a shape in the air. 'If she's neat of figure then all the better. I like a pert walk too, and hair that flies in the wind and is threaded with fire in the sunlight and ashes in the glow of the moon. I prefer brown eyes to blue and a name that reminds me of the scent of flowers carried on the wind.'

'I had never thought you to be so poetical, Zach.'

'Neither have I.'

'You have just described Clementine. Have you fallen in love with her by any chance?'

He opened his eyes, pondering the thought, the image of her fading but his smile still in place. 'Perhaps we should talk about her another day, because the regard I feel for her grows when I'm in her presence. I also feel the need for caution in case I can't trust what I feel. I've never had much practice at loving people.'

'It's rather that you didn't learn how to love when you were a child because when you reached out to people they rebuffed you. If you feel the need for me to counsel you on marriage, my friend, you know where I am.'

'Who better, when you have Julia for a wife.'

A week later, after dinner, Zachariah asked Alexandra to join him in his study. The rose-pink gown she wore enhanced her small waist and the swell of her breast. Her hair was swept up into a glossy knot and her face was a perfect oval upon which her equally perfect features were placed. It seemed odd that she didn't really attract him. In fact, sometimes she repelled him.

With her current hairstyle, Alexandra had never looked more like Gabe's wife. It was practically a copy, with false loops and a thin band across the forehead. As Evan had said, and rather peevishly, 'The whole outfit is suitable for a social dinner, but rather ostentatious for a country dinner at home.'

Obviously, the new maid knew her job.

Alexandra gazed around the room and made a face. 'I understand Clementine is going to refurbish this room. She's looking forward to it and discusses wallpaper constantly.'

'She needs something to occupy her mind besides the children.'

Her eyes engaged his. 'You're vexed with me over something, aren't you? When my foster father was displeased with me he used to place me in a chair then sit on his desk and tower over me, just like you are doing. I found it to be intimidating.'

He moved, placing the desk between them. 'Is that better?'

'Thank you. Why am I here; have you received news of the legacy?'

He shook his head. 'I want to talk to you about your behaviour, Alexandra. I understand you've gossiped with the local women about my household, and in particular about an imaginary relationship between Clementine and myself. This has done her reputation considerable damage.'

'Oh, that . . . I didn't start that rumour and neither did I agree with it when it was raised. Speculation was going on long before I arrived, I believe, and I was unaware of what was true and what was not.'

'I see. Then I hope you will accept my apology.'

'Of course I will, Zachariah.' She smiled at him. 'Is there anything else?'

'Yes there is . . . I thought we might talk a little about your mother. I imagine you'd like to know who she is.'

'Oh . . . I wondered when you'd get round to it. I knew from the beginning that your family was related in my birth somewhere. After all, why else would you have bothered with me? I've seen the picture of my mother in the dining room, of course. I wish you had told me she was your brother's wife when I went rattling on about my mother being a countess. We are very much alike and you must have laughed when I was bragging about her.'

'Yes . . . you are alike. It came as a shock to discover . . . Alice was only fifteen you see, little more than a child. I doubt if my brother knew about you, or her previous, hasty marriage to Howard Morris. Her family would have kept it covered up, lest it spoiled her chance of a good marriage. Although you have the right to know, I would not like this to become common knowledge.'

'People who knew Lady Alicia have already noticed the similarity. The village is a hive of gossip. I know everything there is to know about you, Zachariah, right down to the witch's caul over your head when you were born.'

'Witch's caul? Good grief!'

'The superstitious saw it as a sign that you belonged to the devil.'

Zachariah began to laugh. 'Do I look as though I do? I

thought you'd have more intelligence than to believe such nonsense.'

'You do realize that, whether I get the legacy or not, this makes me half-brother and sister to the children. It will be wonderful to have family to visit.'

Zachariah's heart sank as he lied, 'Yes . . . it will be.' He reminded himself that Alexandra was a young woman who needed family support to fall back on. He must learn to like her, and he must make himself available if he was needed.

He rose and held out a hand to assist her from the chair, guided her to the door and opened it. 'Welcome to the Fleet family, Alexandra.'

'Thank you, Zachariah; it has taken you a long time to decide to accept me. You'll be asking me to walk down the aisle with you soon, and when you do I'll probably accept.'

'If I were you I'd remove my name from your list of eligible men, since that will not happen, Alexandra.'

Her husky chuckle tickled his eardrum. To his surprise she leaned into his body and kissed him on the mouth.

He took a step backwards and over her shoulder he saw Clementine on the bottom step of the staircase. Her eyes widened as she gazed from one to another, as if mortified by embarrassment at catching that moment.

'Oh . . . I'm so sorry.'

Alexandra smiled and as she sailed past Clementine she threw over her shoulder at her, 'That's what comes from listening at keyholes.'

'I wasn't . . . I was on my way back from the kitchen.'

Evan was halfway down the stairs, carrying his engagement calendar. He must have seen what went on.

When an obviously discomfited Clementine turned to hurry across the hall and up the stairs, Zachariah swore.

Alexandra's laughter floated back to him.

'You seem to be having women trouble,' Evan said, closing the door behind himself.

'Miss Tate is a flirt, but I didn't expect her to be so bold. It was unfortunate that Clemmie was in a position to see it.'

'I imagine Miss Tate heard the stair squeak, and made sure Miss Clemmie was in a position to do so.'

'But why?'

'Why do women do anything? Spring has arrived and she's got an itch that needs scratching, so she's baiting her little honey trap and running on instinct. You're a better catch than most, Zachariah. Watch out.'

'She needs to be redirected, since the woman doesn't attract me in any way and I don't want to have to be blunt with her.'

'She can be an enchanting little minx, and she has her eyes set firmly on going up in the world. Your indifference represents a challenge to her.'

'I'm not about to change my attitude, since I have no interest in her. Any challenge she thinks I represent is entirely in her imagination. You'd better guard my back until she transfers her affections elsewhere, Evan.'

Evan grinned. 'It will be my pleasure.'

Seventeen

Alexandra's social event was arranged for the middle of March. Invitations had been sent out, including one to Roland Elliot and his mother.

Not that Alexandra expected them to attend, but she wanted him to know how well she was doing for herself. To tell the truth she missed him, and missed the sense of danger she felt when she was around him, for he'd never made any bones about the attraction she presented for him.

Unfortunately, Basil Cheeves had accepted the invitation, and she thought he intended to propose marriage. It had only been a game on her part, something to make Zachariah Fleet jealous. The thought of being married to Basil was nauseating, and she wished she hadn't encouraged him in the first place. He couldn't keep his podgy hands to himself and he didn't have a brain in his head.

In an attempt to put him off she'd said to his father, 'I'm given to understand my legacy is very small . . . and not as I'd imagined.'

To that Cheeves had smiled, as though he thought she was being modest. 'Sometimes lack of dowry has no significance as a barrier to true love. I want to see him settled and provide me with a houseful of grandchildren.'

How absolutely ghastly that visit had turned out to be.

Almost everybody local had declared an intention to attend her social. The servants had been in a tizzy, until Alexandra had sought permission to take over the arrangements, and had asked Evan to help her. She liked Zachariah's manservant. He had a sardonic sense of humour that made her laugh.

Within days they had a buffet menu, and instructions for decoration. Evan had gone into the domestic agency, to arrange for a chef to supervise the food.

'The occupants of Martingale House haven't entertained since the departure of the former baronet, God rest his soul,' Mrs Cheeves had declared piously, while clasping her invitation card to her bosom.

What was more, another, juicier rumour was circulating that Mr Fleet was in line to be honoured by the King for his many philanthropic works in the form of title and estate. Had Alexandra heard anything?

'Indeed not, Mr Cheeves. Mr Fleet does not bray about his achievements, but plays his cards close to his chest.'

Cheeves had smiled at her. 'Indeed he does. Fleet is as sound a man as anyone could wish to meet . . . and a far cry from the man his brother had been. Mr Fleet is just the type of man the district needs.'

Alexandra had then overheard Cheeves instruct his wife to accept the pert little creature who looked after the children.

'It would be better to keep on Fleet's good side. You don't have to invite the governess to take tea with you, but at least acknowledge her without all the bitchery that goes on amongst your friends. From the hints Miss Tate has dropped, Miss Morris might be his relative from the wrong side of the blanket. No wonder he was annoyed and unfriendly with us . . . though it was kind of him to overlook the insult and do us such a great favour after the snub we dealt her.'

Alexandra managed to prise out the nature of the favour from Mrs Cheeves. George Sheridan again! He seemed to haunt Zachariah. But why?

'No more gossip now, dear,' Cheeves chided in passing to his wife. 'Our friends will look for you to set a good example in the matter.' As if the tittle-tattling old crow would take any notice. Gossip was her life-blood, and the more malicious the better.

Now there was an interesting line of thought to follow. Alexandra grinned at her reflection in the mirror. A hint here and a stir with a stick there, and the collective ant's nest of women in the district would see Clementine as respectable again – well, almost. Illegitimacy was rarely overlooked and the sins of the father were almost always attributed to the child. Though she had obviously inherited her mother's sin along with it.

By that time Alexandra hoped to have received the legacy and be gone, unless the esteemed Mr Fleet proposed to her – though not much chance of that now he was going to get a proper title. The thought awed her.

A sobering thought hit her like a clod of mud thrown up from a donkey's hoof. What if she turned out to be a penniless bastard herself? If that were the case she would have to rely on her looks to see her through with regards to Basil.

She regarded her face from every angle. She'd used a little artifice, the faintest blush of rouge on her cheeks and her lips. But was that curl a little loose? Alexandra pulled her hair arrangement apart and grumbled, 'I thought you were an experienced lady's maid, Ellen. Arrange it again, and this time make sure no ends are sticking out and that curl is secure.'

'I also have Miss Morris and Mrs Beck to attend to.'

'The social is in my honour, not theirs, and I want to be perfect. Do get on with it.'

'Yes, Miss Tate.'

A few minutes later, Evan knocked at the door. 'Ellen . . . Mrs Beck is waiting for you.'

Alexandra traded on his position in the house and their recent friendly cooperation. 'Oh, it's you, Evan. Thank goodness. Ellen hasn't finished my hair yet. She's so slow.'

The maid's lips tightened. 'I've arranged it once, but Miss Tate was dissatisfied with it and thought it was too loose. I was told to style it all over again. No wonder I'm late.'

'I'll see to Miss Tate. You go and attend Mrs Beck.'

As soon as Ellen had gone, Evan brushed the remains of her

hairstyle out, and used the curling tongs to create a froth of curls. He drew them to the back of her head and secured them with the concoction of beads and ribbons that were laid ready on the dressing table.

She liked him, and they were easy and relaxed with each other. 'You're a genius, Evan.'

'I'm aware of my skills, Alexandra. The dress is beautiful and it shows off your figure. You should rouge your breasts a little, since such little gestures evoke desire in a man.' He picked up the small pot of rouge she'd bought from a shop in Dorchester. 'May I?'

She gazed at his reflection in the glass. He was bending over her shoulder, a slightly olive-skinned man of medium height, who was firmly muscled and dark-eyed. Every breath that expelled from his mouth drifted warmly across her bare shoulder and the swell of her bosom, sending a shiver to creep across her skin. There was something very attractive about him. She remembered that Evan had once belonged to an acting company and imagined him playing the villain with his lean face.

Then she remembered him in his Shylock costume and the debacle with the dogs. She laughed. Evan was suited to comedy, and he reminded her a little of Roland.

Unbidden, she recalled the touch of Roland Elliot's hands, his long artistic fingers painting her skin, as gentle and sensual as the wings of a butterfly. There was something about a creative man that drew her, and there was an irresistible desire inside her to be handled. She closed her eyes, feeling the warmth of his body as it touched against hers, and remembering the painting Roland had shown her. She wondered if her breasts now adorned the sitter. How wanton the girl had looked with her wild hair and the brazen invitation in her pose.

He was arranging little curls about her ears. 'You need a man, Alexandra.'

Her eyes flew open and she gave a little giggle and her arm went to her thigh and she pressed against him. 'I daren't ruin myself.'

He ran a finger around her jawline. 'There are ways and means, as well you know it. You might still be intact, my dear, but you're no innocent. A little sexual foreplay wouldn't go amiss . . . a kiss or two. It will make you sparkle and give you something to look forward to. Evan turned the key in the lock and drew up a chair.

'I haven't agreed.'

'You've been teasing me for the past week, so of course you've agreed.' His arms slid round her from behind and his fingers brushed over the swell of her breast through the cloth. He nibbled the lobe of her ear and her nipples pushed against the fabric of her bodice. He loosened the laces and her breasts fell free. 'I can offer you ease and enjoyment, while still leaving you intact. Close your eyes.'

He's a servant, she thought as his hands touched and fondled.

He was also a man . . . and she was sick of being good when her body told her to be otherwise. Lord, he was pressing against her back, as big as a bull!

She should scream for help and have him dismissed.

She could scream with delight!

She wouldn't enjoy it, despite what he said, and the next minute his mouth closed over hers and she gave a little groan. Yes . . . she would.

He must have sensed the way her thoughts were arguing with each other, for he chuckled and inched her skirt carefully up her lap, folding it as he went so as not to crease it. His hands slid up her thighs and she struggled more for show than anything else, until he tightened his arm around her waist.

'Be still and hush now. It's my turn to tease you, and nobody will ever be any the wiser.' When his thumbs probed gently and slid into the warm moist folds of her centre she gave a little whimper and could smell her own musk rising.

He pulled her down, spread-eagled on her back across his lap and his tongue delicately attacked her mouth and her breasts, while he explored what was usually hidden under her gown.

'Oh . . . oh . . .' She whispered in surprise, as a few moments later the exquisite shudder she gave almost disintegrated her. A palm across her mouth muted her cry of release.

He stood, all at once the servant, and bringing her to her feet, arranged the folds of her gown over her throbbing centre. She felt lethargic, relaxed.

'Allow me to lace you into your bodice and shake the folds from your skirt, Miss Tate. You're a born trollop who likes to play with danger.'

She stared at him. 'How dare you insult me! You're a servant, and I could get you dismissed for what you've just done.'

'No, darling, you could not. Zachariah Fleet doesn't trust many people, but he trusts me. And here's a warning for you: leave the man alone. Hussies like you are a penny a dozen and your flirting is an embarrassment to him.'

Tying the last of the ribbons on her bodice together he gazed into her eyes and smiled. 'You have a nice pair of tits, but I suppose other men have told you that . . . Basil Cheeves perhaps. Are you sure you wouldn't like them rouged? No? Well, I'll make myself available when the evening is over, just to finish what we started.'

When she lashed out to slap him, he caught her by the wrist, and then pushed her on the bed and walked away. The lock clicked as he turned the key, and the door closed gently behind him.

Zachariah Fleet was attentive, but was so distant and gentlemanly that Alexandra felt like throwing the bowl of punch at him. It was as though her kiss hadn't had any effect on him, and indeed, as if it had never happened.

Basil Cheeves was almost frothing at the mouth and followed her around like a dog. Her glance fell on Evan in his evening dress. He looked dapper as he blended in with the crowd. He was acting the guest rather than the servant tonight. She gave a faint grin. Perhaps she'd shock him by turning up in his bed.

Then perhaps she wouldn't.

She forgot Evan when Roland Elliot was announced. He looked handsome in his best suit, and every head turned towards him, since he was a stranger to the district.

All she'd ever felt for him came rushing back. She abandoned Basil, who was talking about nothing and was flushed from the amount of drink he'd consumed.

She hurried forward, a smile on her face and her heart leaping in her chest. 'Roland. I didn't think you'd come. I've missed you. Where is your mother?'

'Mother died a month ago. I expected you to be at the funeral.'

She vaguely remembered getting a card. 'I'm so sorry. I had so many engagements to fulfill that I couldn't get away.'

His brow drew into a frown. 'My mother left you some pieces of jewellery. I've brought it with me.'

She drew him across to where Zachariah stood. 'This is my host, Mr Zachariah Fleet. May I introduce Mr Roland Elliot. You might remember that I told you about him.'

'Ah yes . . . the artist from Portsmouth.'

'It's London now.'

Zachariah shook his hand. 'It's a pleasure to shake the hand of an artist when usually I associate with money men. You don't take commissions for restoration work by any chance, do you? I have a portrait that's been damaged. It was scribbled on and then a servant tried to scrub the scribble off.'

'It doesn't sound promising, but I'll see what I can do. If nothing else I might be able to paint a passable reproduction.'

'Good. I'll bring it with me when I return to London. You did say you'd moved to London, didn't you?'

'Yes. My mother left me a small legacy, and since there was nothing to keep me in Portsmouth I sold my premises there shortly after Alexandra left.' He took a business card from an enamelled case and handed it to Zachariah. 'My business has increased considerably as a result. I've had to employ someone, and have taken on an apprentice.'

'You must be very talented.'

Alexandra hugged his arm. 'Oh . . . he is, Zachariah. I'm so happy to see you again, Roland.'

'You look well, Lexie. The country air seems to suit you.'

Nobody else but Roland called her Lexie. She felt guilty for the liberty she'd allowed Evan. She wondered if he'd told Zachariah. She'd heard that men gossiped amongst themselves about such things. But no . . . she would certainly have been informed that she'd outstayed her welcome.

Now she'd seen Roland again it was as though nobody else mattered.

'Where are you staying?' Zachariah asked him.

'At the Antelope for a day or two, then I must get back to work. A business like mine doesn't run itself without my input and I'll shortly need someone to run the business side and take orders.' He gave her a smile. 'I was hoping that someone would be you, Lexie, but it seems that the present company has more to offer you than a hardworking tradesman if it keeps you from acknowledging my mother's death. However, my offer is still open for a short time.' He gazed around him. 'What's the afternoon in aid of . . . some charity?'

She shrugged. 'It's so people can meet and talk socially, and get to know one another.'

Basil Cheeves approached to gaze pointedly at their linked arms. 'Ah, there you are, Alexandra. Who is this man you're being so familiar with?'

'It's my good friend, Roland Elliot. We grew up together and I'm like a sister to him.'

Roland raised an eyebrow. 'Wrong, Lexie. I've never considered you to be a sister. In fact, I proposed marriage to you when we were quite young, and again before you left for Dorset, if you recall. I'm here to persuade you to return to London with me.'

'We will talk about it when we have more privacy . . . Besides, I'm waiting on my legacy.'

'Ah . . . so your legacy has brought the cockroaches crawling out of the cupboard, Alexandra. I too have marriage on my mind,' Basil said.

There was smothered laughter from a couple of the men when Roland eyed Basil up and down and said, 'Obviously an eight-hundred-pound legacy doesn't buy much in the way of cock-roaches in these parts.'

'You are insulting, sir.'

Zachariah stepped between them. 'I think the insult was yours, Basil. It just rebounded back on you.'

Mr Cheeves' voice rose above the hubbub. 'Eight hundred pounds! Is that all the flighty creature is worth? It's a scandal to lead a man on like that.'

'Only if you choose to make it one, Mr Cheeves. The price you put on Miss Tate was a figure plucked from your own imagination, especially since there is another contender for the legacy, and it is not yet determined who will get it. Come now, shake hands and let's enjoy the afternoon, especially since Miss Tate is going to play the piano for us, and Mrs Jennings has offered to sing.'

The expressions on the faces of those present told Alexandra they were already enjoying themselves. Wild horses wouldn't be able to drag them away from the roasting that was taking place. No doubt it would give them something to gossip about after church on Sunday.

The two men eyed each other up. Goodness, she hoped they were not going to fight over her. That would be the last straw.

Roland held out his hand to Basil and grinned. 'A wager . . . the man she decides to wed loses the right to any legacy there may be. In fact, he will marry her for love. The one she scorns collects eight hundred pounds for his trouble.'

Basil's eyes sharpened. 'Do you have eight hundred pounds at your disposal?'

The rat! What had happened to his protestations of undying love?

Roland nodded and said softly, 'May the best man win then.'

Dismay uppermost, she gazed from one to the other. 'Has it never occurred to either of you that I might love someone else?'

'Name him,' someone said.

Her glance went to Zachariah. He was gazing across the room to where a stricken Clementine stood, an unguarded expression of such tenderness apparent in his eyes that Alexandra wanted to cry. No matter how much she'd tried he'd never shown any interest in her and never would. All she'd done was hurt two people she admired, for Clementine had never shown any animosity towards her, unless she pushed her into it.

Evan, the loathsome creature, was standing at his shoulder. Her body remembered how his hands had felt on her and it reacted. Evan had shown her what she was made of, which wasn't much – and he was reminding her to leave Zachariah alone.

Shock hit her. She'd taken the game too far and it had returned with a vengeance to bite her. Was Roland willing to take her without any money to her name; or was it just a game of bluff? There was only one way to find out. 'You know I always intended to marry you, Roland.'

Taking a wad of notes from his pocket he threw them on the table. 'There, she doesn't want you. Consider the transaction completed, Mr Cheeves.'

Basil pocketed the money and smiled. 'That's the easiest money I've ever laid my hands on. You can have her, and good luck.'

There was a muttering amongst a few of the older men. 'You cad . . . shame on you, Cheeves.'

Roland shrugged. 'I think I got the best of the bargain.'

Alexandra felt cheapened by the exchange. 'Not yet, you haven't. Hasn't it occurred to either of you that I have no intention of being bartered back and forth like a sack of potatoes in the market place?'

'Yes, it has occurred to me, Lexie, my love. That's why I'm buying you your freedom, with the only money I have. Remember the story of Pierrot, the poor sad clown who pined for the love of Columbine, only to watch his affection thrown away in favour of Harlequin?'

She recalled the trio of pretty figurines she'd set out on her dressing table. 'What of them?'

'I've decided I'm not going to be the sad clown to your Columbine.'

'It's only a story.' When he turned to walk away she said, 'Don't go, Roland.'

'I've booked two fares on the stagecoach for tomorrow, leaving from Dorchester. If you prefer to stay and you're not there, then so be it. I'll leave without you.'

Gently, he kissed her forehead, and then he turned her hand palm up and placed a purse in it. 'Here's your legacy from my mother. Think of me when you wear it.'

He turned and walked away. Zachariah followed after him. 'I'll see you out.'

Oh God! What if he knew about her indiscretion with Evan and was going to tell Roland?

'Don't count on being Harlequin either, because I doubt if Columbine will turn up,' she flung at his back.

He turned, shrugging. 'There are other women in the world, and at least you now know what your affections are worth. Very little.'

She felt like weeping. All her grand plans had come to nothing.

Everyone in the room was watching her, waiting for her to break down. Well . . . she wouldn't!

She stuck a smile on her face with a paste called pride, and she mingled and talked of nothing in particular for the rest of the afternoon, and she played the piano and sang. All the time

Basil Cheeves was bragging of his good fortune, and she was pretending not to hear while others were laughing behind her back.

Zachariah stepped in. He threw a pile of money on the table and drew out a pack of cards. 'Double or nothing for that eight hundred, Basil.'

Basil's eyes opened wide and a pink tongue licked his lips. He hesitated.

'Don't do it, Zachariah,' Evan said. 'You know you're wretched at cards.'

Zachariah ignored him. 'Best of three.'

Basil grinned. 'You're on.'

Harlequin and Columbine. Hah! Trust Roland to come up with that. He always did prefer the romantic side of things. She didn't know where Clementine had gone, though she was probably skulking in her chamber or in the nursery drooling over children that didn't even belong to her.

But Alexandra smarted, and she felt sick from her heart right down to her ankles. Eight hundred pounds. It had seemed such a lot to start with. Now it didn't. Was that all she was worth?

It seemed so. How scathing Roland had been . . . not that she hadn't deserved it.

A roar went up when Zachariah won. Basil strode off.

Later, when everyone left early, trickling away one by one, Alexandra expected to be summoned to Zachariah's study and taken to task. But the summons didn't come.

After she said goodnight to her last guest she couldn't face anyone so went up to her room. The tears finally came and she began to sob.

There came a knock at the door and Clementine came in. Joining her, the girl seated herself on the bed, drew her into her arms and held her close. 'I'm sorry your feelings were hurt.'

'I deserved it. I've been horrible to everyone. It was the legacy. It went to my head and I made all these stupid plans.'

'What will you do, Alexandra?'

'Go with Roland, I suppose. I love him . . . I really do, but I wanted more.'

'He seems like a nice man, and he has his own business and

he works hard. He's handsome too. And best of all . . . he loves you, which is more than that horrible Basil Cheeves does. Aren't you pleased you didn't accept him?'

'Oh, he never even asked me. He was waiting to see what the legacy was worth, and like most men, just wanted to touch me.

'As for Roland, he made me feel worthless. I should have gone to his mother's funeral. I liked her and we were good friends. Then there was Zachariah.'

When her companion's body stiffened, Alexandra grinned. She was not beyond digging a fork into her yet. Clementine would have some trouble on her hands when Zachariah Fleet decided he was in love with her and let himself off the leash.

'What of Zachariah? Did he . . . show an interest in you?'

Her eyes had such desperation in them that she felt sorry for her.

'I liked him a lot but on the times when I encouraged him he kept his distance. He was being awfully stuffy so I kissed him, knowing you were in the hall and would likely see it if you came in. To be honest, Zachariah didn't really know I existed.'

She decided not to mention Evan, though shame flooded through her, that she could have welcomed his advances . . . and he'd been so cold-blooded about it afterwards.

'Help me pack, then I'll ask Ben to bring the carriage round tomorrow, early before anyone gets up. I'll give you a letter for Zachariah, because I can't face him at the moment.'

She drew in a deep breath, and crossing to the dressing table she picked up two of the figurines and handed them to Clementine. 'These are for you, Clemmie . . . Columbine and Harlequin.'

She dropped Pierrot into the heart of the flames, where he cracked into several shards. 'Nobody wants a sad clown,' she said.

Eighteen

Zachariah didn't read Alexandra's letter. He just slid it into his waistcoat pocket. Clementine guessed it contained an apology.

'Am I to take it that Alexandra has gone back to London with Roland Elliot?' he said.

Clementine nodded. 'She told me last night that she'd be leaving early. She was upset by what happened and she blamed herself.'

'I wish you had told me earlier. I would have liked to talk to her before she left. I rather liked her young man . . . he didn't give a damn for the company he found himself in. I wanted to return his money to him. It would have taken a lot of work for him to have earned that much.'

'With a few exceptions, generally, the company was not very impressive.'

'I'll look them up when I get back to London, make sure Alexandra is settled and give her news of the legacy when I have some.'

'I didn't realize it was quite so much. Eight hundred pounds is a fortune.'

'What will you do with it if it comes your way?'

'I'll probably give half of it to Alexandra, so she wouldn't be too disappointed.'

He smiled at that. 'She wouldn't do the same for you.'

'I wouldn't expect her to. Alexandra didn't want to talk to anyone. She said she was too ashamed.'

'I admit she put a brave face on it afterwards. I admire her for that. Bringing Alexandra here wasn't the best decision I've ever made. She didn't fit in, and she treated you badly.'

'Finding out about her background was difficult for her. I made allowances . . . but I could have been kinder to her. Nobody made her feel welcome, and she reacted to that. She was a good daughter to her foster father, which says a lot for her.'

He placed a hand on her arm. 'You make me feel ashamed,

Clemmie. I want to explain about what happened between myself and Alexandra in the study that day.'

Some devil in her made her say, 'You don't have to try and wriggle out of it, Zachariah.'

'I just wanted you to understand—'

'Oh, Alexandra has already explained it. It's not my business anyway; you can kiss whoever you wish to.'

Exasperation crept into his voice. 'I'm well aware of that, but there's not many women who I'd care to kiss. Alexandra is not one of them. If she explained, then you must know that she kissed me and without encouragement. Did you mean that about me kissing whoever I wished?'

He'd turned the table on her and she took a hasty step back when he chuckled. 'With their permission, I meant.'

'And I haven't got your permission?'

'You employed me to look after the children and be their companion. Nothing more.'

'It's true, but I've come to rely on you for many other things.'

'And kissing isn't one of them, so don't do anything that will make me feel that I need to leave your household.'

He stared at her and grinned. 'That's good old-fashioned blackmail?'

'I won't stay here unless I'm treated with respect.'

He took both of her hands in his and engaged her eyes. 'I hold you in the utmost respect. I always have and I always will. What has brought this on, my Clemmie? Where would you go?'

She shrugged. 'I don't know.'

'Are you telling me you'd leave my children to fend for themselves, when they've grown to love and trust you and look upon you as their mother? I'd never have thought you'd be that cruel.'

Huffing out a sigh she removed her hands and took a step back. 'That wasn't fair.'

'It wasn't meant to be. I fight dirty when I'm pushed to it. Would you really leave me? No, don't answer that. I don't want such a possibility hanging over my head while I'm in London.'

Dismay gathered force inside her. 'Are you going away soon?'

'Within the week, I expect. I'm keeping the new maid on the staff. Her main job will be to attend to you and act as companion and chaperone when the need arises. It might stop a few tongues from wagging in the district.'

'Thank you, Zachariah.' She had an urge to slide her arms around him and keep him with her. 'It will be quiet here without you all. I already miss Alexandra. She was so lively and talented. We are not alike. We don't even look alike.'

'Your maid, Ellen, can play the piano and will teach you if you want to learn, and you will have the refurbishment of my study to keep you busy. I daresay you will see Alexandra again. I don't think she will miss the opportunity of flaunting the fact that her brother is a baron, do you?'

'I did notice the strong resemblance to your sister-in-law in that portrait. Everything is in such a pickle. We are tangled up together like knotted string. How long will you be gone?'

'I don't know. I'd like to spend the summer here if I can. When I return I intend to make some adjustments to your contract. If you have any changes you'd like to make we can discuss them then.

'Now, there's something else I need to discuss with you. Come to the study and take tea with me, would you? It's a fine day, so Julia will take the children out for a walk and keep them occupied for an hour or so.'

The study was warm, with the fire dancing in the grate.

After Mrs Ogden had delivered the tea tray he placed some sheets of paper on the table.

She gazed up at him, surprised. 'Edward's book?'

'Yes. I'd like you to read it.'

'There's not much to read by the look of it. It's mostly pictures.'

'I think you'll be able to make sense of the pictures.'

The boy had possessed the sense to number the pages. The first page had a picture of four adults and two smaller figures standing in a row. They had ear-to-ear smiles. There was a yellow river at the front and a hut, with leaning walls. On a table was a heap of grey stones. She ran a fingertip gently over the children and looked up at him. 'Your family?'

He nodded. 'I imagine so.'

The next picture had had the same background, except there was another man, dressed in dark blue. He had a pistol in his hand and it was pointing at the other two figures. JONAS was written at the top.

Page three showed four figures lying on the ground. Blood gushed out of their chests in a fountain. One of the children was little more than a baby and big tears flew off her face into a puddle. The boy was open-mouthed and he held a stick in his hand. *Screem!* was written under him.

'Oh God, what a brave little boy,' she whispered, tears flooding her eyes.

Page four had thick rain slashes across it. The prone figures were floating on the water. One of them had long red hair. *Wake Papa!* The urgent black letters were thick, as though they were shouting out to them.

The next page only had a river and *Run! Run!*

On the last page there were four figures again. The two smaller ones had eyes but no mouths. They were ragged. There was a ship behind them.

The final page was a picture of a meadow full of different coloured flowers with a child running around and butterflies and birds in the air. Two dogs sniffed at a tree trunk and there was a boy on a pony. They all wore smiles.

Clementine stifled a sob and gazed at Zachariah. 'Your brother and his wife were murdered?'

'If Edward's account is correct and not a figure of his imagination.'

'Do you think the Sheridans killed them?'

'They don't strike me as being killers, and if they are, why didn't they kill the children as well? And who are the other two people? On the strength of this I think we can safely assume that Edward and Iris are my brother's children. We are certainly going to make further enquiries though. Should I question Edward about this, do you think?'

'I think he's told you what happened in the best way he could. You saw how scared he was when he arrived. He'd been threatened and told not to say anything. Yet he found the courage to draw those pictures as a way of getting round that. I would say that it's all he can remember of the incident after all this time. If you question him about it for detail he might stop talking again, and he might make things up.'

He nodded. 'I'll let him know that I've read it.'

And he did, saying to Edward, 'Thank you for the book. I'll

treasure it and keep it in a safe place, so you don't have to worry any more.' He pulled the lad close and hugged him.

The week sped by fast. The children grew used to the thought of Zachariah leaving.

When the day came Julia Beck made tearful goodbyes.

'Be good, my sweet darlings,' Julia said to the children, and was almost in tears as she hugged them. 'Clementine, darling, you must ask Zachariah to bring you and the children to London for a visit one day. No, don't you ask him. I'll tell him myself that he must.'

'It's a long journey for the children to make.'

'Nonsense, dear. They managed to come from Australia without mishap.'

The trunks were distributed into the carriages, overseen by Evan. He would travel with Zachariah, and he loaded a hamper of food, as if they were going off for the day on a picnic.

Clementine and the children watched the comings and goings from the upstairs window. The horses were restless, stamping and squealing and tossing their heads. The children were trying not to cry at the parting, so their voices were thick with the effort.

Wolf panted with excitement as the carriages started off and Happy chased his tail in a circle.

Then the Fleet carriage stopped. Zachariah jumped out and ran back towards the house, taking long, loping strides.

Had he forgotten his hat?

No . . . he'd forgotten the children. He grabbed them up, one in each arm, and hugged them. Then he kissed each of them and put them down again. 'Look after Miss Clemmie,' he said.

'You forgot to kiss her goodbye too,' Iris told him.

'So I did.' He smiled at her. 'May I have that privilege on this occasion, Clemmie?'

She nodded. After all, he couldn't get up to much mischief with the children looking on.

He took her face in his hands and his lips touched gently against hers. He drew her closer and she felt the slow disintegration of her senses as they peeled off to expose each layer beneath. He nipped her bottom lip then kissed her again, giving her a little lick when he'd taken his fill, as though he was removing a smear of piquant mayonnaise from her mouth.

Mischief obviously came in many forms. '*Ummmm,*' she said, so thoroughly robbed of her wits that she couldn't think of anything else that sounded remotely like intelligent human speech.

He gazed down at her, eyes full of laughter. 'Was that an *ummmm* of protest or an *ummmm* of approval?'

She was weak at the knees and became aware of Edward and Iris giggling together: 'Ummm – ummm – diddly – dummm – hum . . .'

'I must get back to the carriage. I only returned to the house because I'd forgotten my hat.'

Ah, so he *had* forgotten his hat. It was still on the hallstand. He did something spontaneous and completely out of character. He ran down the stairs and tapped the brim smartly with his stick. The hat did a somersault. Catching it on the end of his stick, he bowed, and then transferred the hat to his head.

When the children laughed and clapped hands he laughed too. 'Evan taught me that. Perhaps I should join a travelling show, what do you think, Clemmie?'

'I think you're showing off. You'd need more than one trick if you were intent on having a successful career with a travelling show. As for that kiss of yours, I think it might have been an ummm of approval,' she called down to him.

His smile came back to her, slow and warm. 'So I could make a career out of kissing you.'

Iris piped up, 'Polly said that people who kiss each other have to get married, or else it's naughty.'

'You're too young to know of such things, but I'll bear that in mind.'

The door closed behind him and they all rushed to the landing window again.

When he reached the carriage, he waved and leapt inside. The vehicle went rumbling off.

The dogs raced down the stairs and scrabbled to be let out, so they could enjoy themselves by chasing the carriages.

'Don't let them out, else they'll be halfway to London before we catch them,' she said, as the children dashed after them.

July suddenly seemed ages away. She would make a calendar

for the children; then they could learn how to use it as they crossed the days off.

She wondered if she'd spend the rest of her life waiting for Zachariah to return, the life in her body drying up, her hair going grey and her back bending under the weight of her spinsterhood. And would he still be pestering her for kisses?

She smiled. She certainly hoped so!

They had passed through Poole three hours ago, barely crawling. Zachariah had forgotten it was a market day. The road in and out of the port town was choked with horses and carts.

They stopped at his agent's office so Zachariah could tell him he was leaving for London. The office had been busy, the walls covered with the usual posters. One had been a drawing of a man with a beard. There had been something familiar about him. What had his name been? Joshua . . . Josiah . . . Hawkins?

He heard Stephen swearing at a bunch of jostling people when they set off again. Opening his eyes he gazed out of the window, in time to see a mounted man going in the opposite direction . . . Basil Cheeves? The banker's son gave the carriage a cursory glance, and then he scowled when he saw Zachariah at the window.

He glanced towards the horse and rider on his far side and said something to the man, who had a country hat shading his face. There was something about him that also seemed slightly familiar . . . the nose perhaps?

Then they surged forward and were past. The traffic had thinned down considerably and Zachariah heaved a sigh of relief. They would catch up with John and Julia at the Lyndhurst inn.

Dragged from his reverie, Zachariah laughed and said, 'Thank goodness the traffic has eased off. You know, Evan, you can stop the servant and master act now we're alone.'

Evan sighed. 'I've known you for a long time, sir, and it's easier to play the servant than switch roles all the time. I'm not going to be your man forever. Soon I'll have enough money to form my own company of players.'

'You know I'll be happy to advance you the money.'

Evan leaned back in his seat. 'I know you would, but you have enough people dipping into your purse.'

Zachariah shrugged. 'I enjoy the challenge of finance as much as you enjoy the challenge of play-acting.'

'You don't look as though you're enjoying life at the moment, sir. If you don't mind me saying, you look like a man who has taken a fond farewell from his lady love.'

'Then you know a kiss is never enough. Unfortunately, there are lines that a gentleman mustn't cross, not even in his own home, unless he wants to compromise himself. One of those lines tells him not to gossip about his conquests, however small – if he is lucky enough to make one.'

'That would never do.'

'Indeed it would not. Now, tell me . . . what did you do to Miss Tate to send her scuttling off without saying a tearful thank-you and goodbye to her host.'

Evan examined his fingernails for a moment, then looked up at him and grinned. 'As you indicated, a gentleman never tells. Let me just say the lady got a little less than she needed, but more than she deserved, and she left here still intact but with more awareness. She had pretty breasts, didn't she?'

Clementine came instantly to Zachariah's mind . . . although really she hadn't ever left it. 'Ah yes . . . small but neat and firm, with a delightful upward tilt – a delectable handful I should imagine.' He collected his thoughts together. 'Actually, I don't think I noticed them.'

'So it seems,' Evan said drily. 'I thought Miss Tate was a little more voluptuous than you described though.' Evan described her figure in the air with his hands. 'You did understand who I was referring to, didn't you?'

Zachariah raised an eyebrow. 'Of course I did. I'd throw you out of the carriage and bounce you on your arse if I thought you'd refer to Clementine in such a personal matter.'

'So who were *you* describing?'

'Hush now, Evan; there's something bothering me that I can't quite put my finger on.'

'That must be frustrating.' Evan chuckled. Taking out a deck of cards he expertly shuffled them and then began to play patience, using the seat beside him as a table. 'You're terrible at card games, Zach. How did you manage to win that money from Cheeves?'

'I cheated. The cards were Gabe's, and I remember he'd told me he'd marked them.'

'That's what I thought. I threw them in the fire, just in case it was questioned.'

Zachariah closed his eyes, and leaning back into the corner he allowed his mind to drift.

The answer caught up with him as they pulled into the stable yard.

He waited until they were settled down with a tankard of ale, and then said to John, 'I thought I saw George Sheridan riding with Basil Cheeves in Poole. I was hoping he'd left town.'

'Perhaps it wasn't him, just someone who looked like him.'

'That could be true, John, but I feel uneasy.' Nevertheless he ignored his instincts because he had nothing solid to attach them to.

At dinner that evening, they were enjoying the inn's roast beef and dripping pudding when Zachariah found himself gazing at the same wanted poster that had been pinned to the board in his land agent's office. Up close it was a crude, badly printed image of a man with a beard. His uneasiness came back.

Wanted: Dead or Alive. Jonas Hawkins is charged with four counts of murder in the Australian colony, and the kidnapping of two children. Now believed to be in England. The escaped convict is regarded as highly dangerous and has been sighted in Dorchester, Portsmouth and London. A reward is offered for information leading to his capture.

Zachariah poked Evan in the side. 'You know something about theatre disguise. What do you make of that wanted sheet – does it remind you of someone?'

'The beard looks false and that moustache is typical for saloon-bar dastardly villains.' Evan made a corner between his forefinger and his thumb and placed it where the chin would be situated under the beard.

'I'll be damned . . . he looks like George Sheridan,' John said.

Julia placed her hand against her chest and her eyes widened. 'Oh my goodness. Clementine and the children are alone.'

'Hardly; they have Mr Bolton and Ben looking after them.

Besides, why should Clementine and the children be involved?'
John didn't sound convinced about that though. 'The more I look
at the poster the more he reminds me of George Sheridan. It is
him!'

A sense of doom settled darkly in Zachariah's midriff as things
began to fall into place. Could this Jonas Hawkins be the same
Jonas portrayed in Edward's book? There had been four adults in
his picture book – one with red hair. Sheridan's wife, or the
woman who'd stepped on the ship, had dark brown hair.

Zachariah allowed his mind to wander. What if the Sheridans
had been killed along with Gabe and Alice? Jonas Hawkins would
only need to change his name and hire a woman to look after
them until they reached England. Thank goodness the children
had survived.

But Edward and Iris were the only two people who would be
able to identify Jonas Hawkins as the man who'd killed their
father and mother.

Alarm bells began to ring. 'There are too many coincidences,
and something is wrong here. I'm going to return to Martingale
House,' he said.

John said, 'We'll all go back, but I can't leave Julia here by
herself.'

'I'm coming with you, since Clementine and the children
might need me.'

'There is a woman on the outskirts of the village who will
give you shelter, Julia. I imagine Mrs Mason will be happy to
offer her hospitality until we're sure it's safe.'

'We'd better hurry then, else it will be dark before we get there.'
John stood. 'I'll instruct the ostler to get the horses rigged.'

Pushed by a sense of urgency they didn't spare the horses in the
first half of the journey, and they changed to fresh horses when
they reached Poole, leaving their own to recover at the coaching
inn.

They made their way carefully, taking the inland road since
the heath was a dangerous path to take at night, with its bogs
and quarries, and could quite easily cause a horse to break its leg
or tip a man into its mire. They were not far past Wareham when
they came over a rise and saw a red glow in the sky.

'There's a fire, and it looks as though it's on my land. I hope it's not the house.' Fear leapt into Zachariah's heart as he thought of Clementine and the children.

'I'm going straight to the house,' he said.

Nineteen

Clementine didn't know how long she'd been asleep, but she woke with a start.

Now Zachariah and his friends had departed the house had a hollow feeling to it that she'd have to get used to all over again . . . and again, and again, no doubt.

She could hear the clock ticking in the hall. It sounded loud tonight, as though it had an echo to it. When the spring made a whirring sound and struck twice she jumped, and her heart picked up speed.

Something was different. Sliding from the warm nest of her bed she pulled on her robe. Shadows danced on the wall, the light between tinted with different shades of red.

Like flames! There was a faint whiff of smoke in the air, or was it her imagination? She crept on to the landing and gazed down into the darkness of the hall below. The candle lantern on the stair was still alight, but sputtering; everything seemed to be as it should in the house.

Beneath her she heard a scuffing noise. She stared into the darkness, hearing every beat of her heart and unable to decide whether the noise had been inside, or out in the porch.

Suddenly a fist pounded against the door panel.

Clementine's heart nearly stopped and she shouted down the stairwell: 'Mr Bolton . . . Ben . . . wake up.'

The dogs hurtled downstairs from the nursery wing and began to make runs at the door, scrabbling to get out and see the strangers off. They barked furiously.

Eyes wide, Edward and Iris joined her. 'What is it, Clemmie? What's happening?'

'I'm not sure.'

Mr Bolton came from the servants' quarters, pulling on his coat. Ben was on his tail, lighting the way with a lantern.

Heart in her mouth she heard him say, 'Who is it?'

They heard a mumbled voice. 'It's Basil Cheeves. Open up. I was on my way home when I saw the barn in the farm meadow was on fire.'

It didn't sound much like Basil Cheeves, but his voice was slurred as though he'd been drinking.

His face was in shadow when the door was opened. Sensing a romp the dogs sniffed his ankles, gave him a cursory growl, and then when Ben growled an order to them they wagged their tails and pushed past him, scenting the doorpost as they went out. They sniffed the air, then turned towards the barn and followed the scent of smoke, starting to bark when the noise from the fire was borne to them on the breeze.

Mr Bolton said urgently, 'Ben, go and rouse the men from the village. Tell them to meet me in the coach house. If there are enough of us we might be able to make a bucket line down to the stream and save the building, or at least some of the contents.'

Polly joined them on the landing. 'I'll come down and lock the front door. I'll leave the kitchen door open so you can get in when it's over and I'll rouse the house staff in case they're needed and make a kettle of tea. It's thirsty work, fighting fires.'

Mr Bolton headed for the kitchen and Polly headed down the stairs.

The man stayed in the doorway. There was a red glow beyond the trees, and the whiff of smoke in the air.

Clementine drew back in the shadows when he seemed to look directly at them from under the brim of his hat. His head moved from side to side and he almost sniffed the air, like a wild animal seeking out its prey.

She drew the children back further into the shadows. *He didn't look like Basil Cheeves!* Though in this dim light it could have been him, since she was looking down on the figure, she conceded.

A sudden breeze blew out the flame on the guttering candle.

Beside her, Edward stiffened with fear. 'Jonas has come for us; we've got to hide,' he said, his voice a low and painful rasp.

Iris gave a little sob and buried her head against Clementine's thigh.

Despite her instinct to call Polly back up to them, Clementine knew she was too late to do anything to change her course.

Firmly, the maid said, 'If you wouldn't mind, Mr Cheeves, would you go to the coach house if you intend to help fight the fire.'

Clementine breathed a sigh of relief when the man turned away and left. Polly turned the key in the lock behind him with a satisfying clunk. She chided herself for being silly. Of course it was Basil Cheeves – who else would it be? There was no reason why someone should pretend to be him.

Polly said before heading to the door, 'I'll go and rouse Mrs Ogden and the cook, if they're not already up and about. You and the children try and get some more sleep, Miss Clemmie. I'll lock the dogs in the laundry room when they come back, so they don't get underfoot. I'll call you if you're needed.'

Edward tugged urgently at her hand. 'Hide . . . hide?'

The hair on her arms and the nape of her neck stood up. 'It's all right, Edward. The man's gone.'

'Jonas.'

Iris had begun to shiver.

She must get the children back to bed and settle them down. 'Come on back to the nursery where it's warm. I'll tuck you both in bed and then fetch you some warm milk.'

'Don't leave us!' Edward said, and using both hands he began to pull her by the arm in the opposite direction. '*Hide . . . Jonas . . . don't talk!*'

It wouldn't hurt to pander to the boy, who was obviously terrified.

Iris had begun to sob now. 'He'll cut Edward's tongue off.'

'I won't tell . . . I promise.' Edward clapped his hand over his mouth.

'I want Uncle Zachariah,' Iris grizzled.

So did Clementine, but he wasn't here to lend his support so she'd just have to manage by herself. She drew them both into her arms. 'There are a lot of rooms in this house. We'll take some bedding and make a little den for ourselves. We can hide there until dawn, which is only two or three hours away. It will be an adventure, but you must be brave and stop crying. Now . . . where shall we hide?' she said, trying to make it sound like a game.

'In Papa and Mama's room under the bed,' Iris said. 'Sometimes we play there, though I can't remember them.'

'You can't see angels; you just know that they're there, keeping watch.' She gazed out of the window on the way past it. The glow of the fire had turned the sky red beyond the trees and the sound of crackling flames and men shouting at one another came to her ears.

They migrated to their new hiding place, taking the feather quilts and pillows from the nursery. Closing the bedroom door behind them Clementine locked it and placed the key on the dresser, mainly to give the children an extra sense of security. Lighting a candle she placed it back on the dresser, tucked them under the quilt and got in beside them.

The space under the four-poster bed was adequate for the three of them to be comfortable. The children had furnished it with a thick rug and had obviously raided the house for some colourful cushions. It was a safe little hidey-hole that they'd kept a secret, and they probably spoke to their parents sometimes. A couple of boxes would contain some of their parents' personal items, and the dust ruffles that hid the legs of the bed gave it a cozy feel. The children snuggled against her.

'If this was your mama and papa's bedchamber, then I expect you were born in this bed, Edward. They will know you are here and their spirits will keep watch over you until morning.'

'I don't like ghosts, and I love you better than I love my mama because she can't cuddle me,' Iris told her and yawned. 'Do you think she misses cuddling me?'

'I'm sure she does, but I expect she remembers all the cuddles she had with you in the past. Stop talking now and go to sleep, else you'll be a grumpy hen in the morning.'

Iris giggled, and within a couple of minutes was fast asleep, snuggled up against her side.

A wave of love swept over Clementine, as if she was experiencing all the good feelings in existence, and all at once. It churned inside her like a shining kaleidoscope of colours and it made her want to laugh and cry at the same time. 'I love you both so much,' she whispered, then added to it by thinking: 'I love your uncle too.'

The boy began to weep quietly and the only comfort Clementine could offer her troubled little charge was to hold him close until he went to sleep.

She had no intention of sleeping herself, and hoped Edward wouldn't have nightmares.

Despite her resolve to stay awake, Clementine began to drift off to sleep.

A tinkle of glass, followed by the rise and fall of a moaning sound, brought her awake. She banged her head on the underside of the bed when she sat up without remembering where she was. 'Ouch!'

Goosebumps raced up her arms. What was that ghostly noise? Was this room haunted by Gabriel Fleet and his wife after all?

Then the bed ruffles billowed and the candlelight flickered, as though there was a draught. Relief filled her. Somebody had opened a door or a window downstairs and the draught was coming through the gap under the bedroom door.

The glow from the fire still had enough heat in it to paint the spaces between the shadows red, and the windowpanes glistened with ruby streaks. She listened for a while. There were the usual house noises, the snaps of timber in the roof, the scratch of ivy against the wall and the creak on the stair. The clock struck three. She sighed. It was going to be a long night.

She'd hardly lain down again when she thought she heard footsteps above. How easy it was to imagine them coming down the stairs from the nursery with a soft thud . . . thud . . . thud.

There was a furtive sound further up the hall, of a door handle being turned and tested. Her bedchamber! There was something creepy about it. Hinges creaked as a door swung open and then it gave a softer creak as it closed again. That wasn't her imagination. Her door made exactly that noise and she'd asked Ben to put some grease on the hinges.

Her heart began to thump and she jumped as high as a pail full of fleas when Edward placed a hand on her arm. Pulling herself together, she whispered, 'I expect it's Polly looking for us because she couldn't find us in the nursery. I'll go and tell her where we are.'

'Uncle Zachariah told me to look after you and Iris. I don't want you to go.'

'I'll just take a quick look outside the door.' She picked up the heavy brass poker. 'Close the door quietly behind me and lock it. I'll give a little whistle when I want to come back in.'

There was a draught coming up the stairs, setting the remains of the candles in their holders fluttering. It was cold, as though the front door was wide open.

The hallway was long and dark except for the red glow halfway along. She crept along it, breath held as she stopped now and again to listen.

There was a metallic sound at the far end of the hall, as though someone had spun a coin on the floorboards. An awareness of something sinister waiting there for her was overwhelming. Her voice quavered. 'Polly . . . is that you?'

A chuckle came from out of the darkness. She spun, catching a gleam of light touching on metal. He was by the staircase, only an arm's length away.

'Where are those brats?'

'They're not here. They've gone to London with Mr Fleet.'

Bunching her robe in his fist he pulled her towards him, so close she could smell his sweat and the foul, panting gust of his breath.

Jerking herself from his grip she backed away from him, the poker held in the folds of her robe. She needed to get into position to have a good swing at him.

She edged towards the staircase, where the candle still burned in the lantern. He was dressed in black. His hat shaded eyes that glittered in the lantern light, and a kerchief was tied over his mouth. Her blood ran cold when she saw that he carried a knife. 'Jonas Hawkins, I presume.'

'Ah . . . I thought them brats wouldn't keep what they knew to themselves.'

She could have kicked herself. So, he was after the children, and then it would be her turn. Though it would make more sense if he killed her first. She must try and disable him so she could defend the children.

'They're only babies. You've already killed their parents. Leave them alone.'

'That boy's old enough to testify against me.' He lifted the knife and said, 'It will be quick, I promise you, though a bit messy.'

She brought the poker down on his hand and knocked the knife from his grasp. It went tumbling down the stairs. A hand in her midriff sent her tumbling after it. She managed to roll into a ball as she bounced down the stair and by some miracle didn't do any damage to herself except for a bloodied nose, if the warm gush she felt was anything to go by, and probably several bruises. She picked herself up just as the felon came bounding down after her. He grabbed up the knife before she had a chance.

'No!' Edward screamed out from the top of the stairs.

'Ah . . . so you haven't gone to London, brat. I didn't think so.' Jonas turned and started back up the stairs.

'Stop! I'll shoot you if you come any further.'

Edward held the pistol with both hands and his eyes were steady on the murderer in front of him, though the pistol was wavering. She drew on what knowledge she had of pistols, which was next to nothing. Oh God! What if the pistol was loaded? Worse, what if the pistol *wasn't* loaded, and Jonas murdered them all?

Jonas was positioned between herself and Edward.

Clementine groped around her and her hand closed around the poker. She wasn't going down without a fight.

Iris appeared, her expression changing to one of terror when she saw Jonas. She gave a panicky little scream, and then her quivering voice said from the shadows, 'It's Jonas. He's come for us. Quick! Shoot him, Edward.'

'I can't . . . I don't know how. Run away and hide.'

Iris snorted. 'You pull that trigger thing back where your fingers are and it makes a bang and a bullet comes out through that hole in the front.'

'What if I kill Miss Clemmie?'

The conversation would have struck Clementine as ludicrous considering the circumstances . . . if it hadn't come from the mouths of children.

As it was the man laughed and was about to head up the stairs again when Clementine dived at his legs and tripped him. The knife went spinning from his hands off into the darkness. It clattered across the tiled floor.

'Bitch! You're just making it harder for yourself. It looks as though I'll have to use my hands.'

He freed himself from her desperate clutch, pulling her off by her hair. Then he kneed her in the stomach. Struggling to catch a breath she hit the wall and doubled over, her strength almost spent.

'Be still. I'll find a good use for you before you go to meet your maker. I might even allow you to live a bit longer if you do as you're told . . . like the last one.'

The poker was within her grasp. She grabbed it and hit him across the back of the legs as hard as she could.

He turned and punched her, then grasped her by the neck with both hands. 'I told you to be still. It looks as though I'll have to dispose of you first.'

The struggle for air was futile. She tried to rise, but her legs wouldn't hold her and everything seemed to have slowed down. *Run*, she mouthed silently to the children as her heartbeat began to boom in her chest.

But they didn't run. Edward was frozen to the spot.

In the darkening mists clouding her mind Clementine heard the frenzied barking of the dogs. Wolf and Happy burst through the open doorway in a snarling fury.

Jonas kicked out at one of the dogs and it squealed, so the other one redoubled its efforts.

Edward closed his eyes. Pistol wavering all over the place, he pulled the trigger.

There was an explosion and Jonas dropped on top of her like a stone. His hazel eyes were barely an inch from hers and she watched the life drain from them before his hands dropped away and allowed the air through.

She drew in a painful rasping breath before the world went dark around her.

Twenty

Clementine woke to find Zachariah gazing down at her. He looked exhausted.

'The children,' she croaked.

'They're fine and you're safe. Don't you ever frighten me like that again.'

He sounded so cross that relief overwhelmed her. Zachariah Fleet was a kitten compared to Jonas Hawkins. She touched his hand, which rested on the bed. 'You look as though you haven't slept for a week.'

He laughed. 'I haven't . . . well, not for a day or two.'

'Jonas Hawkins, is he . . .?'

'Dead? Yes, he is.'

She shuddered. 'Poor Edward and Iris . . . I thought the pistol exploded in Edward's face.' She tried to sit up, alarmed by the recollection. 'He's all right, isn't he? Tell me he's not hurt.'

He pushed her gently down on to the pillows and curled his long fingers around her hand. 'The pistol Edward was holding belonged to Gabe. When I was sorting out the contents of the trunks Edward must have hidden it under the pillow. It wasn't loaded.'

'Then how did he shoot Jonas Hawkins?'

'He didn't shoot him; I did. I'm sorry the children had to see it, but I had little choice since he was strangling you. They're more worried about you than him. I'd rather have placed him under arrest until we could alert the authorities.'

'At least they won't be looking over his shoulder for him now. They've seen too much killing of people they love in their young lives.'

'That's true.'

'They had a little camp under the bed that I didn't know about. I imagine that was as near to their parents as they could get.' When she smiled at him her face ached. She touched her finger gently against her cheek and winced. 'Do I look ugly?'

'You look as though you've survived a few rounds with a pugilist. Your face is swollen and bruised. Luckily, he didn't break your neck, and it took him longer to choke you than cutting your throat would have, so you're lucky to be here.'

'Can I see?'

'Are you sure you want to?'

When she nodded, he fetched the hand mirror from the dressing table.

She examined her face to find it exactly as he'd described. She couldn't see herself under the damage, but her neck was adorned with several bruises where her attacker's hands had exerted pressure. She giggled . . . then the horror of what had happened overwhelmed her. Tears ran down her cheeks and she began to weep. Pulled into his arms she buried her face in his shoulder.

'Don't cry, my precious,' he said, in a voice so low that she could hardly hear it and thought she must have been mistaken.

After a while she stopped crying and looked up at him. 'Sorry.'

His blue eyes danced with amusement. 'I'm not, since it provided me with an excuse to offer you comfort. Now you look as though you want me to kiss you.'

'I certainly do not.'

'Thank goodness for small mercies; it would be like kissing a suet pudding somebody had stamped on.'

She felt miffed. 'Since when have you been an expert on kissing suet puddings?'

'I might concede you a point on that.'

'May I remind you that I've been threatened with a knife, kicked, punched, thrown down the stairs, thrown back up again, and choked to death, and all on your behalf. I feel bruised all over and I'm very, very angry.'

'And you still have plenty of fight left in you. You were actually ninety per cent choked to death, and by the way, you *are* bruised all over.'

'You and your numbers.' Shocked as his words sank in, she stared at him. 'You examined me?'

He gave a rueful laugh. 'Unfortunately no. I intended to, but Julia wouldn't hear of it. I thought you were dead at first.' He cleared his throat. 'There was blood on you and then I thought

I might have missed your attacker and hit you instead. I'd never have forgiven myself if you'd died. It was close.'

'I don't think I would have forgiven you, either. You saved my life. I did my best to fight that thug off but he was so strong, and the children wouldn't run and hide like I told them to. They didn't even move, but stood there watching. And they looked so frightened. Edward couldn't hold the pistol straight because it was too heavy. His eyes were filled with dread. I couldn't help him because I ran out of strength and felt all floppy like a rag doll.'

He placed his finger over her lips. 'Try not to think about it.'

Gruffly, she asked him, 'What were you doing here, when you should have been halfway to London?'

'It's a long story and best left until you've recovered. Needless to say there will be an inquiry in a few days' time. Your deposition will be needed, and those of the children.'

'May I borrow your handkerchief?'

He handed it over with a sigh. 'I'm running out of them.'

'I'll buy you one for Christmas.'

'That's eight or nine months away. I might need one before then.'

'You've always got an answer for everything, Zachariah.'

'And you've always got a question for the answer, which doesn't mean it's the right question or the right answer. Can you eat something, Clemmie mine? The cook has some chicken soup on the stove that she made especially for you.'

Her stomach growled and he smiled. 'Ah, the answer is in the affirmative, I hear.' He crossed to the bell pull and gave it a tug.

When he returned to her side he reached out to rearrange the little curl by her ear to his liking, a tender gesture that completely disarmed her, so the inclination to turn her abused face into his palm was almost overwhelming.

'Zachariah, please don't do that,' she pleaded, her voice almost a purr with the indecent pleasure coursing through her.

'Why not?'

'Because . . . because . . .'

'Ah, is that why?'

But it was too much to ask. His hand closed over hers again, his glance engaged hers and he chuckled. Stooping, he kissed her, his mouth as light as a feather duster. 'I'll bring the children to see you later today. They have developed a ghoulish interest to inspect your injuries. Don't be surprised if your misadventure turns up in Edward's next *bogafree*, with himself as the hero.'

She tried not to laugh. 'Edward was tremendously courageous. I wonder if he'll include Iris giving him instructions on how the gun worked.'

A low rumble of laughter came from him. 'I was just in time for that little display of female reasoning. What a resourceful little girl she is . . . so calm and in control of herself.'

'Your appearance was a miracle; we'd have been dead by now if you hadn't arrived.'

'And I'd be inconsolable, my Clemmie. Enter,' he called out, and a beaming Mrs Ogden came in followed by Julia and Ellen.

'Eat every morsel.' He kissed her hand and stood. 'Be gentle with her, ladies.'

'Yes, sir, she'll feel better after a nice bath.' Mrs Ogden's mouth fell open. 'Lord save us . . . look at your face. It's worse than it was yesterday.'

'I have looked.' Clementine's voice was watery and she looked as though she was about to cry again. She always seemed to get emotional when sympathy was offered to her.

Zachariah didn't mind having her head resting against his shoulder and her breast pressing against his chest. If only he could have her all – soft and wearing nothing except for the smell of soap and woman and with her furry little nest teasing against him. It would be his time to get emotional then.

He grinned . . . but such delights could wait. He was looking for his handkerchief. Zachariah patted his pockets, only to remember she'd already borrowed it.

But there was a folded paper in his waistcoat pocket. He vaguely remembered Clementine handing it to him . . . a message from Alexandra after she'd left. He didn't know whether he wanted to read it or not. As was his duty he would accept Alexandra for what she was, as part of the family – and should she prove to be the rightful claimant of the legacy, he would allow her access to Edward and Iris.

Dear Mr Fleet

   Thank you for your hospitality. There is something I should tell you, and whether you take it further is your business.

I had the occasion to overhear a conversation between Mr Basil Cheeves and another gentleman, one I didn't recognize, on an occasion when I visited at Mrs Cheeves' request.

The topic was the value of an amount of gold, the property of Gabriel Fleet, which was transported to England in the luggage of your brother's personal effects. They were to take the trunk, remove the gold, then return the trunk to you. The plan went awry when one of your servants took possession of the trunk as soon as it was unloaded from the ship.

Basil Cheeves' companion used to be someone they called Hawk. He was acquainted with your late brother through gambling, and was transported for the crime of stealing betting money from a syndicate to which they all belonged. Basil was involved with the accounting side and your brother borrowed heavily. Hawk evaded the authorities and returned to England. He wanted his share so he could move to America and start afresh, but the account no longer existed.

They blamed it on your brother and tried to kill him on two occasions while he lived at Martingale House. The suggestion was that Basil Cheeves would cause a diversion while the other man ransacked Martingale House for the gold. I thought nothing more of it at the time since they had drunk too much wine and were affected by laughter, and were silly brained like children.

Also I have always found you uncomfortable to approach, only to risk being ridiculed or be rebuffed, so I kept it to myself.

I have no idea if there is any truth to this tale, but I wish for no harm to befall on you and yours. I promise I will stay out of your life, since I believe I was tolerated rather than welcome in your house.

Yours truly,

Alexandra Tate

Her criticism smarted, though he was truthful enough to admit he could have been less standoffish. In fact, he'd never have left Clementine and the children alone had he taken the time to read the letter earlier.

Blood rushed into Zachariah's face. Was there no end to the consequences of Gabe's gambling debts? Basil Cheeves must have set fire to the barn to cause a diversion. And to think he was on the spot, helping to put the fire out.

He wished he'd opened the letter sooner. Cheeves had been in on the plan to rob his house, and it could have resulted in death for Clementine and the children.

He went in search of John Beck and laid the letter before him. 'What is your inclination?' John asked. 'If Alexandra's letter is to be believed, then clearly Basil Cheeves was involved in this invasion of your home. But can you prove that he was? All you have is a letter from a young woman who he embarrassed publicly – a woman who said she overheard a conversation.'

'When I think of what might have happened to the people I love the most, I'm so very angry.'

He missed the smile that sped across John's face. 'That's understandable, Zachariah, since you are blaming yourself for not being here. It won't hurt to put this before Basil Cheeves and see what he has to say. And I think it might be a good idea to talk to Edward, just to see if he knows anything of this gold. If he had his father's pistol he could have the gold hidden away.'

'Clemmie will never forgive me if I upset him. She thinks he's been through enough.'

'A lad will learn how to love from his mother, but he needs to learn to respect his father's word. You might try looking in his hiding hole. I know my boys kept all their treasures in one place when they were growing up. Your hiding place was behind a loose panel in the window seat.'

Zachariah laughed, though growing up in Martingale House had taught him very little about love or respect. 'Julia taught me what motherly love was like, and you taught me to respect you. As for the hiding place, I recall getting stuck in there one day and you pulled me out by my legs.'

John laughed and patted him on the shoulder. 'You needed to have someone to respect before you learned to have some respect yourself. Julia and I are so proud of you.'

Rather than bring Edward down to a room that reminded him of his own unhappy childhood, Zachariah went up to the nursery. Iris was playing with the Noah's Ark he'd bought them, the animals lined up two by two.

Edward was looking out of the window, dreamy-eyed.

'Edward,' he called softly, and the boy turned his head. Immediately his eyes became troubled.

'I want to talk to you a minute. Iris, you can stay with Polly till we come back. You'll be pleased to know that Miss Clemmie has woken up and I'll be taking you to visit her this afternoon.'

Both faces lit up with smiles.

He took the boy into Gabe's bedchamber. 'When I asked you to help me unpack your parents' effects, I didn't expect you to steal a pistol, Edward.'

Edward scuffed at the carpet with the toe of his boot and muttered, 'Sorry, sir. I just wanted something that belonged to my papa.'

Zachariah softened his voice. 'Yes, I know you did, and I can understand that. But guns are dangerous and not designed to be used as toys. You're not old enough yet to have a gun. Your father looked after his pistols and he would expect them to be cleaned and put away until you're old enough to handle them. The pistols were a matched pair and came in a box. Do you have the other one in your possession? What about the powder and ammunition?'

Edward sighed. 'It's under the rug under the bed. There is a loose floorboard.'

'Perhaps you'd fetch it out for me. Is there anything else I should know about . . . some gold perhaps?'

'It's inside the bible. Papa said the word of the Lord was priceless.'

Zachariah nearly burst out laughing as Edward slid under the bed. Gabe must have had his tongue firmly in cheek. A few moments later a polished box with Gabe's initials on it came sliding out. It contained the matching pistol.

Some scuffling went on under the bed, then some huffing and puffing. The lad cried out when he banged part of his body on the bed frame.

'Are you all right, Edward?'

'I've turned the rug back and got the floorboard half up, but it's stuck and the book is too heavy to lift out. I pushed it into the hole.'

'I had better help you.' Dropping down on to his front, Zachariah wriggled under the bed to find Edward struggling with the floorboard. It had a knothole in it. Inserting his finger, he heaved the board out. His gaze went to Edward. 'You didn't discover this loose floorboard by chance, did you?'

'Papa told me about it.'

The bible was heavier than Zachariah expected, as it was wedged in tight. It didn't take much for him to know why.

Eventually he freed the book and pushed it before him as he crawled from under the bed. He pulled Edward out by his legs. Both of them were covered in dust and fluff.

The pages had been hollowed out and it rattled slightly when he shook it. He set it on the dresser and opened it, only to face disappointment. It was full of small round lead balls, ammunition for a pistol.

'This isn't gold. It's balls for the pistol.'

Edward shook his head, then changed his mind and nodded. 'You have to scratch it with a knife to see the gold. Papa painted it so nobody would try to steal it.'

'Your papa always had some good ideas.' Wasting his life and that of his wife for a small amount of gold hadn't been one of them. He took a pocket knife from his pocket and scratched at the surface, smiling when gold glinted through. 'I'm going to put it in my strongbox and you shall have the pistols and half of the gold when you've grown into a man. Iris will have the other half. Best not to tell anyone though, because people can get greedy if they think there's some gold they can steal.'

'Like that man who got into the house? I'm glad you killed him; he was hurting Miss Clemmie.'

'Miss Clemmie is badly bruised, and you must prepare yourself for that. She'll recover in time, but she thought you and Iris were very brave, and so do I. She will need to be loved and cared for while she recovers.'

Edward puffed his chest out with pride. Fiercely he said, 'I wish I had killed Jonas, except the pistol wouldn't fire.'

'I'm glad you didn't, Edward. It's not a good feeling to kill anyone no matter how bad they are . . . However, I had no choice. Shall we go out for a ride? I want to inspect the barn to see if any of it can be saved, and we can see if there are any early daffodils we can pick for Clemmie's windowsill. It will cheer her up.'

'Can I come?' Iris asked, appearing at the doorway. 'I don't want to do girl things all the time.'

Zachariah smiled. 'I'll ask Ben to tie a leather pad to my saddle and you can sit in front of me.'

Edward scuffed at the floor again. 'I love Miss Clemmie and she loves me. She told me so. Perhaps she'll marry me and we'll be her family. She'd like that.'

'No doubt she would, but you're too young to be married.'

'You could marry her instead, Uncle Zachariah. Then she'd be our mama and you'd be our papa.'

Edward certainly had it all worked out to his benefit. 'Did you think that up all by yourself?'

'That's what Polly said to Mrs Ogden when I forgot I wasn't supposed to be listening.'

Zachariah ruffled the boy's hair, trying not to laugh at his earnest expression. 'Did she now? Well, we can't allow the house staff to decide the course of our lives, can we?'

'No, sir, but it's a good idea, isn't it?'

'You obviously think so, but taking a wife is a big responsibility for any man and it needs careful thought. I'd rather you didn't talk about this to anyone . . . especially Miss Clemmie.'

Edward's little hand went over his heart in a gesture Gabe had always used when they'd been small. It was as if the father had revealed a glimpse of himself in his son and sent a little echo to drift out of the distant past and tie them together in the present. He heard his brother's voice distinctively.

'*I'm sorry, Zed . . . I'm so sorry.*'

Zed . . . Gabe had always called him that and he grinned. 'Off you go now, you two. Ask Polly to put your outdoor clothes on so you'll be warm.'

Any doubts Zachariah held about the children now fled. The affection he'd once held for his late brother catapulted him along on a prolonged shuddering wave, so tears filled his eyes at the poignant sense of loss he experienced.

He felt for a handkerchief and couldn't find one. The women of the house had claimed them all! He blinked several times as if he'd just emerged from darkness into sudden light.

Gabe's children would receive all the love and guidance he could give them, Zachariah thought. Alexandra wouldn't be abandoned either. The girl was not of his blood, but it seemed more than possible that she was his niece and half-sister to the children. It had been cruel to bring her up believing a lie when she had the strongest of blood ties to his late sister-in-law. She would be invited to become part of the Fleet family if that's what she wanted.

Then there was his darling Clemmie, conceived during a business transaction between a light-skirt and a bigamist, who had tried to do the right thing by her before he went off to face death on behalf of his country. She refused to believe wrong of either of her parents. And why should she when her father had been a hero who'd died defending his country, and her mother had given her all the love she could afford? She had left her child with only good memories before she died from some disease.

He didn't know how long he'd stood there, gazing out of Gabe's window remembering the oddments of good things that came from his brother.

As for the family connection between himself and Clemmie, it was so remote that it hardly signified. All the same he would employ his usual caution in the matter, as he must.

He mused how odd it was that five abandoned members of the same family had come together. Like debris floating on different tides they'd washed up together on the same shore, as if the time had come for their collective worth to be discovered.

'I won't tell . . . I promise.'

He looked down to see Edward gazing up at him and smiled. 'I only said I'd think about it.'

Edward was almost twitching with excitement, and Zachariah didn't believe he'd keep the conversation private for a moment. He wouldn't put it past the boy to propose marriage to Miss Clementine Morris on his behalf.

Zachariah sighed and hoisted the boy on to his back. 'Come on then, let's go and find those daffodils.'

Twenty-One

Under the guidance of John Beck the children gave separate accounts of what had happened on the night of the fire.

Clementine gave hers, propped up against her pillows and with Julia for support. The magistrate was most sympathetic when he saw her injuries.

Zachariah showed the magistrate Edward's biography, and the boy was complimented on it. 'Well done, lad, you'll have to become a magistrate yourself when you've grown up a little.'

His deposition was marked: *As related by Sir Edward Fleet Bt, and witnessed by his legal guardian Zachariah Fleet and his attorney John Beck.*

After Edward signed it he looked up at Zachariah. 'Is my first name Sir, and what does Bt mean?'

'It's your legal title, one you inherited from your father. We will discuss it when you're a little older, Edward.' *The lad has a big load to carry on those small shoulders in the years to come*, Zachariah thought.

Two more weeks passed before Zachariah allowed Clementine out of bed. Her physical strength had returned and her bruises were fading to a yellowish colour, except for the deeper ones.

She avoided the part of the staircase where Jonas Hawkins had died. The carpet had been scrubbed clean but was now brighter than the other stairs. 'I've ordered new carpet for the stairs,' Zachariah told her.

Clementine became melancholy now and again and cried for no reason when she was alone in her bed at night. She also felt insecure, jumping at the slightest sound, even while knowing she was perfectly safe.

The Becks returned to London after assuring Zachariah that John was perfectly capable of running the business on his own, especially since he owned half the business in addition to being an attorney, an occupation his sons embraced.

'After all, I did teach you about investing money in the first place,' John had said.

'Why didn't you go to London with them?' Clementine asked Zachariah one evening.

Zachariah offered her a smile. 'John can manage the business for a while. I decided it would be better if I waited until you're well enough to travel.'

'You're taking us with you?'

'I can't leave you here. What happened is preying on your mind, so you practically freeze every time you see a shadow moving on the wall.'

She drew in a deep breath. 'Sometimes I see his face when I'm going off to sleep and I struggle and can't breathe. Then I remember the life fading from his eyes and even though I know he's dead, his hands won't let me go.'

'I wish I could have shielded you from that.'

'The children are coping better than I am. They're not moping and they've dismantled their hiding place now the question of who killed their parents has been resolved. It tells me they're feeling more secure.'

'Good, because I do want them to enjoy their childhood without having what happened hanging over them.'

'I'm improving, Zachariah, truly I am. I'm sure I can manage if you need to go to London. After all, the danger has been removed and I have your study to refurbish. That and the children will keep me busy until July when you intend to return.' She drew in a deep breath. 'I know Jonas is not likely to come back from the dead. I just can't understand why he did it.'

'He was an escaped convict, a clever confidence trickster and an opportunist. He'd been an acquaintance of Gabe's since they attended church school together. My brother owed him a considerable amount of money. It was probably from gambling IOUs.

'Gabe and the real George Sheridan found some gold and Jonas Hawkins demanded his debt be repaid. There was an argument and Jonas found Sheridan's portion of the gold. Gabe had hidden his small hoard well and had refused to hand it over. That was the moment when he'd played his last hand, gambling on his own life and the lives of his family. He should have remembered that luck always let him down.

'It would be easy to blame Gabe's death on Jonas. Gabe treated life as a game, and he hid Jonas from the authorities. From

Edward's account, Jonas wore a beard and he shot all of them and pushed the bodies into the river, which was flooding after a heavy rainstorm. Except for Edward and Iris.'

'Why didn't he kill the children as well?'

'They hid, but according to Jonas's woman she persuaded him not to when they were found. But seeing their parents killed was a horrific and terrifying act for the children to have witnessed. Apparently she pointed out to Jonas that the troopers were looking for him, and that the children were his ticket back to England. He shaved off his beard, pretended he was George Sheridan and came up with a scheme for her to pose as Mrs Sheridan. In that way he escaped from Australia without too much trouble, using George Sheridan's identity papers.

'I think he might have disposed of the children in England if we hadn't been waiting for him at the other end. Although Jonas, posing as George Sheridan, had said he'd expected to deliver the children to Martingale House.'

'Yet Edward must have known that George Sheridan and Jonas were one and the same.'

'He always drew Jonas as having a beard. The children were terrified of him and they were scared of the woman as well. Edward doesn't like to talk about it, and had stopped speaking in case the man cut his tongue off, if you recall.'

She shuddered. 'As if I could forget. And Basil Cheeves . . . how did he get involved with Jonas?'

'Through gambling. I've spoken to Cheeves the younger, and his father. They have agreed to rebuild the barn. Mr Cheeves has bought his son a commission in the army in the hope it will make a man out of him. If I'd thought Basil had contributed anything but sheer stupidity to the escapade I'd go ahead and drag him in front of a magistrate. As it is I've decided to hit him where it hurts. I'm in the middle of negotiating a reparation agreement for both you and the children.'

She stared at him. 'But I don't want his money.'

He smiled at that. 'Money is designed to be circulated. Look on the transaction as being an exchange. It's a poor reward when compared to your life, my love. You might want to get married one day. The money will serve as a dowry or you may decide to donate it to charity.'

Her mood took a sudden downturn. 'I don't think I'll marry.'

'Don't you want a family of your own?'

She thought about it. She would be contented just being a mother to Edward and Iris, but would like to be married to Zachariah and have children with him too. If she were given a choice she wouldn't know how to answer.

He smiled as if sensing her hesitation. 'Let's put our cards on the table, Clemmie, shall we?'

Sensing a trick, she proceeded with caution. 'You said you were working on a new contract.'

'With a decent dowry you could attract an offer from a wealthy gentleman in the not-too-distant future and it's possible you might even become Lady Clementine.'

'A gentleman of the finest sensitivity would marry a nursery maid for love alone, but not one from my background. And to hell with being Lady Clementine!' she threw at him. 'I don't want to prowl around looking like a camel with my nose stuck in the air.'

His laughter was a delight. 'What if I happen to know of a man who loves you only for yourself?'

That would be a fine irony when she knew she would never love any other man but him. Her mind stopped in mid-thought and spelled it out for her. *He is referring to himself, you fool.*

She stared at him, trying to read his eyes. He was in an enigmatic mood and she wanted to stamp her foot. She managed to toss a careless laugh in his direction as a barrier against any disappointment that might be coming her way. 'You're not referring to Edward, are you? He's already proposed and I turned him down.'

'I should hope so. Is there something wrong with your reasoning today? I'm referring to the obvious. How honest do you want me to be?'

'Extremely.'

He growled. 'All right . . . because you want to make me suffer I will tell you. It's me, of course.'

'Yourself?' She began to laugh because she was astonished that she'd been right. 'Really, Zachariah . . . why me?'

'Don't try to sound so surprised when that laughter is totally false. My intentions have been clear right from the beginning.'

'As clear as mud, I'd say.'

'Can I help it if you ran a mile every time I approached you? I know my past isn't exactly spotless and I'm not much of a prize and my courting technique is non-existent, since I've never had the inclination to wed before. But I'm proud of what I've achieved when I could have easily ended up as bad as . . . Well, John and Julia Beck saw something in me and I'll be forever in their debt.'

'The past is exactly that, Zach. Would it help if I said I saw something in you too? I think you have a fine sense of compassion and there's a strong streak of the lost boy in you that makes you raise barriers. That's what drew me to you first; the need to break down that barrier and have you trust me. I do love you.'

'Then allow me.' He joined her on the sofa and pulled her on to his lap. She had to believe what his eyes were telling her now, so blue and deep they were. 'I've told you why, Clemmie, my dearest one. I love you . . . adore you . . . I want you with me day and night and I'm desperate to make love to you.'

'Oh!' she gasped, and then grinned at him and teased. 'Well yes . . . I suppose you are. That sounded clear enough.' She placed her hands against her burning cheeks.

He pulled them down again. 'Don't tell me I've been reading the signs wrong and it's only your cheeks that burn for me, my delightful Clemmie.' He laughed and blew gently into her ear so shivers ran down her spine. 'I want a wife I can be wicked with.'

'Do you, Zach?' She cocked her head to one side and regarded him, laughing. 'I'm sure I could be wicked if you show me how.' She looked down at her hands and then at his dark curls. Reaching up she ruffled his hair and laughed. Then hugged him tight. 'I've always wanted to do that.'

A few seconds later he said in a muffled voice, 'And I've always wanted to do this, except I can't breathe.'

'Oh . . . my goodness.' She had him crushed against her heart. When she loosened her grip he slid a kiss over her breast and emerged with a grin on his face.

He took her bruised face in his hands, brought her face down to his and gently kissed every inch before he nipped her bottom lip and captured her mouth with his. A long time later he whispered against her ear, 'I'll show you just how wicked you can be after we are married, my Clementine.'

She almost fell apart at the thought.

She thought she heard the door open, and then it closed again.

'I love you,' he whispered against her mouth.

There was a barely suppressed giggle then somebody whispered, 'Miss Clemmie has got something in her eye again.'

'Don't be silly, Iris. Uncle Zachariah is kissing her. I told you they were going to be married and be our mama and papa.'

'You think you know everything.'

'I do know everything. It's because I'm a boy child, like Jesus in the bible. The Reverend said so.'

'That just makes you plain daft,' Iris scoffed, sounding a little like Polly. 'Uncle Zachariah said it's a fairy tale, and he knows better than the Reverend, don't you, Uncle . . . *Papa*?' Iris giggled.

Zachariah's eyes were full of laughter.

Clementine placed a hand over his mouth before he could answer and he tickled her palm with his tongue before saying diplomatically, 'A man has to make up his own mind over such matters as he grows up.'

They drew apart and smiled at each other before turning to their interested audience.

'Aren't you going to make another kiss?' Iris asked.

'Not while the pair of you are watching. A man should be allowed to do his courting in private.' Zachariah held out his arms. 'Come here, you pests.'

Twenty-Two

1836

At the end of April Zachariah was offered an earldom.

Although it was hard for him to turn down both the honour and the living that went with it, he declined. He didn't want to live in the north of the country. It was too far away from his business and he also didn't want the responsibility of the land, the trappings of rank or the added expense of a draughty old

Tudor house that was displaying signs of rapid decay, if the reports he'd received were correct.

As one of his colleagues pointed out, 'It will cost you your fortune before you can live in it.'

John had laughed as he'd congratulated him on his decision. 'That was an unexpected choice for you to make. Julia and I thought you would accept it.'

'I must admit my vanity nearly ruled the day.'

'Perhaps I'll make a Quaker out of you yet.'

'I doubt it. I turned the honour down because I didn't want the complications that went with it and not because I don't believe in the class system or consider myself less than an equal to my fellow man. I like what I'm doing now. I've reached a position in my life that I've earned. I'm contented. It's a challenge, and I don't want to live within a set of religious rules.'

'Beliefs . . . not rules. Being a Quaker is a way of life.'

'I know, and I thought long and hard about it because I would have liked to please and honour you in that way – but I cannot, and I know you and Julia wouldn't want me to commit myself merely to please you.

'I will tell you now that I always have, and always will, appreciate your wise counsel. I also agree with many of your beliefs. But committing myself to the Quaker life is not for me. I have my house in London and I'm negotiating to buy a country manor that overlooks the sea. I'm going to call it Clementine Manor, but don't tell Clemmie because it's my wedding gift to her.'

'Is it far from Martingale House?'

'Less than an hour on horseback. I intend that we should live there after we're married, where there is no memory of the horror that Clemmie and the children went through. Hopefully, the memory will fade in time. Mr Bolton and his wife will live at Martingale and run the estate until Edward is old enough to assume his responsibility there. I want Edward and Iris to grow up with a sense of family and I want children of my own.'

'A year ago you vowed never to wed.'

'I think you told me that love for a woman doesn't listen to reason. You were right, as usual.'

'And you were right when you decided to take Clementine for your wife. Alexandra did her best to keep you apart, but from my observation of her it was little more than mischief on her part.'

He shrugged. 'Alexandra's manner towards me was annoying for the most part and embarrassing at times. She gave people the wrong impression of our relationship, and I don't think I'll ever forgive her for soiling Clemmie's name with gossip and innuendo. But let us talk of something else. You know, it won't be long before the railways extend to the south-west counties and that will make travel between London and Dorset much easier. And who knows what prosperity it might bring. We should buy some land and property along the route where the railway is expected to run.'

'How did Clementine take the news that Howard Morris turned out to be separate people with the same name, who died on the same day but on different ships?'

'She expressed relief. She said she knew we'd sort it out eventually and wondered why we didn't think of it in the first place.'

'I believe we did . . . we just didn't follow it up.'

'Is Alexandra travelling to Dorset for your wedding?'

'Now her background has been revealed she would rather not be the subject of more conjecture. She's overlooked the fact that her behaviour attracted the criticism in the first place.'

'At least she put you before herself this time.'

'Not at all. She said it would shame her to be regarded as the skeleton in the Fleet family closet when she has done nothing to deserve it except to be born. That is something I can understand because it seems that the Fleet family must always have a scapegoat. She feels that her mother is at fault, and since Alice was married to Howard Morris, there was no reason to give her away when she married again. She forgets that Alice was only fifteen. She would rather her background remained as part of the Tate family now she is married to Roland. She can't be faulted for what happened before she was born.'

'What does Roland think of it? Surely your name would add a little prestige, something to tempt his business clients with in the city.'

'Roland agrees with her, but that doesn't stop him from doing what he needs to do to further his business, and Alexandra didn't stop him from accepting a marriage settlement from me on her behalf. I think she feels she's entitled to it. I do like Roland though. He's got a shrewd business mind as well as being creative, and knows what he wants from life. I can furnish him with a few contacts, but he's already earning a good reputation for the work he turns out.'

'He's just the kind of man Alexandra needs in her life. The last time I visited she was working in the shop front and keeping the books. She has a head for figures, it seems, and was pleased the money went to her. Not that she ever doubted that it would.'

John smiled. 'The woman was certainly full of bounce, and she will get over her embarrassment in time. Now, enough of Alexandra; let us discuss arrangements for our journey. Will we need one carriage or two? Did you allow Julia access to your accounts again, Zachariah?'

'Of course . . . someone had to see to Clementine's wardrobe.'

'Quite so. We will need to take two carriages as well then . . .'

Clementine saw the vehicles turn into the carriageway.

'They're here,' she shouted, and gathering up her skirts she headed out of the nursery and down the stairs.

The children came running after them. Edward made it to the bottom first, via the banister.

'They're here!' Clemmie shouted again as they reached the hall.

Servants came running from everywhere and the dogs came to stand at the door, tails thrashing. Wolf's bark was now deep and threatening. Happy still huffed and puffed.

When Clementine opened the door everyone spilled out and milled around. Servants straightened their aprons and drew on their smiles as the carriage wheels crunched over the gravel. The horses tossed their heads and neighed, thankful for the smell of familiar stables and the possibility of a good rub down to relieve their overheated bodies and tired muscles.

It wasn't the most dignified homecoming, but at least it was genuine.

The children reached Zachariah before she did, attaching themselves to a leg each, and with words bursting out of them.

Edward told him, 'I fell off my pony and scraped my knee. And I've started to write another bogafree.'

'Is the knee better?'

'It went all scabby and Miss Clemmie put some salve on it. I've got a scar now.'

Iris waved a piece of paper in the air. 'I've drawn you a picture of my favourite hen and I'm sad because a fox killed her. Mr Bolton brought some baby chicks home from the market, and he said I may have one of those to look after. I helped the cook make some scones too and we ate them with jam and cream on.'

'I hope you kept one for me,' he said.

'Oh no. It would be stale. I can ask the cook to help me make some more.'

When Clementine laughed at the scene, Zachariah gazed at her over the children's heads. The world stood still for several intimate moments.

She went to him and he drew her into his arms and kissed her briefly on the mouth, then hugged her in front of everyone in an entirely improper manner.

Their wedding day had been arranged for the first Saturday in August. The day was perfect, the sky as blue as Zachariah's eyes.

Her gown was blue too, the palest of tints. The fabric of the overskirt was so fine that it whispered over the silk skirt in the slightest breeze, causing the colours to change and drift. She wore frilled over sleeves to match her tiered collar and her ringlets were secured with posies of silk violets and ribbons.

John Beck was walking her down the aisle. 'You look exquisitely beautiful,' he said as he helped her down from the carriage and they walked through the scattering of villagers who'd not been able to find seats inside the church.

'I'm scared.'

He laughed. 'So am I . . . shall we run away together and cause a scandal?'

'Certainly not! My reputation is already in ruins. What would they say if I ran off with a married man? Besides, we would have done all that catering for nothing, and Julia would never speak to me again. And I love her dearly.'

'Ah yes . . . come to think of it, so do I. Come on then; allow me to take you to your groom.'

All heads turned as they entered the church and Clementine

could feel every pair of eyes on her, like pin pricks. Her stomach received special scrutiny from some of the women.

She smiled at them, knowing they'd be disappointed.

The servants wore beaming smiles and Clementine stooped to kiss Iris and Edward, who were seated with Julia Beck.

The sun struck the windows and she looked to where Zachariah waited for her with Evan by his side – then to the rector who stood waiting. His smile said he enjoyed conducting weddings.

She drew closer and Zachariah took her hand in his. Calm filled her as the choir began to sing.

The beauty of the service affected Clementine and tears filled her eyes as he promised to love her always.

Zachariah sighed. Reaching into his pocket he brought out the first in his new supply of handkerchiefs and handed it to her.

'I see you finally found yourself, Zachariah Fleet,' she whispered, gazing at the new design of his entwined initials.

'I had to find you first.' He lifted her hand to his mouth and the grin she offered him was irresistible when he said, 'I love you.'

Lightning Source UK Ltd.
Milton Keynes UK
UKOW04f1733091115

262387UK00001B/7/P